Hawt Flash

Midlife in Aura Cove Book 1

Blair Bryan

Read More By this Author
Order Direct & Save 15%

Use code AURACOVE15 at checkout.

Scan the QR code to explore all my books, unlock exclusive deals, and more!

Prefer to tap? Click HERE.

OR Find My Books at Your Favorite Bookseller

Books By Blair Bryan

Books by Ninya

———

Want FREE Books? Enter to Win a Gift Card to My Bookstore https://tealbutterflypress.com/pages/join-our-email-list-and-win

There's a new winner every week!

For every woman of a certain age who believes the best part of her life is over.
The magic you've been waiting for is on its way.

PROLOGUE

The woman hurried, toward the hangar where her private jet awaited, her long white hair rippling like a cape behind her, hiding her voluptuous figure. Pausing, she shivered, deliciously. It had been ages since she'd felt this quickening, the almost-palpable shift in the air that was the harbinger of an extraordinary event: *an awakening.*

As a bolt of lightning burst behind her, she glanced back to make sure she wasn't being followed, mentally chastising herself for allowing her excitement to get the best of her.

The restoration of her family's triad of power – *her* power -- was almost at hand! As the waxing blood moon fattened in the sky, the pool of crackling energy that hovered just beyond her reach also swelled, collecting the dispersed energy of her female predecessors. Half a century passed since she'd first laid eyes on the bundled baby; the decades had crawled by so slowly, leaving her to bide her time in idle pursuits of pleasure. Waiting.

Her jaw clenched as she considered the blunders and errors that were made, mistakes she could have averted if she'd been allowed her rightful place at the side of the little girl upon whom all her hopes and plans depended. But now a calm knowing relaxed her features. The day of reckoning was coming: only a few days more and her great-great-granddaughter would turn fifty.

ONE

Katie mumbled under her breath as she sheared perfect squares out of the supple wool suit fabric. Her special *fabric-only* scissors slashed through the stiff cloth like butter. Each clip made a crisp slicing sound as the blades of this meticulously maintained and sharpened tool scissored together. It was the pair she hoarded and hid from her kids when they were little, the only scissors sharp enough to stand up to the task of shredding her husband's ridiculously expensive suit. The pile of wool grew as a smug giddiness crept inside her, filling the crevices between her anger. Watching them transform from precious cargo sheathed in paper-thin dry cleaner's plastic into a massive pile of gray fluff and fuzz was deeply pleasurable.

"More satisfying than any time we've spent between the sheets in the last few years." She said it aloud and punctuated it with a snort. "God, I'm so damn funny today." Katie had taken to talking to herself and the dog when her last child left the nest four years ago. The sprawling showplace home they lived in was so cold and quiet now without the kids. It was a habit she acquired to fill the cavernous spaces in her home and in her heart.

It took a solid hour to cut the suit into gratifying squares. There was an extra perverse thrill knowing it was his good luck charm, the gray wool one she helped him pick out when he landed the job interview at the firm in Florida.

Their day of picking out menswear together for the interview now felt a million miles away. She remembered being stuffed into a delicate upholstered Louis XVI armchair, awkwardly clutching a glass of champagne the tailor forced into her hand while Jeff pawed through the racks of suits, engrossed in options.

"The suit makes the man," Jeff had explained when she gasped at the price handwritten on the luxurious cardstock of the tag. Six thousand dollars? Instantly annoyed, he shushed her with his glare. "I knew you wouldn't under-stand. This is the big time, baby. I have to look the part."

She rolled her eyes at his nickname, which used to make her weak in the knees but had lately sounded phony.

"I'll need an entire closet full of them once I become partner."

The word partner still held the sting of rejection they'd both felt when he'd been overlooked for partnership at the firm in New York. Even though he'd graduated from Columbia, Katie discovered Jefferson was a mediocre attorney at best. He was quick to pass the blame to her, though, and offer a plethora of excuses for the slight. The most hurtful one being Katie wasn't quite the caliber they expected from the wife of a named partner. She wasn't a dinner-party-throwing Atkins evangelist rocking a blowout 24/7. Katie was curvy and relied a little too hard on shapewear to keep her voluptuous curves in check.

With his future career aspirations cut off at the knees, she'd convinced Jeff to leave New York when their oldest was just entering high school. Between the bitterness from the slight, the punishing long winters, and being confined to their minuscule rental, Jeff was eager to make a fresh start. After a few beers one night, they'd taped a map of the United States to the wall and thrown two darts. His landed on Chicago and her heart leapt. Her parents lived there with Yuli, her beloved grandmother, and they would jump at the chance to help her with the kids. Hers defied gravity and swerved to land on St. Petersburg, Florida, a place she'd never been.

"Chicago's a hard no for me. Having your parents in our backyard and sticking their noses in our business constantly? No, thank you. Your relationship with them is already off-the-charts dysfunctional. I mean, who talks to their grandmother every day?"

A visit to St. Petersburg, Florida, sealed the deal. After sharing an order of peel-and-eat shrimp from a food truck on the beach, Jeff drove their rental car down the streets of Aura Cove, a small beachfront community twenty minutes outside St. Petersburg. Katie couldn't explain the feeling of peace that enveloped her when they crossed into the city limits of Aura Cove. It felt like home.

"This is it, baby! We're going to live here one day. Believe it! I am going to manifest Aura Cove for us. You wait and see."

He was so certain, a month later, they'd rented the only

house they could afford in the area, and it felt like fate when Jeff landed his interview at the firm.

"Look, I understand your need to look professional, but we could spend a week in the Maldives for what this one suit will set us back. We could send Beckett to football camp, and the payments for Callie's braces are starting next month, not to mention the moving expenses are still on our credit cards. I mean, the timing isn't great right now."

"It's an *investment,*" he explained in the condescending tone that had become his default setting. "You wouldn't understand," he dismissed. "I mean, look at yourself!" He hissed under his breath, "It's obvious I'm going to have to choose all your clothing for you from now on. I will not lose out on another partnership opportunity because of my frumpy wife." He waved his hand up and down at her. "Would it hurt you to take some pride in your appearance? It's not that difficult."

His criticism stung as she glanced down. Dressed simply in a wrinkled maxi dress and sandals, her ebony hair was gathered into a loose braid that flowed between her shoulders. Fighting back embarrassed tears, she wrapped her arms around her soft middle that resulted from the mom's diet. Coffee, cheap four-buck chuck from Trader Joe's, and whatever was left on the kids' plates before she scraped them to wash dishes. Katie was proud of her thrifty ways. They enabled her to put Jeff through college after she dropped out of Northwestern when she was pregnant with Lauren. Then they helped pay for Columbia, the Ivy League law school that forced them to become New Yorkers far longer than she'd wanted. With the insane cost of living in New York and three little mouths to feed, she worked two jobs to make ends meet. It had been a slog, but all along the way Jeff promised her the sacrifices would be worth it, so she buckled down and got through it like she always did.

But that day, at the menswear atelier, with his six-figure student loans still hanging over their heads, to drop this extravagant sum on one suit was difficult for her to swallow. Katie knew better than to argue when he was in a mood. She clamped her lips shut, cutting off the objections she had, and watched him amble to the dressing room, whistling without a care in the world, oozing with entitlement.

Jeff had an *Alice in Wonderland* effect on her. With one compliment, he could make her rise with confidence and become greater, but with one stinging word of criticism, she would shrink until she almost disappeared. It was a dynamic whose lineage could be traced back to her unplanned pregnancy in college when she was too young and too exhausted to object to it.

Jeff was a different man when he strode out of the changing room that day, the small-statured tailor quickly following behind, nipping at his heels with a measuring tape flapping from around his neck. The power suit transformed Jeff. He stood taller and commanded more of a presence in the room, his hands balled into fists at his hips, standing in the Superman pose he heard made him appear more powerful. It was a technique he gleaned from the Tony Robbins cassette tapes that cost another fortune, but that Jeff insisted were crucial to his self-development.

She was ashamed to admit it now, but Katie initially

flushed with pride at seeing her handsome husband adorned in the finest worsted wool. It was an emotion that quickly dissipated while she watched him preening in the mirror from her seat on the uncomfortable antique chair. It was obvious, Jeff was enamored with his own reflection, smiling wider, turning and twisting in the mirror, admiring himself like a modern-day Narcissus. Luckily, the reflection was a mirror instead of a pool of water or he would have suffered the same fate.

That day, seeing him in the suit, she imagined the dream of the Aura Cove life Jeff promised was within their grasp. She pushed away the embarrassment and the little digs that seemed to be part of every conversation and focused on the fact that all their dreams were going to come true. When he hurt her feelings, she consoled herself with pride in the work she'd done for their family and a pint of Ben and Jerry's. She told herself, *You can't have it all. No one can. This is good enough. I am happy enough.*

Jeff was right. The suit gave him the confidence to nail his interview, and he was immediately offered a position in the up-and-coming law firm, one that promised a guaranteed track to being named partner. During the next nine years, she could count on two hands the number of times they'd had sex since Jeff's move to the swanky glass and steel high-rise in downtown St. Petersburg. Katie blamed the hours he'd been required to put in to get the brass ring. Jeff was a competent lawyer whose biggest accomplishment was conning an Ivy League law school to accept him. In Florida, his luck changed drastically, and a couple of high-profile cases fell in his lap with profitable outcomes for the firm. After paying their dues in a small rental while the kids were in high school, his newfound success gave them the resources to manifest their dream home in Aura Cove four years ago. Then his prediction came true. Exactly ten years after they'd first driven down the streets of Aura Cove, dreaming about their future, he became a named partner at Lewis, Garfunkel, and now newly added Beaumont.

Becoming a named partner in his law firm was supposed to be the culmination of all their years of hard work together. A shared triumph. Katie waited in the wings for praise for her sacrifices to provide for the family while he was studying for the bar and putting in the long years to earn his partnership. She picked up the slack because he was just *so busy* and couldn't be bothered with trivial things like getting dog food or sitting though their three now-grown children's parent-teacher conferences and extracurricular activities.

He puffed up like a peacock, seeing his surname being added to the sign in the sleek lobby. Two weeks ago, she walked in on him masturbating to the letterhead. Letterhead! His full name was spelled out in the pretentious block lettering at the top of a thick cream cardstock in his hand. Jefferson D. Beaumont, esquire. That should have been the first sign.

Back in her kitchen surrounded by the high-thread-count wool squares, Katie sighed, frustrated with herself. Continuing to shear the fabric, she shook her head, angry that she didn't pick up on the signs as she sipped on a glass of wine. Sure, it was only ten-thirty, but it was close enough to noon. Okay, technically it was noon *adjacent,* but in her current state, she was more than willing to overlook this small momentary lapse of judgment.

Just an hour earlier, her fingers wrapped around a crumpled receipt that, at first glance, was another innocent ball of forgotten paper stuffed without thought into the pocket of his sport coat left for her to dutifully retrieve. Katie habitually checked his pockets before sending the garments to the dry cleaner, after the hissy fit Jeff threw when a tube of lip balm claimed two of his Finamore dress shirts. Shirts that cost more than any article of her clothing in their shared closet. She never dreamed the unassuming wad of paper had the power to destroy her life.

She rubbed her palm on it to flatten it back out. It was a late checkout from her favorite hotel, the one he always booked for their anniversary. There was a prickle of knowing as the hairs on the back of her neck stood up and her hands began to shake. Time stood still as she squinted to study it, trying to make out the tiny font.

Tears blurred her eyes as she scrambled to find her reading glasses and brought the receipt closer to her face. The bill had been paid with a credit card whose last four digits she didn't recognize. Two line items were daggers in her heart. Champagne and room service. $194.77. One made her burn with smug self-righteousness. In-room Cinemax. $29.

"Maybe it's not me after all. Who orders pay-per-view porn during a secret tryst? Sex addicts. That's who." Arlo, her dog at her feet, howled in agreement. His caramel hair was long and tangled, and he needed a groom.

Katie stared down at the paper, unable to tear her eyes away from the evidence. In her crazed state, she rubbed the heel of her hand over it again and again as her thoughts swirled, wincing when she noticed the dark spots tucked between the bluish veins on her hands. Marks she first tried to classify as freckles, but now had to admit leaned hard into age spot territory.

"Why do a woman's hands age faster than the rest of her body?" she asked, then answered herself. "That's easy, because women do all the work! Am I right, boy?" She reached down to pet Arlo, then scratched his favorite spot under his chin. "You're the only man in my life who hasn't been a total disappointment. You're mommy's best boy, aren't you?" she asked, using her goofy high-key dog modulation that made one of his ears perk up. He was a mutt she'd rescued from death row at the local pound. A dog that she loved and Jeff loathed because he shed.

"God knows we can't have a single hair on your perfectly pressed trousers! Jerk!" She picked up a handful of wool fabric squares and let them fall like snow from her fingertips back down to the table.

A secret credit card. The unfamiliar digits stung. It was the reddest of the red flags. The new information burned inside her, tumbling and roiling in her belly, a revelation that held a secret power she was failing to contain. Needing to release its power into the world and free herself from its poison, she aggressively punched the digits of her best friend's phone number. When Frankie picked up on the first ring, like she always did, Katie blurted, "He's got a secret credit card." The words, now free and the secret unlocked, hastened the flow of tears welling in her eyes and tracking down the lines on her face.

"Oh, Katie," Frankie consoled. "No."

"Yes. Very much yes." A bitter sigh escaped her lips, and she swallowed the knot in her throat.

"And this is why I'm dead inside. NTM," Frankie said.

"NTM?" Katie was confused.

"Never trust a man," Frankie spelled out. "Did you know there was an actual study done at some fancy university that found males were more willing to punish others for their own personal gain than their female counterparts?" Frankie huffed in outrage. "I didn't need a study to come to that conclusion! I lived it!"

"Focus, Frankie. We can get back to hating them collectively as a species later." Katie let out a strangled laugh, then burst into tears. "I'm such an idiot." She cried, "Looking back, there might have been a few hints, but I ignored them."

"Like what?"

"There were a few late-night texts he explained away, and a couple months ago he started going to the gym again. And then one afternoon, I went to his office to surprise him with lunch, and he was already out with his legal assistant, Brittany. I waited in his office for two hours for them to come back. It was humiliating."

"That shit bag," Frankie muttered. Her tone was infused with the outrage Katie felt, and her unfettered loyalty endeared her even more to Katie.

"Denial ain't just a river in Egypt," Katie deflected with humor, using a twangy Mark Twain drawl, then burst into tears. "God, what do I do?"

Frankie was always good in a crisis. "I know what *I* would do, but this is your life. Whatever decision you make, I've got your back."

"I don't think I can turn a blind eye to it anymore." She exhaled deeply with resignation. "I mean, it's one thing to have suspicions, but completely different to hold the proof in your hands." She gulped, staring down at the receipt. "I think I want a divorce." Katie found the wine bottle and dumped the rest of it into her glass, and then chucked it toward the garbage can, where it hit the refrigerator and shattered into a million pieces.

"What was that noise?" Frankie asked.

"Shoot," Katie said under her breath. "It's nothing. I just dropped a glass."

"Are you okay?"

"Of course not," Katie argued. "No one's okay when they discover their husband is cheating."

"I'm sorry, honey," she offered and then changed tactics, switching into damage control mode. The sympathy in her tone made more tears fall down Katie's cheeks. Frankie wasn't normally empathetic; she was a logical Scorpio with a thirst for revenge. "I'm not the one you call when you need someone to hold your hand." Frankie always admitted her shortcomings easily, and that was part of her charm. "But when you need someone to drive the getaway car or help you bury the body, I'm your girl."

"Okay, listen to me very carefully. You need to be smart here. First, you have to get your paperwork together. Make a plan. Do you know where all the financial documents are at?"

"Of course. I'm the one who pays all the bills."

"Okay, good." She exhaled. "Get copies of everything, bank statements, credit cards, investments, retirement accounts, everything you have owned jointly. I'm going to text you the name of *the* attorney. She's a real ball-buster. Ruthless as hell. You know he's going to find some big gun to represent him, and he already has a tremendous advantage from knowing the ins and outs of the legal system. Jeff is going to exploit every loophole he can find. You have to protect yourself."

"I know." Katie cradled the phone between her shoulder and her neck while she swept up the glass. It was important that everything looked copacetic if one of the kids popped in for a visit. She wasn't ready to face the thought of them seeing her flaws, that this perfect life she killed herself to provide for them was just a fairytale, except this one didn't have a happy ending anymore.

TWO

The information burned, and after two hours of sobbing and sobering up later, Katie pulled herself into a standing position and walked into the marble-ensconced bathroom. The beveled mirror reflected a woman she now barely recognized. For the last ten years, she went through life on autopilot with hardly a glance in the mirror most days. Katie had other priorities, but now, full of self-doubt and accepting blame that wasn't hers, she internalized the destruction of her marriage.

Studying her reflection, she briefly wondered if her creeping up in age or lack of a decent skin care regimen was to blame. She inventoried herself. Her round, heart-shaped face was flushed and red, and her green eyes were bloodshot and swollen from tears. She leaned in and tugged at a clump of hair. The crisp white of the hair of her forelock was showing again. It was a patch of brilliant white that started at her widow's peak in her otherwise raven hair Jeff forced her to religiously dye to black every two weeks. The fresh growth was stubbornly white, as was half of her right eyebrow.

"We are projecting an *image*." His demand was patronizing the first time he thrust a drugstore box of black hair dye into her hands. Katie remembered flushing with shame at his insensitivity toward her genetic abnormality, but she eventually caved. It was always easier to just go along with whatever Jeff wanted. Go along to get along.

When they first started dating in college, he picked out her clothing for special events. They would shop together, and he would pull various looks for her to try on and model for him in the cramped dressing room. At the time, she thought it was sexy—a shopping spree with her attractive boyfriend—but when they got pregnant and then engaged, and she discovered the debt that his shopping sprees incurred, she resented their frequent visits to the mall. Where he would make his demand and she would hand her credit card to the cashier, each swipe making her more anxious and afraid.

"No, no, no," she told herself. "He does not get a free pass. Growing older is not an excuse for infidelity." Katie cursed the universal principle that made men more attractive with age, but thinned the hair of women and widened their hips.

On a mission now, she yanked the door to the bathroom closet, gathered up the box of hair dye that arrived monthly thanks to an Amazon subscription, and tossed it into the trash. The box hit the bottom of the metal can with a satisfying clang.

"Never again. I will never change for another man again," Katie declared as she turned side to side in the mirror, noting the softness of her belly. It was the result of a lifelong truffle habit and the evidence of years of finishing whatever unhealthy things her teenagers were eating. Their metabolisms could take the influx of calories and sugar. Katie's could not. Her weight crept up for years while she taxied them to appointments and sporting events. Although her nest was currently empty, her metabolism never got the memo. The weight stuck, as stubborn and resistant as the white streak in her hair. As she took stock of herself in the mirror, seeing herself again with fresh eyes, it was obvious she'd let herself go.

She did a quick jumping jack. Then a full set of ten. Her extra flab jiggled, and she felt her butt cheeks slap together in an impromptu round of applause.

"Hey, at least I have one raving fan." It was an odd accomplishment, but one that she recently learned was highly valued in the hip-hop videos her son, Beckett, loved to subject her to when he stopped by for his weekly visit. That mostly included several loads of laundry and eating everything in the refrigerator. He adored gangsta rap, and Katie would never admit it to him, but the beats *were* kind of catchy. She secretly added them to the Spotify playlist she created for her ambitious jogging debut. A debut that never happened.

She pulled off her clothing and put it in the hamper.

"And I'll never have to pick up his dirty socks from the ground ever again!" She added that one to the win column. Jefferson was a slob, leaving wet towels on the travertine floors daily. His time was too important to waste on trivial things like laundry. It was yet another concession she made to keep their marital train on its tracks. They were adding up. Now she could see all those concessions didn't matter at all. The train derailed despite them.

Her life had gotten away from her, the way life does after you jump through its hoops. Dating. Check. Baby. Check. Engagement. Check. Marriage. Check. She got a few of them out of order but completed her to-do list by the time she was twenty-five. She didn't pause long enough to ask if the traditional woman's checklist of life was even what she wanted to do in the first place. Without asking if there was another option, another road she could take. She walked the one that everyone was already on like a zombie, afraid to take the darker, lonelier fork where she considered only herself.

His betrayal had the effect of re-centering her internal navigation point. Amid her insecurity and uncertainty, a brilliant idea bloomed.

"I need to get out of here. It's time to do something for me." At the doorway of the bathroom, Arlo was sitting on his haunches and barked in agreement.

"That's right, boy!"

The well-lit, walk-in cherry closet was filled with rows of Jeff's expensive suits and obnoxious dress shirts. He'd gotten even more fashion-conscious since inking the partnership deal and had started mixing and matching outrageously patterned dress shirts with sport coats his personal stylist insisted he needed. They made him even more insufferable. Katie pulled on a pair of dark boot cut jeans that hugged her curves with a high enough waist to keep her muffin top contained and then pulled an olive green woven top over her head. The green was a color she loved, and it brought out her enormous green eyes. She sucked in her belly, watching her ample chest rise, and added a belt. From the basket that sat on the entry table, she plucked a pair of sunglasses and her olive green Baggallini purse that Jeff couldn't stand, a zippered contraption that kept every detail of her life organized. It wasn't pretty, but it was functional. When her attendance at a social event was required, it forced her to load all her necessities into the pretentious Dolce and Gabbana handbag that Jeff had given her as a birthday gift.

"And no more crappy birthday gifts that are really for him! Another win!" she said to Arlo. "And just in time!" With a milestone birthday—her fiftieth—merely days away, Katie found herself unusually introspective, the reflective place you pause at the midpoint of any important project. It's the time when you reassess what is working and what isn't, and Katie had to admit she had been dissatisfied for years. Measuring the place she was against the place she wanted to be, she acknowledged the divide for the first time.

Inspired to make a change, she drove her car down the clean streets of their subdivision containing immaculately groomed executive homes and through the gate, waving at the security guard manning the entrance. At first, she drove aimlessly, just happy to get out of the house. On her wrist, her apple watch vibrated with an incoming call. She glanced at it, seeing Jeff's name with a heart emoji that now made her nauseated. With an eye roll, she pushed the red ignore symbol and sent him straight to voicemail, a defiant act that was out of character for her. She had been groomed to make herself constantly available to him. For the last twenty-six years, whenever he called, she ran to the phone like a trained seal. Sometimes with a screaming child glued to her hip, lately while the sauce burned.

"No more." She laughed as a tiny power surge jolted to her center, making her feel unstoppable. An electric pull nudged her forward. Driving the twenty minutes from Aura Cove to St. Pete's Beach, Florida, she whipped it to the left and then, on impulse, straight into the Volkswagen car dealership. She rolled down the rows of beetles in every color. It was a car she'd coveted her entire life since the first glimpse she got in her teens.

"Ooh! Mommy likes!" She stopped the basic black sedan that Jefferson had insisted on and popped out of the car, landing in front of a green convertible bug. She circled it, bending down to look into the console.

"And it's a stick," she remarked to herself. Katie learned how to drive a stick from her dad when she was sixteen. During jackrabbit stops and starts in the Kroger's parking lot, she discovered the give and take that driving a manual transmission required. The shifting made her feel like a race car driver and her first car was a manual Chevette—an ugly little rust bucket she adored because it was freedom personified.

She was rounding the car, her fingers caressing the curves of it like a lover when a sweating, portly sales-person appeared.

"Hello there!" His greeting jerked her from her reverie to the present.

"I've always wanted to drive one of these."

"Well, you've come to the right place." His eyes glinted with the transparent greed of a man who works on commission. "Did you want to take her out for a test drive?"

"No. I'm just looking." Katie dismissed him at first, then reversed her decision seconds later. "You know what? I changed my mind. I actually think I would like to take it for a test drive."

"Fantastic." He clapped his chubby hands together. "Let me get the keys." He walked away as Katie leaned in closer. The interior was ivory and burl. It was an indulgent, beautiful car, and she couldn't wait to drive it.

A few minutes later, he reappeared. "I'm Dave."

"Nice to meet you, Dave. I'm Katie."

"It's a manual transmission. Have you driven a stick before?"

"Yes, but it's been a while," she admitted.

He tossed the keys to her, and Katie snatched them from the air before sliding into the leather driver's seat. The car sunk as Dave's formidable form lowered into the seat next to her. Katie turned the key in the ignition and the vehicle roared to life (as much as a beetle can roar). She shifted into reverse and backed out of the stall and then shifted to first gear. The muscle memory came back surprisingly fast as she worked both her feet on the clutch and gas, but they lurched forward as the engine died.

"I just need to get the hang of it again," Katie explained. She turned the ignition once more, and the car leapt forward, still not smooth, but at least it didn't kill the engine. She slammed the gas pedal harder and then shifted to second and then third as the engine signaled the need for more power.

"There you go," Dave praised her as he patted the

dashboard. "You're buying a piece of history. Did you know Volkswagen discontinued the beetle in 2019?"

"What?" Katie's mouth hung open in shock. "Why?"

"Electric vehicles are the next big thing. After seven decades, Volkswagen called it quits. That makes this vehicle even more rare since they manufactured the last stick shift Beetle in 2015. You would own a piece of history."

"You said that already, Dave," she reprimanded, a bold characteristic that seemingly came out of nowhere and surprised her. "But what I really need to know is how much will this *piece of history* cost me?"

"I can have you in it today for fourteen-five plus tax, title, and license."

At a stoplight, she pressed the convertible button. There was a mechanical whirring noise as the top folded in on itself and settled on the back of the back seat. The sun felt delicious and warm on the crown of her head. With a little gleeful whoop, Katie slammed down the gas and shifted to first gear, then second, then third, then fourth, as the wind whipped her hair into a frenzy. She glanced over at Dave's wispier comb over, flopping in the breeze, stifling a giggle. His thick hand clutched the handle of the door and his feet braced on the floorboards while she flew through traffic on the freeway.

Back at the dealership, she filled out the paperwork, negotiated an incredible deal on her trade-in, and drove it off the lot an hour and a half later. When she got back to her house, she smiled when she saw Callie's car parked in the third stall.

Katie walked inside the house breathless and wind-blown, humming to herself.

"Hey, Mamacita!" Callie said warmly as she walked toward Katie with her skinny arms outstretched. Dressed in a sundress and pink Converse shoes, from their gene pool, Callie came out a clear winner. She inherited Jeff's creamy skin that contrasted perfectly with her mom's raven black hair and emerald eyes that were lined and framed by dark lashes. Her long, straight hair was parted in the middle and hung down her back. "What have you been up to? You look windblown and red-cheeked."

"Hey, sweets," Katie said, enjoying the hug. "I was just doing a little shopping." She pulled back with a wink and hiked a thumb to the driveway where the beetle sat parked.

"No way!" Callie shrieked. "I've always wanted one of those. Can I drive it?"

Katie shook her head at her daughter's blatant audacity. "Can you at least let the new car smell dissipate a little before asking me that?"

Callie laughed the rejection off with her straight and perfect smile, the result of four years of braces and head-gear. "That's not like you."

Katie pursed her lips together, wondering out loud, "So, what *am* I like?" It was a strange question, and one she had never considered before.

"Predictable and boring." Callie laughed. "No offense, Mom, but you're a rule follower."

"Oh, yeah?" Katie felt the challenge rise in her chest. "Maybe I'm turning over a new leaf. Maybe it's time for a new set of rules."

Callie's eyes widened, and she glanced from side to

side. "Who *are* you and what have you done with my mother?"

"After surviving raising your brother, don't you think I deserve a little something special?"

Callie's hands and eyebrows raised in unison. "You got me there. Beckett cleared the way for me. As long as I didn't light the house on fire or come home high, I was golden."

"You weren't perfect either, sweetheart. Your dad and I aren't stupid. I know it's impossible to believe, but we were young once, too," Katie mused.

"Mom, you're practically an antique."

"I prefer vintage," Katie corrected. "I'm like a fine wine."

Callie rolled her eyes and opened the fridge, then pulled out a Tupperware dish of leftover lasagna and popped it into the microwave.

"Just coming to fuel up, or did you miss me?" Katie asked.

"A little of both," Callie answered with a grin. "Summer school has been brutal."

"You're getting close to the end, sweetheart. Graduation is only a year away. I'm so proud of you."

The corners of Callie's mouth turned up in a smile. "Thanks. It's hard to believe, after next year, I won't have to register for classes ever again or spend a fortune on overpriced textbooks that I can't resell."

"It truly is the end of an era," Katie agreed as tears welled up at her lashes.

"Mommmm." Callie walked toward her and hugged her tight. "Awww. You're such a softie. I love you."

"Love you, too," Katie repeated and then swiped at the tear that raced down her cheek.

"It's good to see you treat yourself," Callie said. "You sacrificed so much for us when we were growing up. I don't know how you did it. Raising kids is so exhausting, I don't think I want any," she teased.

"What?" Katie exclaimed. "You promised me *seven* grandchildren." She walked to the bookcase and plucked out a faded notebook and filed to a page in a handwritten journal Callie had created in kindergarten. One large stick figure was surrounded by a set of seven crudely drawn smaller stick figures. The words at the top Katie read aloud, "When I grow up I want to be," she paused for emphasis, "a mother."

"Mom, I was *five* years old."

"It's still legally binding," Katie exclaimed. "This is an agreement in writing. I think it will hold up in court."

Callie shook her head and then grinned as the solution appeared. "Dad will help me wiggle out of it."

Her off-handed comment was a stab to the heart. Against all odds, Jefferson Beaumont was becoming a halfway decent criminal defense attorney in Saint Petersburg, Florida. His morally flexible reputation was legendary and attracted the toughest cases from the guiltiest criminals, some rumored to have ties to the mob. His billable hours from the Gabriano family alone helped them build their dream home in Aura Cove.

"Your dad is good at that," Katie turned away and agreed. Emotions had a way of displaying in her eyes and on her face. She wasn't ready for the kids to know. She had a lot of things to do before that revelation would be made. It would devastate their lives. The façade of the picture-perfect family Jeff insisted on and Katie worked to provide was about to come crashing down on all of them, and she wasn't ready to burst the idealistic happy little family bubble quite yet.

THREE

Later that evening, the sunset cast warm light into the sunroom that flooded into the kitchen, where Frankie was mixing up a very special batch of martinis. Made with a shot of Dulcolax, she added the lid to the stainless steel tumbler. Frankie had shaken, not stirred the ingredients together, then poured the cloudy mixture into a glass. Katie fished out an olive from the jar and dropped it in, having second thoughts.

"Don't worry, the olive brine will mask the flavor," Frankie explained with a wicked grin, adding another splash of it to the glass. She was tall and thin with a shock of fire-red, frizzy hair laced with more glittering white stands each year. No matter what she ate or drank, it never affected her thin frame. Her blue eyes were bright in her face and her cheeks speckled with freckles.

Katie's shoulders stiffened when she got a notification that the garage door was opening. She exhaled and then plastered on a tight smile, praying it looked natural.

"It's showtime!" Frankie cheered, her eyes glittering

with mischief as she handed Katie the martini glass she'd prepared with a wink. "Bottoms up, Jeffy."

"Who's car is that in the driveway?" Jeff asked, coming through the door with his briefcase and carelessly dropped it and his keys on top of the cabinet in the entryway. He extended one hand toward his wife and snapped his fingers at her impatiently, ignoring Frankie's presence completely. An act that made Katie's blood boil and chased away any second thoughts she had.

"Mine," Katie pushed away the irritation and purred sweetly, placing the martini glass in his hand like she always did. Enjoying a couple of drinks with dinner had become their Friday night custom since law school. It used to be the cheapest rotgut vodka they could afford with garish pimento olives floating in a sea of bitterness, but over the years, they had graduated to the good stuff—Grey Goose and blue cheese-studded artisanal olives. Knowing this martini was a little different, Katie counted on Jeff's propensity to gulp his first one down. He didn't disappoint, draining the glass in one long, bitter swallow.

"Did you do something different?"

"No. I've been using the same recipe for years, darling," she answered, crinkling her forehead in forced concentration. Frankie pinched her lips together as her eyes darted over to lock on Katie's.

"Are you sure? It tasted a little funky," he remarked with a scowl as he smacked his lips and tongue together, trying to decipher what was different. Then he raised the glass, indicating Katie should rush over for a refill like she was bar staff at a posh wedding. Absentmindedly, he tugged at the Windsor knot at his throat. His teeth were impossibly white in his deeply tanned face and his skin was smooth and unlined, the product of his bi-monthly visits to the Botox fairy. As he aged, he was still attractive at a distance, but when you got closer, there was a plastic quality that made him look like he was trying too hard.

"I'm so sorry, sweetheart," Katie gushed her apology as she walked across the travertine floor to take his glass. "Let me make you a fresh one. Why don't you change into something more comfortable and I'll bring it right over to you."

"You read my mind." Jeff shrugged out of his electric blue suit jacket, revealing a flashy paisley shirt with French cuffs and cufflinks as he walked into their bedroom.

"Well, my work here is done," Frankie whispered to Katie as she looked at her watch. "In about thirty minutes, Jeff's night is going to get really shitty." She cackled at her own joke.

"I can't believe I let you talk me into doing this," Katie murmured.

"*You* didn't do anything," Frankie offered. "You're still riding on the high road. I, however, am not, and I'm totally okay with that." She opened the door and called out over her shoulder, "Text me when it kicks in! I'm going to need the play-by-play."

Katie laughed at her audacity. "Okay, fine, but I'm drawing the line on video."

"Buzzkill." Frankie laughed, then pulled the door shut behind her as Katie made Jeff a fresh drink.

"Did you take my gray Armani to the dry cleaner like I asked today?" Jeff's voice rang out from their closet.

Katie pinched her lips together to stop a wicked grin from escaping, envisioning the garbage bag filled with pieces of it currently inside the trunk of her new car. "Of course, dear, I know your routine. I know how you like to have it ready for court on Tuesdays. It's your lucky charm. I wouldn't dare forget."

"Of course, you wouldn't." He came back into the kitchen and leaned in for a perfunctory kiss, his lips tight and unyielding. She felt a surge of heat, a tingle of strange déjà vu, and in her mind, the image of a woman flickered.

Confused, she fanned herself with a kitchen towel. Now that she was knocking on the door to fifty, she'd experienced a couple of hot flashes. They always popped up out of nowhere, leaving her sweaty and flushed.

While his back was turned, she wiped his kiss from her mouth with the back of her hand in disgust. Jeff settled into his favorite leather recliner a few moments later, and Katie scurried over to him with his drink and a coaster the minute he sat down. Holding up the remote, he rifled through Sports Center, stopping at an advertisement for the big pay-per-view fight.

"So, let's circle back to the car?" he began from his post in front of the television. He kicked the footrest back in and sat forward to make his case against it.

"What about it?"

"It's a little juvenile, don't you think?"

"I've always wanted one. The kids are gone now and we can afford it, so what's the harm?" Katie pressed.

"Because you're almost *fifty*. A Volkswagen bug is far more appropriate for a college student or a hitchhiker in the seventies. Jesus, Katie, it's ridiculous."

Not as ridiculous as the glowing shade of white your teeth currently are. Ross has nothing on you. Or that paisley dress shirt. Now that's ridiculous.

He sipped thoughtfully at the second drink, distracted again by swiping through texts on his phone. "This one is much better. Looks like you're not a total disaster in the kitchen after all." His snarky comment normally would have rolled off her, but now she was observing each interaction with fresh eyes. The rose-colored glasses had been stripped away, and she was hyperaware of the derogatory words he chose. For years, her day-to-day life with him had required a certain amount of sleep walking. She had tuned out and focused on raising the kids while he strained to achieve, but the receipt had woken her up. It took every ounce of her freshly discovered willpower to bite back the comments she yearned to unleash.

She glanced around their beautiful home. Her gaze lingered on the marble countertops and crisp white cabinets she'd chosen with their builder during the remodel just last year. Every decision she agonized over, finally being given the opportunity to design her dream kitchen from the flooring up. Katie loved to cook, and the appliances cost a small fortune, but every time she turned the burner and the gas crackled to life on her Viking range, it gave her complete satisfaction. She researched them for six months before finally making a decision. Jeff didn't care about the functionality, he just wanted it to look like one of the showplace kitchens featured in *Architectural Digest.* A kitchen in a magnificent home that was fitting for a successful man, an up-and-comer like Jefferson

Beaumont. In his world, appearances mattered. They reinforced the image he strived to maintain.

Jeff reclined again with his feet up, engrossed in his phone that was never farther than arm's reach away. Clients called night and day, and at five hundred dollars an hour, he took every call. His dark hair turned prematurely silver, and over the last year, after a lengthy consultation with a twenty-something image consultant, she convinced him to wear it longer. His dark glasses and dark brown eyes still turned heads. The result was a carefully curated plan to look trendy yet educated, with the glasses adding a few bonus points to his IQ by design.

"Look, I'm not opposed to you getting a new car, but why don't you go see my guy at the Lexus dealership?"

"Because I don't want a Lexus," Katie argued.

He quietly stood and brought his empty glass to her for another refill. Standing with the massive marble island between them, his expression turned puzzled. He wasn't used to Katie disagreeing with him. He cocked his head to one side, studying her, and she felt her pulse quicken at her throat.

Careful. Keep him completely in the dark while you get your ducks in a row.

Changing tactics, she sidled up to him with his third martini, her voice like warm honey. "Can I keep it?" She forced herself to kiss his neck to butter him up. Twenty-six years with Jefferson Beaumont taught her that most arguments could be solved with a little sugar.

He murmured and closed his eyes while she stroked him below.

"You would be my hero," Katie cooed while fighting

the urge to vomit, knowing those were the secret words that fed his ego the most.

"If it means that much to you. I'll allow it."

She wanted to spit the words back at him.

I'll allow it? Who does he think he is? He doesn't get to allow me anything.

The fury built in her belly. For the first time in a very long time, she felt the fire, the burning need to stand up for herself and fight. Neglected embers in her marriage had been smoldering for a very long time, and the hotel receipt had become a flashpoint. The point of origin that would combust it all. Fire could be cleansing, though. Burning her current life to the ground so something new could begin was oddly freeing. She turned away to hide her expression and pulled out a cutting board. Keeping him in the dark was crucial right now.

Katie pulled steaks from the refrigerator to let them come to room temperature before grilling them. She glanced at her watch and hummed as she seasoned the marbled ribeyes with salt and pepper.

Ten more minutes.

Right on cue, across the room, she heard Jeff's belly rumble for the first time.

"Whoa," Jeff declared. "Did you hear that?"

"Hear what?" she asked sweetly, pressing her lips together to keep the grin from spreading across her face.

Another loud burbling sound shot out, and she heard a loud fart muffled in the recliner's leather. Jeff bucked forward and forced the footrest down, his arms wrapped around his belly.

Another low gurgling noise with a high-pitched squeal

was emitted from him. She saw a light sheen of sweat bead up on his forehead. Two minutes later, he popped up from the chair and ran to their ensuite bathroom. Katie raised her glass of red to his retreating form and sipped at it with a knowing smile. She tapped out a quick text to Frankie: "Mission Accomplished" with three poop emojis.

She walked to the closed door, the slight scent of poo wrinkling her nose, and rapped softly with her knuckles.

"Are you okay in there, sweetheart?"

He groaned in agony. "I had a bad feeling about that food truck. Mexicans. Probably illegals."

Katie rolled her eyes, feeling guilty he was using his natural default—racist rhetoric to explain away his weak stomach.

"Oh no!" he cried out as she heard loud splashes from his watery bowels and had to clamp her hand over her mouth to stop from squealing with delight.

"You eat without me. I think I might be in here a while," he shouted through the door. She heard more loud dumping noises as diarrhea hit the water while Jeff cried out and the stench intensified. "Oh, God!"

"Oh no! You poor thing," Katie cooed. "I'll make you a nice bowl of bone broth." She turned on her heel and bounced out of the room.

As she retreated, she heard him cry, "Oh God, here we go again."

She ran on stockinged feet to the patio door at the other end of the house and collapsed on the patio furniture. The waterfall in the pool and the fountain ringed by palm trees gurgled loudly nearby, covering the sound of her shrieking hysterics. Katie rolled forward and gripped her stomach while tears ran down her face. It took a full five minutes to get herself under control enough to return to the kitchen for the steaks.

"Looks like tonight is your lucky night, Arlo! Tonight we feast like kings!" At the sound of his name, he jumped down from the couch and followed her out onto the deck. There, he promptly circled three times, then plopped down on the rug in front of the door, enthralled by the scent of fire-roasted meat.

She burst into more laughter, her stomach shaking and abdominal muscles strained and tensed. Squealing and laughing hysterically, she gasped for breath. Her cheeks tingled and were tight from laughing for so long, and her side ached. She crossed her legs and grabbed her crotch. You could never trust the Kegel muscles of a woman who'd birthed three children.

FOUR

orcing herself not to disrupt their normal routine and arouse suspicion, it took every ounce of determination and a couple of extra glasses of wine to crawl into their marital bed that week and sleep next to him. Katie had inched to the edge, thankful for the vast real estate of the California king. Hovering on the edge of the mattress, the thought of touching him made her recoil. She yanked the blanket toward herself and hugged it to her chest, understanding it was the symbolic first of many battles they would have in the near future.

Unable to settle enough to rest, she rolled over and studied him while he slept, his mouth open and snoring softly. His face softened in slumber, his jaw slack. The crow's feet at his eyes traced faint fine lines down his cheeks, and after studying the face of the man sleeping next to her she'd loved for most of her adult life, she was surprised her heart felt empty and hollow. There was no sad, sentimental tug of her heart toward his, and the revelation stunned her. When had it stopped? She couldn't pinpoint the exact moment when things shifted, but somewhere between the raising of the kids and the building of his career, there was a disconnect. Now she felt like he was a stranger sleeping in their bed as she tossed and turned next to him.

At Frankie's urging, she'd called and gotten a consultation with Davina Thorne. She'd been proud of herself initially when she made the appointment. She was finally being proactive, but as the hours melted away in the darkness of that long night, her stomach knotted up. It would be a dirty, no holds barred fight to the bitter end. That much was certain. She'd suffered through enough of his post-mortems on big cases to know there wasn't much Jeff wasn't willing to do to win.

She rolled onto her back, and after another hour of staring at the ceiling while he snored next to her, she downed a couple extra melatonin to help herself finally drift off to sleep. When she woke up the next morning, thankfully, Jeff was already gone. The sun was high in the sky as Katie sat on their deck overlooking the strip of ocean that had initially sold her on the property. It was about as far as they could get from their shabby law school apartment. For Jeff, owning a beachfront home was another jewel in his crown. An outward sign of his financial success. For Katie, it was more spiritual than that. The ocean called to her from their very first visit. Staring out at the vastness of it, and the constant rise and swell of the waves, it was a gentle reminder that life goes on and she was but a grain of sand in the world. Most mornings, after enjoying two cups of coffee on the veranda, she would walk Arlo barefoot on the sugary sand. Today, she didn't have the luxury of time.

Sitting under an umbrella on the patio, she sipped a cup of coffee to shake the last vestiges of grogginess. The Florida humidity was already climbing and curling her wavy hair. As she sipped, she focused on her meeting at ten. Katie sighed. It was the first step in what she knew would be a long and contentious court battle. The only redeeming factor was the kids were over eighteen, so she wouldn't have to fight Jeff for custody.

In her closet, Katie changed clothes four times before deciding on a pair of dark jeans, a sunny yellow cardigan, and a pair of gray heels. She only wore heels when she was heading into battle. Adding three extra inches to her height usually added three extra inches to her confidence level, and she knew she needed it today.

It was a short twenty-minute drive into the heart of downtown St. Petersburg, and she eased the bug into a parking spot in front of the office. Posh shops and eateries were tucked between towering high rises. Behemoth glass and metal structures rose high into the bright blue sky dotted with clouds. At the end of the street was a park that overlooked a marina where sailboats and other seafaring vessels floated on expansive docks, waiting for their masters to return.

She glanced at her reflection in the mirror and tried to smooth her hair, which had frizzed up from the humidity of the warm morning, and got out of the car. Once on the sidewalk, her heel got stuck between two stone pavers and she lurched forward, losing her balance, and fell down to her hands and knees. Red-faced, she popped up quickly and glanced around, relieved that no one had seen her stumble. She didn't notice the woman with the long white hair across the street.

After a short ride to the eleventh floor in an elevator, she was seated on a low-slung sofa for a brief wait in a bright, monochrome lobby filled with plants and modern art. A few minutes later, a twenty-something with a chignon and a pencil skirt led her into a sleek, white oak-trimmed office. The wood grain was bleached and bright, and it was as far removed from the good ole boys' dark mahogany and tufted black leather that Jeff's firm favored. The assistant beckoned to an acrylic ghost chair that sat in front of an immaculate desk.

"Tell him either he is forthcoming with the information from all of his accounts by the end of business tomorrow, or we subpoena his records. We both know your client isn't as squeaky clean as he pretends to be," a throaty, aggressive female voice boomed from behind a chair that was swiveled toward the window. "Judge Mathis will rip his balls off and shove them down his throat. She isn't as lenient as others on the bench with men who hide assets." Katie heard a garbled response on the other end that she quickly cut off. "Cut the shit, Jack. We know about the Caymans."

Katie clutched at her necklace to center it and tried to calm her nerves, patiently waiting for the conversation to end. She glanced around the room, seeing no family photos or cut flowers. Modern and clean, Davina apparently favored a glass and iron aesthetic with layers of plants all bathed in beautiful light flooding in from the wall of windows behind the desk.

"We will not sit idly by while you lie to our faces. You either hand over the information we requested or my forensic accountant will get started and we will file an order to bill your client for his services. A word of warning, though, he's *very* thorough."

Her timbre was dominating and strong, with a drill sergeant's harshness. In a lower register, it demanded respect, and Katie had to admit Frankie was right. This was exactly the kind of tigress she needed in her corner. She knew Jeff had a stable of attorneys on speed dial used to twisting the truth for their own gain. Rallying around one of their own was one of their favorite pastimes. More than once, Jeff had gleefully recounted one of his colleagues' messy divorces, chronicling how they had twisted the law as far as they could without breaking it. Their strategy was to financially ruin and cut off the wife until she was forced to take a lower settlement. The first burst of fear bubbled up, and Katie tamped it down, smoothing the front of her cardigan while she waited.

"Look, your client has twenty-four hours to turn over the records or I'll move for an emergency hearing. We're done here."

The conversation ended abruptly, and the chair swiveled toward Katie. Without skipping a beat, she opened a file on her desk and quickly glanced at it. "Katie Beaumont?" She rose and offered a well-manicured hand with blood-red fingernails. "I'm Davina. Tell me how I can help you today."

"Well, I think I need a divorce."

"You *think* you need one?" Her head cocked to the side and her dark eyes drilled into Katie's. The intense scrutiny of the other woman made her shift uncomfortably in the seat. "By the time you get to me, you'd better know." She sat back down, leaning into the cream leather chair, and waited for Katie to continue, her eyes narrowing. Katie felt vulnerable. Being studied by an intelligent woman was like being under a microscope. All of her flaws would be easily discovered and cataloged, and Katie felt her confidence melt away.

Finally, finding her voice again, she squeaked out, "I do. I need one," Katie corrected and cleared her throat, continuing, "My husband...he's an attorney."

At that news, Davina's bored, ambivalent expression morphed into legitimate interest. Smelling blood on the water, her ears perked up, and she leaned closer to Katie, resting on her forearms.

"Beaumont?" Her gaze flicked to the ceiling as she turned the name over in her mind, searching for familiarity. She folded her hands together, deep in thought, then seconds later bolted upright in the chair and added, "As in Lewis, Garfunkel, and Beaumont?"

"Yes," Katie confirmed evenly.

"Okay, well, now you have my full attention." She opened a file and flipped open a yellow legal pad. "Give me the details."

"He's been unfaith..."

"Irrelevant!" Davina interrupted as she scribbled notes, and Katie jumped. "Florida is a no-fault state."

"Okay." Katie looked down at her three-inch heels and damned them for pinching her toes and over-promising and under-delivering a sense of confidence. Everything about Davina Thorne was sharp and severe. Her blonde hair was carved into a straight asymmetrical bob, the edge of which looked like it could slit your wrist. Her perfectly tailored cobalt blue power suit hugged a body that spent a lot more time in the gym than Katie's had.

"Continue," she demanded, gesturing her hand in a circle, prodding Katie to speed things up. "Are there children involved?"

"No, we have three kids together, but they are all over the age of eighteen."

"Are any of them in college?"

"Yes. Our youngest, Callie."

Katie watched her scribble more notes on the yellow legal pad.

Davina's eyes bored into hers, assessing and judging. "Let me guess, he controls the checkbook, pays all the bills."

"Actually, no, I've been handling our finances since we were married." Katie sat taller in her chair. "With the exception of the secret credit card I just found out about, I have the passwords and all the information about all of our accounts."

Davina's scarlet red lips pursed, and she nodded, biting the inside of her cheek, then blurted, "Hmm. I'm surprised."

"Ouch," Katie admitted with a wry smile, trying to make her frustration known using her most effective coping mechanism: humor.

Davina's thin lips turned up at the corners slightly at the joke. Her brown eyes drilled into Katie's again relentlessly.

"You're going to need to develop a thicker skin if you

are going to survive this. In my experience, things can go nuclear in a split second." She snapped her bony fingers together, producing a sharp popping noise. "Is he aware of your intentions?"

"Not yet."

"My advice is to keep it that way for now. Keep him completely in the dark while you get your affairs in order."

"Double ouch," Katie joked again, self-deprecatingly, hoping to see Davina's lips crack with another smile, but Davina remained stoic.

"I guess that *was* a poor choice of words," she admitted, then slammed the cap back on her writing instrument and set it down with authority. Davina stood and walked to the front of her desk and leaned against it with her arms crisscrossed on her chest, her red talons drumming against her arm. Gold Jimmie Choos covered her dainty feet.

"I can see that you're a nice person," she started explaining.

Her words didn't feel like a compliment to Katie. They stung.

"However, I am not," Davina admitted with a wicked smile. "Nice impedes being effective. I blame our parents' generation for raising women to be weak, always deferring to men for approval. No one likes me, and I take it as a compliment." She flashed another smile that held a hint of sadness, then assessed Katie again. "I refuse to hold my clients' hands and baby them through the process. If you need someone to do that for you, look elsewhere."

Her blatant honesty was refreshing. Katie had never been in the presence of such a brash woman before, and she felt her fears dissipate in the presence of Davina's animalistic female power.

"However…" She paused, then continued with a confident smirk, "I win settlements faster and for more money than any other divorce attorney in the Tampa Bay area," she boldly claimed as Katie nodded.

"My retainer is ten grand. To be honest, it's hard to tell how this one will go. Likely, he will fight us every step of the way, and as a result, it could deplete significant joint assets. I don't want you to go into this without knowing that fact. We will be systematically destroying the life you took decades to build. There is a chance at the end of this, the only asset that will remain is your freedom. Is that going to be enough?" Davina's eyes flashed, and dread filled Katie's belly. She'd never thought that far. The idea of dismantling the life she fought so hard to build and coming out the other end with nothing at fifty was hard to swallow. Katie fought through the fear and knew she had no other choice.

"If you want to move forward, I will have my assistant prepare the letter of engagement, and we can file as soon as the end of the week."

The speed startled Katie. The fact that she could destroy twenty-six years of marriage in a matter of days was a difficult concept to fathom. Katie swallowed hard against the lump forming in her throat. Tears welled up in her eyes, and she balled her fists to stop them from falling.

"Stop that," Davina blurted so abruptly it shocked Katie into compliance. She softened her tone. "I can guarantee he did not shed a single tear while chasing his bright, new, shiny thing around the office."

"How'd you know?"

"With attorneys, it's about proximity and opportunity. Let me guess, his legal secretary?" Katie nodded silently and Davina continued, "it's time to get into barracuda mode. Do you have one of those?"

She shook her head wryly. "Nope. That's why my best friend told me to call you."

"You've made the right decision. I'm not going to sugarcoat it for you. I will always tell you the truth, even when you don't want to hear it."

"That's why I need you."

"Divorce brings out the worst in people," she continued. "You are going to see and hear things that will crush your soul and have you questioning your ability to make good decisions. I am here to wage the battle while you are emotionally processing the end of what you thought would be a lifelong relationship. I will work my ass off to guarantee you are fairly compensated for all the sacrifices you made along the way. Your efforts to take care of him and to raise your children were not for nothing. That is what I will do for you. I will not stop until you receive a fair return on the investment you made in Jefferson Beaumont."

Katie took a deep breath and nodded. Normally, she liked to sleep on big decisions and employed a twenty-four-hour rule, but Davina Thorne was solid and her gut said she was the one. Her intuition had become a tiny voice inside her, dampened by years of settling. It was always accurate, but over the years she'd tuned it out, this time she decided to tune in.

"Where do I sign?" Katie asked. Her hand shook as she

quickly scrawled her signature on the contract and on a check for the retainer, glad that Jeff didn't keep a close eye on their joint finances. There was a small measure of peace found at the moment of decision. Instead of second-guessing and ruminating about her options, she leapt forward, feeling a tiny burst of pride in her ability to make a bold decision in her life and it was addictive.

FIVE

I t was tedious: the wigs, the colored contacts, and the disguises required to slip back into the general public and out of the celebrity limelight the woman was accustomed to, but it was a game she'd become very adept at playing. While she *could* change her hair color or eye color with a snap of her fingers, the use of magic took a toll and wore her out physically. It was far easier to employ cheap tactics and dress up to move among the ordins without detection. Wearing non-descript colors and blending in, she would force her instantly recognizable shock of white hair into a cap and then top her head with a wig, usually a mousy brown one. A color that was unremarkable in every single way.

The woman had already lived a hundred and thirty-five years and was forced to conceal her longevity. Ordins were dreadfully mundane with tiny minds that couldn't handle the truth. To protect her secrets, she had carefully dissected her life into two distinct lifetimes. There was a clear-cut before and after. During her first lifetime, her aristocratic father had given her the birth name Zoya, but after her awakening when her second lifetime began, she was compelled to reinvent herself again and claim a new name.

Getting older? That part was easy. Outliving the ones you love? That was the hard part. The embittered loneliness was like living in a bubble, and she found it helped to find ways to distract herself.

She pulled the golden handle of the glass door to the swanky new bar she'd read about and walked in, finding a single open seat at the end of the very full bar. She drummed her gloved fingers impatiently on the dark wood as she watched the lone bartender run from patron to patron, consumed with pouring beer and shaking up mixed drinks. Annoyed by the crowd that kept him at bay, she flicked her fingers toward the door, and instantly, the bar began to clear out.

Her latest distraction had skin that was a deep caramel color, a shade she couldn't resist since it was deliciously taboo in her early teens. She eyed him as he poured an amber-colored liquid into a glass and then lit it on fire. His jawline was chiseled with an impeccably groomed beard, and she felt a gathering of energy between her legs.

Yes. This one would do.

"What can I make for you?" His question oozed warmth and flirtatiousness when he finally landed at her end of the bar. Her eyes drank in his full lips, and she felt a familiar fluttering as the energy surged out toward her limbs.

"Vodka gimlet?" She beamed at him with a bright smile.

"Coming," he said with a wink, and her lips quirked upward.

"Not yet, you aren't," she quipped and was rewarded with a flash of white from his sexy smile. Like taking candy from a baby, it was almost too easy. Zoya usually preferred a bit of a chase, but tonight was all about scratching an itch.

"The key to an outstanding vodka gimlet is the finest vodka and fresh limes," he instructed as his eyes locked on hers again. Pouring two ounces into the shaker, he placed the lid on the top and shook it cradled in his long, capable fingers. She leaned forward, savoring the sight of his eyes lowering and lingering on her bust line. Through the decades, men's fervent adoration toward décolletage never wavered. She counted on it. They were a tiresome lot—all of them—though not without their redeeming qualities between the sheets.

She tugged on the fingers of her black satin glove and dropped it into her lap, looking him up and down appreciatively, sizing him up like a rarity at an auction. Enjoying the way his tuxedo pants curved around his trim waist and fuller hips, her thorough once-over made her unabashedly lick her lips in anticipation, like a tigress before feeding time. He was delicious.

He offered the drink to her, and her fingers lingered, brushing against his. She felt the jolt first and then closed her eyes to receive the message. Her long lashes fluttered in response, and time froze. Flashes like lightning pulsed into her brain. It was always a puzzle, translating the images she received into useful information.

Handcuffs. A dog. A motorcycle. A heart monitor. 377.

What a pity.

She sipped at the gimlet, dipping her chin in a way she discovered in her late teens was irresistible to the male species. Not bad. He had a few useful skills. Maybe he could be a wonderful plaything, a fun little dalliance to pass the time as she waited for Katia's fiftieth birthday to arrive.

"You're not from around here, are you?" the bartender asked, flashing a stupid grin that she couldn't deny probably worked for him ninety-nine percent of the time. His hazel eyes with green flecks were gorgeous beacons, bright in his dark face.

"I'm from everywhere and nowhere," she answered. It was the truth, a quality she leaned on infrequently. People didn't want the truth. They wanted a fairytale, and she was good at playing along. His smile was genuine, with teeth that were white and straight. She shivered, remembering the days before orthodontia, where you were at the mercy of genetics and, much like choosing thoroughbred horses, you needed to get a good look at gums before signing on the dotted line.

"Ah, a worldly woman of mystery," he complimented her earnestly, and it made her heart quicken. The sweetness of youth, like a peach that was ripened on the tree one moment, then wrinkled the next. But he wouldn't make it that far. He would be forever young. "What's your name, beautiful?"

"Zoya," she responded using her long-abandoned birth name, as she often did when she met anyone with fewer than five hundred days left to live.

"Your accent?" He hemmed and hawed. "It is Russian?"

She spat on the ground in disgust, and his eyebrows waggled. "Ukrainian." She sipped again and enjoyed the way his button-down shirt pulled at the buttons when he flexed. Zoya batted her eyelashes at him. It really was so easy. Child's play, you might call it, and this was a beautiful man-child.

Six

A few days later, after sharing a bottle of wine with Frankie, the truth was starting to set in.

"I feel like such an idiot," Katie admitted.

"Stop it. You were an amazing wife to a man who didn't appreciate it. You will be better off when this is all over."

"I know, but right now, it hurts."

"You know what always makes me feel better?" Frankie said as her blue eyes crackled with mischief and her eyebrows waggled up and down. "A little revenge." She pulled out her laptop and Goggled. "How to make your ex-husband miserable." Reading for a long minute, she said, "Eureka! I think I've found it."

She turned her laptop to face Katie where, on the screen, a basic black website screamed, "Don't accept cheap Chinese knockoffs! Liquid Ass is made in America!" Frankie turned it back toward herself. "Seems kind of fitting, doesn't it? Liquid ass for a real asshole?"

"What is it?" Katie's nose wrinkled and her lips

twisted up in a grimace. Frankie was a little rough around the edges, but unabashedly herself and one of the most honest people Katie had ever met. Jeff called her white trash and a host of other derogatory names Katie would never repeat. Not because it would hurt Frankie's feelings, but because it hurt her own.

Frankie read aloud again, "Liquid Ass is a foul and overwhelming funny prank product. Once unleashed, this power-packed, super–concentrated liquid evaporates, filling the air with a genuine, foul butt–crack smell with hints of dead animal and fresh poo. Each spray of this soul-shattering liquid summons the ass genie to manhandle your senses." She looked at Katie over the top of her reading glasses, snickering as her lips moved while she read to herself and then dissolved into a pile of giggles as she read aloud again.

"The testimonials are gold. Listen to this. After six months of hearing the teenager who lived in the apartment above me shout obscenities into his Bluetooth headset until three am, I was exhausted and desperate to find a solution. I tried talking to the little prick and his crappy parents, but nothing ever got accomplished. Enter Liquid Ass. I drilled a few holes in the ceiling's perimeter and shoved Q-Tips dipped in the foul liquid up into his bedroom, and I sprayed it into the vents three times a day for an entire week. The stench was so foul, I had to stay at a friend's house. While this plan required time and dedication, I'm pleased to report the screaming stopped the first day and, after only a month, his family broke their lease and moved out."

"Wow. That seems pretty extreme," Katie argued. "Do

people really do things like that?" She was in shock. "It seems a little juvenile."

Frankie continued, undeterred. "Lucky for you, your best friend has the same immature thirst for revenge as a teenage boy." She thought for a moment. "How about the Beamer?" Frankie offered with a sly grin. "I was thinking a little squirt into the air vents, or maybe under the seats? Let it marinate all day in the sweltering summer heat? That's it, I've decided for you. We're ordering a bottle."

Katie laughed, then admitted, "He does love that car more than he ever loved me."

"You leave it up to me." Frankie pulled out her credit card and punched the digits in. "I'll take care of every-thing. I'll drive down the dark roads of juvenile retribution while you continue to ride tall on the high road. He won't know what hit him." She snickered with glee as she finished the purchase.

Katie sipped on her wine and then laughed at herself when fresh tears welled up at her lashes. She swiped them away. "Sorry, Frank, I'm all over the place."

"No apologies necessary. Jefferson never knew what a gem he had," Frankie consoled, giving her friend a squeeze. "What else can we do to make his life as painful as yours is right now?"

Katie thought it over and then got a flash of inspira-tion. "Oh! I've got an idea. How about we set up an ad on Craigslist for free labradoodle puppies that rings direct to the unlisted number he only gives out to high-profile clients?"

"Now that's the spirit!" Frankie encouraged her while

opening a fresh bottle of wine. Katie took over the laptop and started to create a listing:

Free Labradoodle Puppies. Four females and six males. Homes must provide a safe, fenced yard and lots of love. Call to tell us your story and bring home your next fur baby!

She snorted with glee as she punched in Jeff's private number. The one that bypassed his secretary and assistants and rang directly to him, twenty-four hours a day, seven days a week.

An hour later, at six pm, she was shocked to see the notification he was parking in the garage.

"He's home," Katie groaned.

"What a buzzkill." Frankie quickly popped up off the chair to dispose of the empty wine bottle. A few minutes later, a clearly agitated Jeff walked into the house with the phone cradled between his shoulder and his ear.

"Where did you get this number?" he demanded. Then a few seconds later, "No, I don't have any labradoodle puppies."

He pushed the button to hang up the call, and it rang again.

"Jefferson Beaumont." His tone held every speck of pretentiousness a name like Jefferson Beaumont could hold.

"What? No! I don't have any labradoodle puppies." His voice trailed off as he walked into the master bedroom to change clothing.

Katie's eyes met Frankie's wide ones and held. She

pulled her into the pantry, where they shut the door and then dissolved into a fit of repressed giggles. Clamping hands over their mouths to stop the sound from escaping, they inhaled deep breaths through their nose. After two long minutes, a new incoming call set them off again. They shook with laughter, stitches ripping up their sides. Frankie held up her hand and Katie high-fived her as another phone call pealed just outside the pantry door and a frustrated Jeff answered.

"You're going to make me pee," Frankie whispered, and then another round of fresh giggles made tears run down both their faces. "I know your birthday is coming up, but damn, this feels like it's a present for both of us."

Four more calls later, they heard him demand, "Where did you get this number?"

"Katie!" His barking anger cut through their glee, sobering them up instantly.

"That is my cue to leave." Frankie said, "But don't you feel just a tiny bit better?"

"I do." Katie nodded with a smile that made Frankie grin.

"We did God's work tonight."

"Katie!" The volume increased as his steps got closer. Katie quickly wiped her eyes, shook her body like a dog to release the tension, then walked Frankie out of the pantry.

"The secret is cornstarch for the softest chocolate chip...."

"Katie!" he interrupted again as the phone rang at his hip. Katie bit so hard on her lip that she tasted blood. Frankie waved as she breezed out of the house, leaving them alone in the kitchen.

Listening, she focused on his brow where a frown should furrow, but seeing it smooth and bordering on feminine was a huge turn-off. She reveled in the obvious irritation in his voice. Every time the phone would ring, she heard him give a polite introduction, followed by an angry retort, and saw a downward tug on the corners of his mouth. Over and over, she heard him slamming down the phone in-between calls, only to have to pick it up again.

"What's going on?" Katie asked sweetly.

"My phone number has apparently been published in a Craigslist ad for free labradoodle puppies. The phone's been ringing off the hook for an hour."

"Oh no!" She twisted her face up in a look she hoped read as empathic shock. "Not your *private* number!"

"Unfortunately." The phone rang again. "Jefferson Beaumont."

It rang over and over all night long, and Katie shook with repressed giggles so hard she had to get out of bed and lock herself in the bathroom. She snickered and roared with laughter as tears ran down her face. It would have been easy to just put the phone on silent, but it was also Jeff's lifeline to his high-paying clients who would make life difficult for the firm if they could not contact their attorney. The phone rang nonstop from seven pm until eleven pm every five minutes. Jeff would always answer sweetly, then morph into a hateful shrew. It was such a waste of his valuable time, and Katie struggled to contain her glee. He'd already had his secretary order a new phone number, but it would take a day to communicate it to his clients, and in the meantime, Katie delighted in his misery.

They were petty little jabs, but they helped ease the

ache and kill the pain of what the reality was. She was preparing to set off a bomb in her life. This life was a lie she'd bought into wholeheartedly, and she cursed her trusting nature. Hours after the phone had finally settled down, Katie was staring at the ceiling, stroking a sleeping Arlo's belly, ruminating in fear and worry. She knew the easy street they had been living on would soon be littered with sinkholes. It was a beautiful fakery that she didn't realize was all a charade until she found the receipt. How much more time would she have wasted if she'd never found it? Days? Months? Years? Decades?

She supposed discovering the truth was a relief. Once she got through the divorce, she could become whatever she wanted to be. Katie could start on a path of her own choosing, but where would that path lead? Where would she even begin? She'd been living on autopilot for so many years. The idea of taking the controls into her own hands was terrifying.

"I'll be fifty tomorrow, boy," she'd whispered to Arlo. "Can you believe it? I can't. The first half went so fast." Getting antsy and desperate to escape the toxicity, she slipped out of bed, threw on some clothes, grabbed her keys to the bug, and drove them down the empty streets of Aura Cove. Putting the top down, as it was still near eighty degrees in the middle of the warm summer night, she belted out the lyrics to her favorite 80s playlist as Arlo howled in the seat next to her. She felt the fear dissipate as she pulled into a parking space at her favorite place in the world, her grandmother's truffle shop on Main Street— Kandied Karma.

Back in Chicago, when Katie turned fourteen, she

worked the counter at the original Kandied Karma, the luxury chocolate boutique Yuli built after her husband passed away. It gave the old woman something to do, and within two years, her profits soared. Her truffles found their way into the homes of celebrities, thanks to a long stint on Oprah's Favorite Things list. Yuli made a serious business selling her decadent handcrafted truffles that chic restaurants and coffee shops in Chicagoland clamored to serve.

Katie's teenage summers were spent delivering truffles all over the tri-state area and waiting tables in the candy shop. Yuli was a plain, no-nonsense woman with unflappable Midwestern grit and a boxy body to match. Her white hair was often whipped into a bun at the base of her massive neck, and she'd developed a dowager hump from leaning forward too much in the kitchen. But her eyes were a rich golden hazel that noticed everything, calculating with a deep intelligence cloaked in humility. Yuli was a brilliant businesswoman whom Katie often used as a sounding board. She was proud of her Ukrainian heritage and only called Katie by her given name—Katia.

Yuli was happiest in her apron in the shop's kitchen, cranking out delectable varieties of chocolates and truffles in amaretto and dark chocolate orange flavors. Katie loved taking care of the customers. Hearing patrons exclaim, "This is just too pretty to eat!" filled Katie with pride, but Yuli would sigh and roll her eyes in irritation when they made this bold declaration but then, seconds later, bit into them anyway.

It delighted Katie when her family followed her to Florida to be near her children. Jeff called their move

suffocating, getting even more frustrated when Yuli hit the
ground running in the tourist mecca of Aura Cove. She
invested the profits from the sale of her Chicago store and
funneled them into a sunny storefront on Main Street. In
four short years, she made bank on the winter influx of
chocolate-obsessed travelers being so close to the vacation
destination, St. Pete's Beach. Katie still worked at the
counter several days a week and helped Yuli with deliveries. It wasn't the high-powered career that most women
were in pursuit of, but Katie simply loved the quality time
she got to spend with Yuli. The extra pocket money from
tips was just a bonus.

Yuli's truffles were legendary. Deep dark chocolate, as
close to black as possible, infused with botanicals and
herbs grown in her backyard. With laboratory preciseness,
Yuli measured each precious ingredient, handing it to
Katie to place into the double boiler. Yuli meticulously
hand-painted each of the forms, taking the time to create
delicate sculptures out of chocolate.

Most of the ingredients were available locally, but
some of them had to be ordered from carefully curated
shops overseas. Vanilla beans had to be ordered direct
from Madagascar. Herbs had to be ordered months in
advance from apothecaries in eastern European countries
that had more stringent quality controls on organic foods.
The shop's freezer had a special section with amber-
colored bottles methodically labeled in perfect rows. Yuli
even installed a dedicated electrical circuit to keep the
temperature optimal for her hard-to-find organic
ingredients.

That night, the shop was silent, except for the hum of

the refrigerator. Coaxing a cup of coffee from the French press, she pulled out the double boiler from the pantry and put it on the commercial Wolfe gas stove that crackled to life. In her happy place, Katie breathed in deeply, letting go the tension, and relished the sizzle and scent of browning butter. She pulled out the dropper from the exotic truffle oil and tripped over Arlo, accidentally splashing much more than the required eyedropper full into the butter.

"Oh no!" She looked down at the mixture, wondering if she should toss it out and start over. In the end, her frugality won out, and she surged ahead, adding the dark chocolate and stirring until it melted. Taking it off the heat, she added the crystallized ginger, stirring constantly to incorporate it just like Yuli had shown her. She swiped a tasting spoon through it and, after a few quick blows to cool it off, took a taste. A flush of heat surged up her torso and made her cheeks redden. She fanned her face with her hands to cool down and continued stirring.

"Can't even taste it," she said, and Arlo lay down with an exaggerated huff, bored with her already. "So good." She swirled in the heavy sweetened cream, shut off the gas, and added the amaretto liqueur. Dipping another spoon into the mixture, she tasted it again before pulling it off the stove completely to cool. She felt another blast of heat radiate from her core to her limbs, certain her proximity to the stove was the reason.

Seeking relief from the hot flash, she walked the chocolate into the blast chiller. Ten minutes later, she was cooled down and so was the chocolate. She scooped out perfect circles with her melon baller that never saw the inside of a melon. Then she dropped the creamy balls into cocoa and finely crushed almonds and set them onto parchment paper in long straight rows, humming to herself. When all the truffles were stacked in the chiller, she cleaned up the kitchen, and at four am, she and Arlo made the short drive home. When she pulled into the driveway, it surprised her to see a brightly colored box sitting on her doormat in the dark.

"A birthday present?" Katie squealed, running to pick it up. "For me?" Once inside the house, she looked at the card. It was a thick ivory cardstock attached to the box with ribbons of curly gold. In calligraphy written in Yuli's handwriting, it simply said, *"And then there were three. Taste & See."* Nestled inside the box were three truffles. The white truffle was the prettiest—aqua in color and dusted with iridescent edible powder. It looked like a mermaid and was almost too pretty to eat. The next one was a milk chocolate truffle with gold leaf filigree, and the final was a dark chocolate truffle with a decadent red cherry on top.

She made a fresh cup of coffee and set the truffles on a dessert plate, taking them out to the lanai to watch the sunrise. First, the dark navy of night lightened the sky, and then the sun broke the horizon line at the sea and cast golden light onto every surface. She picked up the white chocolate truffle and bit into its soft, creamy center. When it hit her tongue, her body rocketed forward then back as electric currents raced down her arms and to the tips of her fingers. She braced against the chair, feeling the impact of an internal explosion that left her reeling and breathless. A flush of burning heat walked up her spine, then combusted into a fire as every cell of her skin tingled.

Disoriented, she shook her head to clear it. "Whoa. That was a serious hot flash," she gasped out to Arlo, who was seated on the floor next to her, his feet tucked underneath him.

She took a bite of the milk chocolate truffle, and her torso convulsed forward again, her eyes forced shut from the intensity of the sunrise. When she finally opened her eyes, the world was brighter and more beautiful, the colors deeply saturated. She squinted from the intensity of the light, and her eyes burned as they adjusted to it. The sunrise was now in full effect, washing the sky with rich peach and earthy pink hues that sharply contrasted with the puffy white clouds and baby blues of the morning. There was a subtle glow as light raced down the lines of every object in her view and rendered a 3D quality to the world around her that made her gasp in wonder. Her heart hammered away, and her every sense was more alive. The air smelled like wet paws and the rich chocolate truffles, a conglomeration of scent so overpowering she sneezed. She shielded her eyes from the rays of the morning sun that felt like they were searing her flesh.

Katie fanned herself and struggled to gain her composure.

"Not even a biscuit? How rude!" A deep male voice she didn't recognize came from under the table and startled her.

She cocked her head intently, listening, quickly discounting what she thought she heard, and took another sip of her coffee. Her eyes darted around the lanai and pool, then rested on Arlo, who licked his mouth and began to pant.

Laughing at herself, she muttered, "I must be losing my mind." She admitted, reaching down to pat Arlo's curly head, "I swear I heard you ask me for a biscuit."

"I did!" he answered so matter-of-factly Katie jumped, staring down at Arlo's wide eyes in shock. "What?" He seemed to shrug, another strange human trait that bewildered Katie.

"You can talk?"

"Yes, silly girl," he answered, then licked his paw. Katie jumped up and ran to the pantry to grab a bully stick for him. The intensity of the disgusting scent it gave off triggered her gag reflex, and she had to pinch her nostrils together to keep it out. Bile pooled in her belly, and her mouth watered. She threw the offensive stick several feet away, and Arlo chased after it. Holding it stationary with his paws, he licked and licked for a solid minute while Katie sucked in huge gulps of fresh air to clear her sinuses. "Stop staring at me," he demanded. "I know the idea of chewing on a dried bull's penis *sounds* revolting, but trust me, it's a delicacy. Downright delectable. I can't help myself."

"Sorry." Katie averted her eyes and heard him groan with pleasure while he chewed. She picked up the remaining dark chocolate truffle and popped it into her mouth. Her teeth bit through the succulent cherry, and another whiplash sent her reeling back into the chair, leaving her weak-kneed and exhausted. "What in the world is happening to me?"

"The awakening," Arlo said half-heartedly between licks. "That's all I can tell you."

"The awakening?" Katie asked. "What is…"

The patio door swung open and silenced the rest of her question, as a freshly showered Jeff appeared, jarring Katie back to reality. "Where's my coffee?" he demanded, like she was his personal barista. A gold watch she'd never noticed before ringed his wrist. His pink-striped shirt with the pristine white cuffs was a little over the top, even for him. And the pinky ring? Puke. The only one who could pull that off was Elton John. Katie's nose wrinkled in disgust. His first three words already annoyed her.

"It's still in the pot, dear," she said sweetly, refusing to pop up like a toaster pastry and get it for him.

"What's with you this morning?" he muttered, unaccustomed to serving himself. Katie was too exhausted to move. After a long pause, he went inside and then returned a few minutes later with it. His cologne hung like an oppressive cloud around him, causing Katie to sneeze. She wriggled her nose and leaned back to get away from it, but the cologne had begun a full-on assault on her senses. There were three more sneezes in quick succession that caused Jeff to step back.

"Are you getting sick? I can't afford to get sick this week. I have opening statements tomorrow."

Katie rolled her eyes, and she swore she heard Arlo make a *humph* sound while he gnawed on the bully stick under the table. "It's your cologne. Did you have to take a bath in it?"

He ignored her question, settling into the front page of the New York Post, one of the last remnants of their previous life. She studied him as he sipped his coffee. His eyes were brighter, the crow's feet at the corner of his eyes deeper. She begrudgingly admitted he still had a magnificent head of hair. His manicured fingers drummed on the table as he read and sipped on his coffee, ignoring Katie completely.

For once, she was grateful for the oversight. Inside, she was drowning in a sea of sensations. It was hard to exist in a world that was filled with noises and smells and colors so bright they reminded her of the obnoxious colored lights on the strip in Las Vegas. It was overkill, and she struggled to put more than two thoughts together.

Tap! Tap! Tap! The drumming of his fingers reverberated through the air like thunder, driving her to the brink of insanity. She reached out and pressed his fingers down on the table and felt a jolt that reminded her of the time she'd licked the connectors of a nine-volt battery when she was little. A reflex made her body jerk back. Collecting herself, she glanced down to see him studying the "Page Six" column. "The Autumnal Equinox Ball at the Castanova Compound is only a few months away. Mark my words, this is the year I manifest an invitation."

Jeff had been angling for an invitation to that event for years. Obsessed to the point of writing affirmations on the bathroom mirror, which Katie overheard him recite to himself when he was shaving in the mornings. The party was *the* premier celebrity event of the entire year and was more exclusive than an invitation to the White House. The Castanova Compound was a secluded island only accessible by a private airstrip.

It was an event that sounded about as much fun to

Katie as a Brazilian wax. He read the rest of the article and then closed his eyes, pinching together his thumb and first two fingers in a weird meditation gesture he used to center himself. His loud exhales grated on her nerves.

Ten minutes later, she was relieved when he folded the newspaper, then stood and leaned down to give her his habitual parting peck on the cheek. She closed her eyes as his rough lips met her cheekbone and images rocketed and flashed into her consciousness, zinging by too fast to interpret.

Jeff in a hotel room, naked and grunting on top of his blonde legal assistant, Brittany. A bank statement and palm trees. A safe deposit box filled with stacks of cash. An ultra-modern kitchen with a million-dollar view. She gasped when he pulled away, instantly exhausted.

What the hell was that? Is this what a heart attack feels like?

Jeff whistled as he walked to the door without a care in the world. Katie shook off the overwhelming fatigue, picked up the briefcase he'd left under the table, and followed him to the foyer where Jeff was tugging on his loafers on the bench. Shaky and unsteady, she leaned against the wall and held it out to him.

"What would I ever do without you?" he asked sweetly as he stood with his arms open and, exhausted, Katie fell into them like she had so many years in their marriage. His touch sent bolts of electricity through her, and her body convulsed as more images flashed behind her eyelids. A pregnancy test. A water hut in Bali. A surprised whimper left her lips as she became limp in his arms.

"Katie?" Jeff cried as he set her down on the bench.

Her head lolled to the side, and she felt nauseated. "Are you okay?" Her hearing was dampened, and it sounded like Jeff was underwater.

Her eyelashes fluttered, then opened. The room that had been so vibrant in rich color was now grayed and muted. "Probably just a hot flash." She was weak, desperate to get back into bed and sleep it off, whatever it was.

"You're getting to that age," he said. "I'm surprised it's taken this long."

"Gee, thanks," she muttered.

"Let's get you to bed." He reached out to touch her again, and she braced for impact. This time, she was grateful to feel nothing. Not even a tingle. He helped her to the doorway and then pulled back the comforter. She curled up in the fetal position and felt the comforting weight of her blanket before falling into a deep sleep.

SEVEN

At noon, Katie's eyes opened, and she was disoriented and groggy. Thick from the lingering vestiges of sleep, her limbs felt heavy. She blinked a few times, trying to find her bearings. Pressed close to her was Arlo, who was a bed hog and insisted on lying snug against his favorite human. Katie stroked his ears absentmindedly, recalling his deep voice.

"Do you like that, boy?" she asked, and his tail thumped on the bed in response. "Say something to me," she asked, and his tail wagged harder on the bed. "C'mon, say something. You can do it," she coaxed as his pleasured body wriggled in delight. But no words were uttered. She glanced around the room. It appeared as it normally did. Tasteful warm gray walls and ivory trim, a color chosen by the decorator Jeff hired. She'd wanted a soft aqua but had been overruled.

"I'm such an idiot. Don't tell anyone I thought you could speak." She laughed at her own joke. Arlo's ears perked up, and he howled.

Today was the day. Davina's office was serving Jeff papers at the firm. It was a bold, calculated move Davina talked her into, unaware it was Katie's fiftieth birthday. Katie's vindictive streak reared its ugly head, and she made the rash decision to indulge it as her birthday gift to herself.

At first, she'd been unsure it was the right decision, but after so many years of being invisible, she'd agreed. Today, she would force him to acknowledge the mess he'd made. It would mortify Jefferson to have their dirty laundry aired in front of the partners, his colleagues, and legal assistants. It was the kind of tawdry gossip that would invite judgmental whispering and stain his image forever. But now, in the clear light of day, knowing the confrontation was mere hours away, she second-guessed her decision.

She sat up in bed, looking over at his pillow that was concave by the self-important head that lay on it, and realized this was the last time she would have to share a bed with him. Tonight, she would sleep alone.

Every day she'd waited since she'd found the receipt, her heart hardened more. A little at a time, she was turning to stone inside. She walked through twenty-seven years of memories they'd created throughout dating and marriage, weighing each one for the truth against her skewed perception. Was he really thrilled the night she told him she was pregnant with Callie, or was he already pulling away then? Had he been secretly retaining options for a new life, one that lined up with his desire to be carefree, rich, and single? Was he toying with the idea of bidding on one of those sleek warehouse loft apartments he couldn't shut up about after seeing them online? It stunned her how cavalier he was about jeopardizing the family they had taken decades to build. She had become an inconsequential servant to him, and the truth of it stung.

"Does he even see me anymore?" she asked Arlo as she rubbed his underbelly. Anger bubbled up, wrapped in justification. "That bastard does not know what is about to hit him, does he, boy?" Arlo whined in sympathy and followed her out to the kitchen for a late breakfast. Katie added a scrambled egg to his kibble. "One more long day, we tell the kids, and then the hard part is over," Katie lied to herself as she wrapped her fingers around a steaming mug of coffee. Needing a little pick me up, she hit it with a shot of Rumchata and breathed in the calming cinnamon scent. She cleaned up the kitchen, tucking the remains of Yuli's special birthday truffles into the freezer.

Today was going to be the beginning of the end, and it made her reminisce about the beginning of the beginning. She was so young when they met at a Northwestern mixer. They were the cookie-cutter perfect 'it' couple that made other people feel like they were missing out on something valuable. It was a secret superiority she remembered indulging in. Long nights after making love, he would bring a tub of mocha chip ice cream and two spoons to bed, and they would polish it off and then give in to their libidos again. The urgent fluttering would gather in her center that was besotted with his touch. It felt like two people couldn't possibly love each other more than they did. When she unexpectedly got pregnant with Lauren, the decision to marry him was easy. She wanted her daughter to have two parents. But her bouts of morning sickness were so oppressive, they forced her to drop out of her classes at Northwestern the week after Jeff proposed.

Their wedding day was a warm June afternoon when she was thirty pounds lighter with a toddler in tow. Then two more kids, law school, and a move to the Big Apple used up every available resource she had—time, effort, attention, and money—as their life together was entirely focused on accomplishing Jefferson's goals.

"I wish I could go back and shake the heck out of the stupid, naive girl I was," she grumbled, watching Arlo devour his bowl of food.

Her stomach flipped. There were so many emotions coursing through her. It wasn't a simple process to leave your husband. As much as Davina droned on about the legalities and practical considerations, like finding a place to live and telling the kids, it was the idea of being alone for the first time in her adult life that struck her.

"What if I end up a penniless recluse, boy?" she asked Arlo, who hovered at her ankles. "What if I die and hunger forces you to gnaw my face off from starvation?" He whined, then plopped down. "No? You're probably right. One of the kids is bound to come by needing something." She gasped, "Oh no! The kids!"

Although they weren't kids anymore, she still thought of them like they were. Callie was the youngest at twenty-four and walked the line between being a bleeding heart and level-headed. She was earning a degree in animation at the University of South Florida. The most like Katie of all her children, she was hardworking yet empathetic. Beckett was the middle child and the most unpredictable. At twenty-five, he fell in love almost daily, waxing dramatically about authenticity and creating angsty poetry he performed at Slam Night for snaps. He was the wild card. Their oldest, Lauren, was a twenty-seven-year-old daddy's girl. They shared a love for the finer things in life— boutique hotels and extravagant foodie experiences. Katie felt like a cast-off shoe in their presence, always ending up dribbling the organic honey down her dress or swiping a cuff through the port wine reduction, while Jeff and Lauren ganged up and teased her.

The truth was, she didn't know *how* they would respond. They were adults, after all, no longer dependent on her or Jeff for survival. They were all living on their own and beginning their own pursuits of happiness. She had sacrificed and put their needs first, doting on her children and relishing every stage of motherhood. After reading a million parenting books when she was pregnant, Katie was determined to give them a childhood they didn't need to recover from. It was as healthy as it could have been, with Katie so plugged in and involved and insisting on open communication, no matter what the topic. And as they got older, she loosened the reins and gave them the freedom to make mistakes and solve their own problems. She was proud of the adults they were becoming and she wanted more for them, more than her own mother had wanted for her. Each generation was to have an easier row to hoe. At least, that was the story she told herself and her driving force. It was easy to sacrifice when you loved your family as much as Katie did.

"Who am I now without Jeff?" she asked Arlo as she tugged his ears, an act that brought him such pure unadulterated pleasure his tongue lolled out of the side of his mouth.

The idea fluttered panic in her belly. It was a fear that she never dreamed she would have to face, but here she was, facing it.

Soon you will know who you truly are. The answer startled her. Katie's heart raced, and she grew lightheaded. In a panic, she searched the room for the source of the words, then laughed at herself.

"Girl, you gotta get a grip. You tell one person you're hearing voices and you'll get locked up in the looney bin."

On her wrist, Katie's watch vibrated, and she looked down to see Davina's name and answered the phone quickly.

"He's being served at three pm. You've confirmed he'll be there?"

"Yes," she answered, not trusting herself to say more, and knowing that lawyers practically charged by the word, so short and sweet was her game plan.

"Do you have a place to go tonight in case things get ugly?"

"I'm not leaving my home," Katie said, her voice low even though no one was there to hear it. "We can negotiate like civilized people. I was married to the man for a long time. He will not want to stick around when he's free and clear to shack up with his office tart."

"Have a backup plan," Davina advised. "We'll meet next week."

———

Katie knew precisely the exact moment the papers were served. She received four phone calls and eleven texts in the span of seven minutes. She ignored them all, sitting in the first burst of genuine anxiety. Her heart quickened when she saw his name flash across the caller ID. Her breathing turned shallow, and she had to force herself to close her eyes and recenter. A decision had been made. The die was cast, and now she could only move forward. There was no going back.

After she was in a calmer state of mind, she scrolled to his name in her favorites and made the call. While it rang, she mentally made a reminder to regulate him back to the general contacts as soon as possible.

"That was quite the stunt you just pulled!" His tone was steel when it came on the line.

"Whatever do you mean, dear husband?" she asked, forcing sarcastic cheer into her voice. She couldn't help herself. A part of her enjoyed his visceral reaction.

"You know what I'm talking about," he bit back at her. "Seems a touch dramatic."

"Just making sure the punishment fits the crime."

"What crime?"

"The one that has you screwing your legal assistant at swanky hotels."

He cleared his throat and waited like she knew he would. He often waxed poetic to the kids as they grew up. "With silence comes power. When you are in a negotiation, say your peace and then stop talking. Most of the time, the other party will give in."

"I know what you're doing, Jeff, and it won't work on me anymore."

"You're being unreasonable. Can't we talk about this?" He was scrambling, and Katie enjoyed hearing her unflappable husband struggle to maintain his composure. "You're willing to throw away almost thirty years of marriage? How could you hurt the kids like this? You're being selfish."

"You have got to be kidding me. Do not bring the kids into this!" Katie was furious. "Do not try to make this my fault. *You* broke YOUR vows, not me!"

"What do you mean?" He feigned innocence.

Katie felt sick. "Stop the charade. You got caught. It's over." She exhaled and then said, "I should have seen this coming. You always take the easy way out. Cheating leaves all your options open. I'm sure you thought when you tired of your plaything, you could still come home to a home-cooked meal and someone who picks up your dry cleaning, but not anymore. We're done."

There was a long silence, and Katie waited. Her heartbeat thrummed in her ears. Every sense was alive and on high alert.

"We can handle this amongst ourselves." His intonation down-shifted into businesslike and made the hairs on the back of Katie's neck stand up. "We can file for an uncontested divorce and keep most of our joint assets intact. I'll handle everything, and I won't even bill you for my services."

Katie laughed out loud at the absurdity. "You must think I'm a complete idiot." Exasperated, she flung her head back and stared at the ceiling, trying to calm the rage that threatened to boil over. "You have lost your mind if you think I am going to be grateful for the *gift* of your legal expertise that my hard work subsidized." Internally, his reaction shut a door and locked it shut.

"You're being unreasonable. Of course, you would have an emotional reaction. Women always fall apart under pressure."

"I guess we'll have to see about that," Katie spat out at him, disgusted by his reaction. "I don't trust you anymore. I hired an attorney, and she is going to look out for my best interests."

"Davina Thorne is going to bleed you dry, and at the end of this, you'll still be a frumpy housewife who is only fit to man the counter at her grandmother's chocolate shop." His default coping mechanism was to lash out with words. Words were always his most lethal weapon. Reducing her and belittling her, chipping away at any confidence she accumulated until she was a fraction of the woman he married. He thought he was carving a master-piece from her block of womanly marble. Under the guise of making her better by transforming her from the inside out, he chiseled away every day at her with his 'advice.' Year after year until he whittled her down to a cracked stump. Forced to see the truth for the first time, she did the only thing her instincts told her to do. She yanked the hammer and chisel from his hands.

"That is what alimony and spousal support are for, dear husband. I'm floored. I never thought I'd have to teach a brilliant legal mind about the finer points of family law in Florida."

She was wired, running high and hot on the first burst of power she'd ever felt in her marriage.

"I will not leave my house," he demanded. "I built it from the ground up."

Typical Jeff, taking all the credit for the house he paid the mortgage on, but she lovingly designed and maintained. She shook her head in disbelief.

"Fine, you can move into the guest suite on the second floor, and I'll keep the master."

He cleared his throat again, clearly frustrated. "Let's talk about this when the dust settles. Emotions are running too high right now. You always let them get the best of you."

"I suggest you talk to my attorney. I have nothing more to say to you."

She pulled the phone away and punched the end call button, satisfied she'd cut herself loose from an anchor that held her down her entire adult life.

"Happy Birthday to me," she said to Arlo, who barked in reply.

EIGHT

Zoya sat alone in the darkness, the golden antique skeleton keys resting in the palm of her hand. When she'd turned fifty almost a century ago, they'd arrived by courier with the deed to the island and instructions for a chartered flight. She was desperate to flee Chicago in those dark, terrifying days after her sweet Salvatore was murdered. The loss was so profound, she simply didn't care if she lived or died. Over the next two weeks, she plotted her escape, an escape of the more permanent variety, but the very day she was planning to do it, her second chance appeared on her doorstep, seemingly dropped from the sky like manna from heaven.

She remembered landing on the island for the first time in the chartered plane with Yuli. The flight had been silent. They occupied opposite sides of the aircraft, but the third passenger on the plane was Zoya's rage. She couldn't look at thirteen-year-old Yuli with anything but searing hatred. Harnessing the unbridled hope of youth, Yuli tried to connect for years, but each interaction was a painful reminder to Zoya of who was missing. She could not find a way to forgive, and eventually, Yuli stopped reaching out.

In Chicago, Yuli grew up alongside Salvatore's only son, Dominic. She was a quiet teenager who would often go days without speaking. Her nose was always in a book, often hiding behind them while shoveling food into her mouth, starved for something that neither Zoya nor herself could articulate.

Feeling sorry for the sad, silent child, Salvatore often brought home books for her. When Zoya overheard him speaking to Yuli in the soft tones he usually reserved for her, the rage only intensified. Yuli would never be called beautiful, but she had the plumpness of youth and Zoya was filled with unfounded jealousy. It seeped in and choked her heart off from the ability to love, driving her to make Yuli's life as painful as possible.

The day they'd arrived on the island felt like a distant dream. After the paralyzing fear and loss of the love of her life, she was gifted ease in the form of a beautiful home on the edge of the sea. Eager to find the lock for the keys, she walked the acres of the secluded estate. On their sixth day on the island, she found a small, nondescript metal building covered in overgrown weeds and tall sea grasses. She gasped when she turned the key in the lock and it opened. The door creaked as she pushed it open, and a soft glow illuminated the darkness when she stepped inside.

As her eyes adjusted to the low light, a hum shot down her limbs and energized her body. Carved into the stone of the wall was a short poem:

Women's history is rewritten by the men in power.

Here lives a collection of our important hours.
Painful days must be re-lived.
To prevent them from happening ever again.

Beautiful memories should only be felt.
If viewed more than once, the music box will melt.
Our family history is nothing to fear.
But you must heed the lessons inside the boxes
here.

Even though the exterior of the building was small, the interior was expansive. It defied reality and stretched out as far as her eyes could see. There were stacks of shelving that filled the entire room, and on each shelf rested a collection of unique music boxes. In every shape and size, some of them seemed to glow from within, and others were dark and dusty. As she walked closer to them, she felt a magnetic pull and energy zinged up and down her spine. She saw four numbers on each shelf and instantly under-stood they corresponded to a year from her ancestral history.

Her hand trailed down the smooth wooden shelves as she let their energy pull her toward the 1900s. A soft smile turned up the corners of her mouth when she found 1905. There, a pink crystal box was glowing so brightly, she knew it had to be from her daughter Nadia's birth. She yearned to open it. The pull was magnetic as she reached out, plucked it from the shelf, and hugged it to her body. Faintly, she heard herself humming and her heart filled with warmth and burst with love. She gazed down at the facets on the crystal box with a sad smile and considered opening it, but her eyes drifted back to the warning poem etched into the wall. Understanding she could only view it once or it would be destroyed forever, she forced herself to put the box back on the shelf and continue further down the rows.

She stopped with a gasp at 1925. She reached out to lift the box, and a pin under the lid pricked her finger, making her yelp and jerk back in surprise. The music box was crimson and black and covered in intricate webbing. She carefully pulled the box from its resting place. A shudder passed through her as she remembered the events of the worst day of her life. The muscle memory of it made her cry out and a knot formed in her gut. Even after all these years, the final moments of her beautiful Nadia's existence on earth ripped her heart out every time. People often said time would heal, but it never did. Instead, the hole in her heart only deepened.

Time had robbed her of the happy memories of her daughter. The way Nadia's voice sounded. The curl of her hair. The years had softened her recall as her memory became muddy in a maddening way. The only clear memories seared into her soul were the traumatic ones, and all time seemed to do was amplify her rage. In her arms, the box now felt filled with lead and she tumbled to the ground, unable to hold on to it any longer. She sat down on the cold concrete floor, staring at it. Tentatively, she reached out a hand to touch it. A wail escaped her lips, and the box became frozen to the touch. It instantly seared the tips of her delicate fingers with frostbite that made her pull her hand back with a yelp. She yearned to open it, to see the face of her daughter one more time. Afraid to get burned again, she reached out, but her hand hovered just an inch from it. She tapped it and the burn was gone. Becoming braver, she bent down to pick it up and was surprised when it lifted easily and practically floated back to its place on the shelf.

In the days following the discovery of the family archives, she spent time every day walking down memory lane and learning about her lineage. It had been an intense education.

Now, she'd had the keys for almost a century. Having seen the inside of every box, Zoya knew them all intimately. She savored the solitary viewing of the joyful moments unwilling to lose them forever, but often wallowed in the painful ones watching them over and over, hoping to glean knowledge from them.

She walked to Katia's section, and one gold leaf box shined brighter than all the others, emitting light. It would make the perfect gift for Katia's birthday, opening a pathway for her to formally introduce herself. Her way. Zoya already knew she'd have to fight a lifetime of Yuli's programming, but she had a few tricks up her sleeve to get into Katia's good graces.

She packed it carefully inside a cardboard box nestled in a sea of opalescent tissue paper, and on top added a scroll of parchment paper with instructions for Katia. She hummed to herself as she added more tissue and then taped the carton shut. The box warmed up in temperature, emitting the comfortable heat from the memory trapped inside. It was a magical characteristic she'd always marveled at. You never knew what you'd feel when you came in contact with one of the boxes. It was like the music boxes were alive.

Holding the warmed cardboard box in both her hands, she closed her eyes, conjuring up Katia's front door in her mind's eye. She saw the bright white trim and the aqua half-moon welcome mat. Next to the leaded glass front door, there was a bed of plants, including a massive palm tree that spread out its fronds to the sky. She concentrated fully, her lips moving quietly as she chanted. A few moments later, the box disappeared from her hands and landed with a thump on Katia's doormat, waiting to be discovered. Still meditating, Zoya struck out her hand, and with one index finger extended, she made a pressing gesture. At the front door, an invisible finger pressed the doorbell, and deep within the house, Arlo howled. Zoya opened her eyes and then brushed her palms together. Mission accomplished. Now, all she had to do was wait. When she was a little girl, her father always told her in frustration, "Patience is a virtue. Practice it." It was a lesson she never learned. Zoya was great at a good many things, but being patient was not one of them.

NINE

Back at Katie's house, the doorbell whipped Arlo into a frenzy. His harsh barks filled the air, making it impossible for Katie to ignore the delivery. She padded from the kitchen in the new lemon-yellow marshmallow slides she'd just purchased for herself. Jeff put them into the same category as Crocs—ugly and unwearable—but she didn't care about his opinion anymore. They were like walking on a cloud and worth every penny. At her marshmallow-clad feet, Arlo jumped up, trying to get her attention.

"Okay, okay! I see you." Katie leaned down to scratch the patch of curly fur under his chin. "Calm down, sir." She snuggled her face closer to his, and he licked her cheek with a sloppy kiss that made her giggle.

Standing again at the door, she glanced through the leaded glass, expecting to see a delivery driver, but there was no one. Puzzled, she turned the deadbolt and opened the front door. On the half-moon doormat sat a simple cardboard box, no label, no writing. No hint on it to help her figure out where it came from or what was inside.

"What in the world?" She bent down to retrieve it and carried it into the kitchen with Arlo on her heels. Retrieving a knife from the kitchen block, she sliced into the tape on the side and opened it. Stuffed with iridescent tissue paper, she got giddy at the prospect of receiving a gift. "Ooh!! I bet it's from one of the kids," she told Arlo, who shook his head from side to side and let out one forlorn howl.

She pulled the tissue paper out of the way and then retrieved a parchment scroll. Cutting the twine that held it together, she unrolled and smoothed it on the countertop. Her mind recalled with irony it was the same action she'd done with the receipt two weeks ago. Pushing past the mental jab, she read the words.

Half a century has a way of softening your memories. Here is a sweet token of my love and appreciation for you, my Katia. When you open this music box, you will relive the most beautiful day of your life. Enjoy the trip down memory lane, but heed this warning:

Beautiful memories should only be felt.
    If viewed more than once, the music box will melt.

I have waited for this day longer than you can imagine. Happy Birthday.

Zoya.

"That's weird. Who's Zoya?" She returned to the
carton and pulled out a gilded, gold leaf-covered box,
surprised it was warm to the touch. The intricately hand-
carved lid sat atop a satiny mahogany base. "Damn, this
thing is heavy!" Whining, Arlo's tail was tucked, and he
ran in circles underfoot, distressed. Frantically, his noises
got louder, turning into cries as he rooted around at the
baseboards near her feet.

Distracted, Katie shushed him. "Just give me a minute,
boy." She turned the box over in her hands and marveled at
its craftsmanship. Setting down the box, she hunted for her
reading glasses. Arlo's whining intensified even louder,
transforming into low growls and jarring barks. He nipped
at her ankles, clearly distressed, following her from room
to room until she finally found her reading glasses on top
of the refrigerator.

"Dude! Cool it!" she barked at Arlo, who huffed and
then finally settled at her feet. Glasses on, she bent down
and peered at the box for several long seconds. She read
the parchment four more times to clearly understand the
instructions.

With the thrill of anticipation filling her, she hesitated
once more before lifting the lid. A tinkle of music spilled
out. Like the pop-up books Beckett favored as a child,
delicate balsam wood lifted and shifted together,
conforming to a tiny familiar apartment. She gasped when
she leaned closer and saw the number on the tiny door.
Carved from deep rich walnut, inside the box's interior was
a replica of their first apartment in New York when Jeff
was in law school. She leaned closer to it, her bright
yellow frames perched on the end of her nose. She picked

it up and tilted it from side to side, enamored with its delicate beauty. On the right-hand side was a tiny gold crank, and she slowly turned it as the music spooled out faster. She cranked until she couldn't anymore, afraid to overdo it and crack the delicate innards of the box. She set it down and climbed on a stool at the kitchen island, then leaned forward, resting her chin on her forearms.

Prisms of rainbow-colored light pulsed out of the box into the air in time to the lyrical sweetness of the tinkling music. The vision of her kitchen glowing mesmerized her. The wash of color and hard edges were softened by a sweet yearning that spread from her center to her fingertips. Then she felt the sensation of constriction and being tugged into the box. The tinkling crescendoed, filling her tiny ears with notes swirling and dancing around her. Confused by the sensation, Katie looked down at her arm, awash in golden light. She felt at ease, like being two margaritas deep at her favorite Mexican restaurant.

Now fully inside the music box, she glanced at the ground as the sidewalk disappeared and transformed into sugary white sand underfoot. In the distance, she saw a tiny version of herself kneeling next to a miniature Beckett, handing him a kite. Then the déjà vu of the memory hit like a wave, propelling her back to Christmas break when Lauren was eight, Beckett was six, and Callie was five.

She'd booked a condo on the beach for Christmas break, and Jeff stayed behind. At first, his refusal to participate left her angry and frustrated.

"Let's celebrate Christmas on the beach this year! We can build a snowman with sand!" she told the kids, who were as giddy as she was at the prospect of going somewhere new. They spent so much time crammed into their apartment in the city. Even in the summers, parks were few and far between in New York.

"It's not prudent or fiscally responsible to take a vacation right now. Cancel it. We can go later."

"I have to get out of this city!" she'd cried. "I hate it here. Yuli sent me some money for Christmas, and I want us to take a vacation with the kids."

"There will be time for that later. I'm a new associate. I can't take that kind of time off right now. Not to mention, it's indulgent and unnecessary to waste a month's worth of rent for seven days of fun."

"No." Katie dug her heels in. "I promised Yuli I would use her gift for something *I* want to do. This is important. Can't you see I'm dying here? Winter in New York is miserable. Gray, drab, and cold, and I swear it makes people even more angry and irritable. I want to feel the sun on my face and see the ocean, and I really want you to come with us. But I'm going to do it, with or without you."

His eyes narrowed on her, and she felt her resolve melting.

"Please, come with us. Make some memories with me and the kids."

"I can't," he said. "I just got a new case."

"Fine."

He probably thought she'd change her mind like she always did, but Katie refused. She felt a tug on her heartstrings pulling her there. She created a calendar with the kids, and together, they crossed off each day leading up to the trip. Jeff withdrew even more, finding more excuses to stay at the office, spending extra time there in the days between Thanksgiving and Christmas.

He wasn't even around to kiss them goodbye the morning of their departure. Katie packed her rented car and drove the sleepy kids through the flat plains of upstate New York for seventeen hours straight to the Florida coast. She'd packed the car with suitcases filled with shorts and swimsuits, adding a football and three kites she'd found at a vintage store. Road-weary and exhausted from the long drive, she had to bite back a sob of relief when the condo was in sight.

"Hey, sleepy heads, we're here." She shook the kids, rousing them from sleep, exhausted herself and bleary-eyed from driving all night. "Just grab the most important things we need tonight, and we'll unload the rest tomorrow after we've had some sleep."

A few minutes later, seeing Beckett struggling to untangle the kites, she laughed. "I'm not sure kites qualify as vitally important, buddy."

Beckett grinned, both of his front teeth missing.

"I was thinking more along the lines of socks and underwear," she offered, and he groaned.

The next morning, after a blissful eight hours of sleep, she'd made chocolate chip pancakes. Lauren had carefully measured the ingredients into the bowl for her, and Callie was heavy-handed with the chocolate chips, but Katie didn't care. After a sugary start, she said, "Who's ready to try the kites?"

"Me! Me! Me!" They clamored to the door, each clutching a kite to their bodies, barefoot and wearing shorts, their albino east coast legs a shock to the eyes.

Callie scrambled up the path through the tall swatches of sea oats on either side of the condo, running to the water's edge with the unfettered abandon and enthusiasm only five-year-olds possess. Katie followed behind with the swim bag filled with towels and sunscreen and a cooler filled with juice pouches and fruit snacks.

After finding a home base, spreading towels on the satiny sand, and lathering the kids with half of a bottle of sunscreen, Katie donned a visor and picked up one of the kites.

"Beckett, my man, let's do this." He jumped at the chance, fitting his smaller hand into Katie's, and walked her down the beach away from other tourists spread out on blankets.

From her vantage point in the music box, Katie's heart swelled, flushing with sweetness from the memory of his little hand in hers. Shortly before the trip, he'd entered first grade, and after bending to peer pressure from his new friends, he became embarrassed when she reached for him. Now that he was a grown man, she knew that vacation day was one of the last times he would hold her hand, and she understood mothering was a series of infinite heartbreaks. You never knew when you would experience a last time with your child. That was the bittersweet tug-of-war between the joy and agony called parenting.

She felt the wind pick up and watched as younger Katie's visor whipped off her head and blew toward a group of hopeful seagulls who squawked at it when they realized they couldn't eat it. She left it there. "You run as fast as you can, and when I tell you to let go, you do it, got it?"

Little Beckett's head nodded up and down enthusiastically. "Yes, Mama."

Katie unraveled the string to give him room, then turned her back to the wind, letting the breeze do most of the work. "Run, Beckett, run!" she shouted, and he took off like a shot. "Okay, now!" He let go of the kite and it lurched forward gently, being tugged up by the force of the breeze.

Beckett ran back, and she knelt down on the sand, circling her arms around him. She handed him the circular string holder as the kite continued to pull up and up. "Keep the tension on the string," she advised, "and let it out slowly." She placed his hands on either side of the tightly wrapped wheel of string. "You're doing it!" she praised, and he stood taller with pride as the kite rose higher and higher, dipping back and forth into the wind. "We just need to hold it tight." She let go of the line completely. "Look at you! You're flying solo already!"

"Girls, half the battle is facing the right direction," she instructed Callie and Lauren. "If you can't feel the direction of the wind, you can do this." She licked her index finger, and the girls giggled and tried it themselves. "Which side of your finger is the coldest? All you have to do is stand opposite that side." After a few dive bombs, all the kites were flying through the air—a pterodactyl, a butterfly, and a colorful origami bird. Floating higher, they bobbed and wove into the deep blue and cloud-filled sky. A sense of accomplishment was written in the unfettered joy on her children's faces.

Katie relived the moment as it played out in front of her inside the music box, the sweet tinkling soundtrack entrancing her. Catapulting her back to it, she relished the absolute joy she felt that day. She wallowed in complete contentment as the sun set later that evening. Katie saw herself build a fire on the beach in the hole the kids helped dig with the firewood she'd purchased from a local grocer. Their faces reflected the rich warm glow of the campfire as they roasted marshmallows to make s'mores. An hour later, their eyes softened with exhaustion, and after dumping buckets full of seawater on the fire, she'd led them back to their tiny condo. Tucking them into the bunk beds and futon in the living room, they were dead asleep as soon as their heads hit the pillow. It was a perfect day with absolutely nothing missing, not even Jeff.

That day she made a promise to herself that she wouldn't beg Jeff to engage with the kids anymore. She was going to create a life filled with happy memories, with or without him. It was freeing, cutting a thread away that had been a source of contention between them. It didn't matter if he made the kids a priority, because she would, and while he would always have an invitation on the future adventures she would plan, she had a feeling he never would exercise it.

Back in the kitchen, the music tinkled to a stop as Katie felt tugged outward and wobbled back to the stool. It took a few long moments to get her bearings. Outside it now, her eyes gazed at the box longingly, tempted to crank it up again. She wanted to feel her entire being flooded with light, love, and the warmth of comforting memories again. This desire yanked at her heart and it took every ounce of resolve to fight against it and heed the warning on the parchment. With a heavy sigh, she finally closed the lid and swiped at her cheeks, surprised to find wetness there. Laughing at her own sentimental heart, she placed the box in the center of her custom built-in curio cabinet that flanked the fireplace Jeff insisted on when they built the house. The fireplace looked beautiful in the photographs from their featured article in the *St. Pete Sentinel*, but they never actually used it. In the span of an hour, the music box had become her most cherished possession.

TEN

Two days of tip-toeing around each other later, Katie was shocked to learn that Jeff still planned on keeping up appearances and would attend her belated official birthday dinner. It was an annual event celebrating two birthdays in her family since she and Yuli had been born on the same day. Katie looked forward to it every year, but she was anxious about this one. Pretending nothing had changed in their lives was becoming more and more problematic.

"Fifty years," Katie said as she tugged on shapewear that hugged her curves. She pulled a dress with the tags still on it out of the closet and tugged it over her head, relishing the feel of the satiny fabric as it fell like a water-fall down her body. She wrestled with the zipper, contorting her body into circus-worthy shapes until she'd nearly dislocated her shoulder in the process. Relief rushed in as she felt it finally give and zing into place at the base of her neck.

"Ah-ha!" she exclaimed, triumphant yet red-faced

from the effort. She leaned in, looking at her face closely in the mirror, turning her chin to the left and right, then back again. Her fine lines were non-existent and her skin glowed.

"Not too shabby for half a century!" She raised a glass of Dom Pérignon champagne to her own reflection. It was the special bottle they'd kept in their climate-controlled wine chiller, given to them as a gift when Jefferson made partner. She swiped some age-defying foundation under her eyes, brushed on a pretty pink blush, and then applied two layers of coal-black mascara. "Damn, girl. You are lookin' good!" She chortled to herself, taking another long sip of the bubbly. Her pores were smoother than she remembered, her eyes sparkled, and the skin under her chin that had been softening with age for the last several years felt tighter. There was warmth blooming in her center from the champagne and self-love she felt washing over her when she pressed her hands down her waist, marveling at her smoother curves. It had been a hot minute since she had felt at home in her body.

There was a gentle knock on the door. Grasping the flute of champagne, she turned to open it, annoyed to see Jeff standing on the other side, dressed for dinner.

"Is that the Dom the practice sent over when I became partner?"

"Yep," she said as she drained the glass with a bright smile, then turned and filled it to the top again without offering a drop to Jeff. The selfish gesture stunned him, and for a solid minute, he couldn't speak. His eyes traversed down her body, making Katie fidget uncomfortably.

"There's something different about you," he said as he followed her out to their bedroom, where Arlo was splayed out on the comforter. "Get down!" he shouted at the dog, who growled and then jumped to the ground, landing too close to Jeff's foot. Jeff rewarded him with a swift kick to his haunches, making the dog yelp in pain.

Katie ran over and scooped him up into her arms, protecting him from further harm. "Do that again and I will end you," she snarled at Jeff, who just shrugged his shoulders like it wasn't a big deal.

"Weak men abuse animals," she blurted. Katie was on a roll and couldn't stop herself. "And while we are at it, this is my personal space, Jeff. Next time, do not enter my bedroom without an invitation."

The request visibly shook him, and he stepped back, his face muddled in a state of confusion that Katie savored. Stuttering, he asked, "How... how are we going to play this with the kids and your parents?"

"My vote is the truth," Katie said.

"The truth? It's such a tricky thing."

"No, it's really not," Katie said and then continued, "Maybe it is for *you*, but it's very simple for me. You were having an affair. Our marriage is over, but we love them all very much. At least now my dad will have a legitimate reason to hate you. He's never exactly been Team Jeff."

"And Yuli's going to have a thing or two to say." Jeff shuddered. It was true. Her father hadn't been Team Jeff, but Yuli outright hated him. Her disgust was so evident she didn't even try to hide it on her square face. She was a brick house, solid and unyielding, and Jeff shared the hatred. Over the years, for Katie's benefit, they had declared a truce, staying as physically far apart from each other at family gatherings as possible.

"I don't think they need to know all the sordid details of our private life."

"Our private life?" Katie spit out at him. Rage bubbled up that had been building for years. "Our private life?" she repeated as she strode to him in long steps, her voice getting pitchy. "I am done making excuses for you in front of the kids. They are adults. They can handle the truth."

She studied him and finally realized what he was striving to protect. "This isn't about the kids at all, is it? You're worried it will hurt your precious reputation. God, you make me sick! After all the sacrifices I made for you and for our family? If you wanted out of this marriage, you should have had the balls to tell me instead of sneaking around behind my back."

Jeff retracted, scrambling for control. "Maybe this isn't the best idea. Maybe we should tell the kids by themselves first."

"You know, I always thought you were the strongest man I'd ever met. Now I see that, underneath it all, all the posturing and dress up, you are a pussy." The word emboldened her. It was one she usually avoided, but, hey, when the shoe fits.

"Vulgarities?" Jeff spat back. "I always knew you were trash, just like Frankie."

Forcing away the tears that wanted to spring up, she answered, "We're telling them all—tonight. One and done. It's not up for discussion." Katie yanked the bottle from its marble chiller and walked into the kitchen as the front door opened and Callie and Beckett sailed in chattering with each other.

"Hello, my loves."

"Wow, Mom, you look incredible. Did you lose weight?"

Almost two hundred pounds, Katie wanted to say but bit it back. It was accurate, but too soon. She opened her arms and squeezed them tight to her.

Lauren walked in next, still talking on her phone. They waited a full three minutes while Lauren held up her finger, asking them for quiet as Callie rolled her eyes. She'd followed in her father's footsteps and was a junior associate at a firm downtown.

Finally, she ended the call and turned to Katie. "Happy Birthday." She held out a skinny, wine-shaped bag and then turned to her father with a huge smile. "Daddy!" She ran over and melted into his arms. Her preference for him always stung.

Next, after a quick rap on the door, Katie's parents, Kristina and David, shuffled in with Yuli behind them, her steps strong and sure.

"Happy Birthday to you! Happy Birthday to you! Happy birthday, dear Katie and Yuli! Happy Birthday to you!" They sang and then wrapped her and Yuli up in a group hug.

"You look beautiful, dear," Kristina said as David kissed her cheek. He walked with a cane now, age hunching him into a gentle C-shape. After his last hospitalization, it was harder for him to pick up his entire foot, reducing his gait to a shuffle. Next to him, Yuli was surprisingly spry. Katie noticed for the first time Yuli was lighter on her feet than her parents, who were twenty years younger. It was an odd and unsettling revelation she tucked away to speak to Yuli about later.

"Thanks, Mom," Katie said as the first bubbles of fear fluttered in her core, forcing her to re-think her initial decision to tell everyone all at once.

"Happy Birthday to us, my sweet Katia," Yuli said with a smile. Katie saw a twinkle in her eye that wasn't normally present. She was typically stoic, the result of hard work and burying your husband before you were ready. When Yuli was happy, the only clue was the slight upturn of her usually straight lips. She was dressed simply in a long black muumuu that was more like a sack and left the woman looking as wide as she was tall.

A few minutes later, Katie exhaled and gestured to the dining room table. "Why don't you guys have a seat? Jeff and I have an announcement to make."

With murmured grumblings from the kids, they reluctantly pulled out chairs and sat down. Katie glanced around at the faces of everyone she loved, gaining the strength to continue. Slowly, Katie turned to the kids and began. "We want you to know your father and I love you very much. You are the best things we've ever created together, but some events have happened, and your father and I have decided to separate." Callie gasped and abruptly stood, her chair clattering to the ground as she ran to the bathroom with Kristina close on her heels. Yuli's face was filled with joy, and she clapped her hands together. Waving her hands up into the air and chanting in unrecognizable words that Katie was certain were prayers of gratitude, her utter glee was apparent. Katie fought the urge to join her celebration and focused on the kids.

Beckett asked Jeff, "What did you do?" a pointed question that made her heart swell in the presence of his absolute loyalty.

"He didn't *do* anything," Lauren answered for him immediately, defending her father. "Right, Dad?" Looking up at her father, her brown eyes were glossy and filled with hope.

Jeff cleared his throat. "Sometimes people drift apart." Katie shot him a look, and he froze.

Sometimes your husband's dick falls into his legal assistant's vagina. The words seemingly pulled out of thin air sat at the tip of her tongue, begging for release. Katie had to swallow them down to prevent them from escaping. Clinically naming genitalia in front of an audience (that included her children) was not something she normally relished.

"Sometimes people come into your life for a season, and your mother and my season is over," Jeff continued. Yuli muttered to herself and rolled her eyes.

"You don't just give up on Mom! She's done everything for you," Beckett said.

"You son of a bitch!" David raged, finally finding his voice. He was a quiet man, complacent and easy going. "The sacrifices our Katie made."

"Dad." Katie ran to his side. "It's not good for your heart to get so worked up." She wrapped her arm around his thin frame and navigated him back to the recliner.

Not skipping a beat, Jeff tried to paint himself in a

better light. "We've *both* worked hard to provide a great life for all of you."

"Right." Beckett was annoyed and unconvinced.

"Dad," Katie said to David, smoothing the wrinkled skin on his forearm. "I have to check on Callie. Promise me you'll stay here and not get in the middle of anything."

"I'm not an invalid!"

"I know that, but right now, I need you to remain calm."

"Fine," he muttered and crossed his arms across his chest.

Needing to check on Callie, Katie rapped on the guest bathroom door with the back of her knuckles. "Honey. Can I come in?"

"Sure," Callie said and opened the door, her eyes red-rimmed from crying. Kristina motioned Katie inside, giving her daughter a tight squeeze. After a long pause, Callie spoke. "Why, Mom? What's going to happen to you? What's going to happen to our house? Where are we going to go for Thanksgiving?"

"Whoa, those are all valid questions, honey, and we will figure them out as we go. Come here." Katie pulled Callie's trembling body close to her own. "No matter what, you have two parents who love you, and that will not change. I'm sorry this news upsets you. I wish there was another way. But don't you want me to be happy?"

"Of course I do."

"The truth is, I haven't been happy in a really long time," Katie admitted.

"You haven't?" Kristina and Callie asked in unison. Callie sniffled, looking up at Katie.

"I haven't," Katie confirmed. "Now that I'm fifty with half of my life behind me, it's time to make myself happy. I can't live through you and your brother and sister anymore. I deserve more for myself."

Kristina nodded in understanding. "No one knows what goes on inside a marriage, sweetheart," she said to Callie, trying to smooth her crushed feelings, and Katie's heart swelled with love for her mother's defense. "But are you certain?" she asked, meeting Katie's strong, steady gaze for another long minute. "Okay. I can see that you are." Exhaling, she continued, "Then you have our full support."

"Thanks, Mom." Katie let out a long breath. "Callie, I know this is going to take some time to accept, but it's happening. I love my family. You, Beckett, and Lauren are the best decisions I ever made, and I do not regret one moment of my life spent mothering you. But now it's time for more. It's time for me to step into a better-fitting life, but no matter what, I promise you, my darling, there will always be room for you in it."

"I know," Callie said. "But change is hard."

"It is," Katie agreed. "And to be honest, I've feared it most of my adult life, but I know without a shadow of a doubt in my heart of hearts, this is the right decision for me."

Callie sobered up in the presence of the strong timber of her mother's newfound confidence.

"Let's go see the others. It will be okay." Katie said.

They walked with arms around each other to the kitchen, where the rest of the family sat quietly around the table. "Maybe dinner isn't such a good idea after all, considering what we just shared with all of you?" Katie offered. "How about we get together next week when some of the dust settles and we can talk?"

Their heads bobbed up and down in agreement, and then they shuffled out one by one. Lauren hugged Jeff and then slipped away. It was an obvious slight that hurt Katie's fragile heart. Beckett's shoulders were thrust back, his jaw clenched.

"I love you," Katie whispered into the crook of his warm neck. "It hasn't been good for a long time between your father and me. I hope you understand and can find it in your heart to forgive me." He pulled back with a tight nod.

Callie lingered with Kristina and David. Katie offered them a sad smile and then helped get the rest of her family settled in their car. The news had rattled Kristina and David, seeming to shrink them. Katie reached over and pulled the seatbelt across her fragile father's lap. "Give 'em hell, ladybug. You need anything, you come to me."

"Thanks, Dad. You're the one man I could always count on. They don't make 'em like you anymore."

The sentiment brought tears to her lashes. She closed his door and then opened the door to the back seat, where Callie gave her a quick hug and then scooted into the back of the car.

Finally, Yuli pulled Katie in close for a bear hug. "You are stronger than you realize. Life is just getting ready to open up for you." Katie pulled back as the older woman brushed her enormous hand that was remarkably soft across her cheek.

"I'm sorry Jeff and I ruined our birthday celebration."

"You've ruined nothing. All is as it should be."

"I hope you're right."

"You'll see. Yuli knows."

"I have so many questions," Katie pleaded, looking into her grandmother's warm eyes.

"And I have many answers, my dear. We will talk soon."

She stood in the driveway and watched their brake lights disappear. Jeff had let himself out, slithering away on his yellow belly without so much as a goodbye. The hard part was over now. Everyone she loved knew of the impending divorce. She didn't have to hide anymore; it was the most bittersweet moment of her life. A weight, she didn't realize she'd been carrying for years, lifted. With a sad smile, she brushed a tear away, then gathered up her bag and keys and drove with the top down to her favorite tapas restaurant. It was her birthday week, dammit, and Katie was going to celebrate it.

ELEVEN

The next morning, Katie tugged on her shoes and went for a walk. The streets of Aura Cove were deserted in the early light of a new day. Turning out of the cul-de-sac her home was tucked into, she walked down the quaint streets of the tourist town. Glancing over her shoulder, she felt uneasy, like she was being watched as she walked past Kandied Karma in the heart of the tiny bustling downtown. She walked past gift shops, a realtor, and a photography studio. Stopping, she studied the plate-glass window where happy families smiled back at her in their sun-kissed beach family portraits.

Were these families actually happy? Or were they just sleepwalking through their lives, too? She wondered what her life looked like on the outside to strangers.

"Stop caring about what other people think and live your own life," she muttered under her breath.

Katie turned away to start walking, catching movement out of the corner of her eye, when at her hip, the phone rang.

"Hey, sweetheart, we just wanted to see how you're holding up after everything that happened last night." Kristina's soft voice filled Katie's ears. In the background, she heard her father's pipe up. "Ask her if she needs any money." David avoided phone calls at all costs. Instead, he placed his wife on the other end as an interpreter, shouting out his questions and demands as Kristina played middle man.

"Tell Dad I'm fine. I'm actually out on a walk right now, getting my steps in. This revenge body isn't going to build itself." She picked up her pace and headed back home.

"That's nice, dear." Her tone was soothing and sweet. "What's a revenge body?"

"Nothing, Mom." Katie wasn't about to explain the finer points of being single again and dating after divorce to her mother. "Did you need something?"

"We're worried about you. Now that you've had some time to sit with it, are you sure? People change their minds all the time. I'm sure you could give your marriage another chance if you wanted to."

"Mom, I love you, I do. But yes, I am one hundred percent sure." To put their doubts to bed, she told her parents the unvarnished truth. "Jeff was unfaithful."

There was an audible gasp on the other end of the phone. "What a jerk!" Kristina said, then covered the receiver with her hand and shouted out, "David, Jeff was cheating on Katie!"

"I always hated that no-good son-of-a-bitch!" She heard her dad's muffled words as he railed in the background. "I knew he was a shyster!"

"Well, he sure fooled me," Kristina admitted. "That man talks out of both sides of his mouth. I feel like such a fool."

"If it makes you feel any better, he fooled us both."

"It doesn't," Kristina answered sadly. "I'm so sorry." Her mother's apology was dripping with pity, and Katie felt herself recoil from it. She didn't want it. Eager to hang up the phone, she cradled it between her shoulder and her ear as she used the mailbox key to open her slot in the free-standing group box at the end of her street. Nestled inside an L.L. Bean catalog was the small box of smelly revenge Frankie ordered that made her grin. Maybe this *was* going to be a good day after all.

"Got a big day ahead?" Kristina asked to make conversation.

"Actually, I've got something important to take care of right now. Please give Dad a hug. Love you, Mom."

She hung up and hurried back to her house, then tiptoed inside, listening for any signs of movement. Hearing none and confirming that Jeff was still sleeping, she texted Frankie. While she waited, she turned off the security cameras Jeff insisted on that ringed the house.

Twenty minutes later, she met Frankie outside with the bottle.

"Come to mama," Frankie said, rocking a messy bun, a Rolling Stones t-shirt, and a pair of long cutoff jean shorts. "Gimme!" She rubbed her fingers together in delight.

"And while you're busy with that, I found another little way to your revenge-thirsty heart." Katie waved a tube of Gorilla glue in the air.

"Gas cap?" Frankie asked, waggling her eyebrows with a mischievous glint in her eye.

"Exactly," Katie answered. "Who knew revenge could be so fun?"

"I did," Frankie said. "I knew. Welcome to the dark side, my friend." She laughed a deep, maniacal, "Mwahaha!"

Katie pressed the unlock button on Jeff's key fob, and Frankie slid into the buttery black leather upholstery of his Beamer. Through the window, she saw Frankie pull the dropper from the package and squeeze it into the air vents. Katie stood outside the car and busied herself opening the gas cap. Within seconds, the foul stench must have hit Frankie's gag reflexes, and she jumped out of the car, dry heaving, then ran to the bushes and promptly vomited.

"I don't think I've ever been as satisfied with an online purchase," Frankie said when she returned, her eyes watery and red. "And in case you ever wondered, this is how much I love you, Katie Beaumont. I'm not done yet. I'm going back in." She offered Katie a wicked grin and made quick work of adding more droppersful of it to the passenger vents. Then she bent down and dribbled it onto the underside of the seat. Katie watched through the windshield as the thirsty rawhide of the leather visor wicked away the liquid from the dropper. In the car, Frankie yanked her t-shirt up over her nose and mouth, attempting to breathe through it.

Katie knocked on the glass and tapped at her watch. "We have to hurry. He'll wake up any minute!" She raced back to the side of the car and carefully spread a thick line of glue all the way around the gas cap, and then also ringed the cap in her hand before twisting it back on and shutting the little gas door. Frankie emerged from the car again, coughing and dry heaving. It took a full five minutes of fresh air before she could get herself under control. Holding the key fob above her head, the alarm beeped twice as Katie pressed it to lock the doors before they walked calmly back into the house.

"And now we wait," Frankie said, washing her hands, still taking in huge gulps of air to clear the rancid smell from her lungs. "That stuff is the real deal. I feel like I can taste it."

"Ick!" Katie crinkled up her nose in disgust, unsure they'd done the right thing, but it quickly passed when she laughed out loud at the vision of Jeff at a gas pump struggling to get the gas cap off. Sweating and straining in his four-thousand-dollar suit.

"I'm only sad I won't get to see it with my own eyes, Arlo," Katie said, and he barked in agreement, following her around the kitchen. They enjoyed French toast on the lanai and lingered over Irish coffees.

An hour later, Jeff slid open the patio door to make an announcement. "I've got a meeting." He was already showered and ready.

"You don't have to inform me of your schedule anymore," Katie answered back before he slid the door shut.

"Ooh! It's go-time!" Frankie popped up and quickly gathered the sticky plates and silverware together. "It's like Christmas Eve, and I've been a good girl, Santa!"

"You have not!" Katie countered.

Frankie gasped and pretended to clutch pearls at her

throat. Then an engaging grin spread across her freckled cheeks. "Okay, fine. You might be right."

A few minutes later, an angry Jeff returned to the house, slamming the door behind him. "Disgusting," she thought she heard him say. Her ears perked up in excitement as she overheard his first few words. Her eyes widened and locked on Frankie's as she sucked her lips in between her teeth to stop the spread of glee that wanted to work its way across her face. Frankie reached out and gripped her hand and shook with repressed laughter.

"It's happening!" Frankie whispered as she did a little booty shake. Her excitement apparent.

In the study, they heard him make a call. "Dante? It's Jefferson Beaumont. What the hell did you do to the Beamer yesterday when you detailed it? It reeks so foul, it's like something died in there."

Katie heard him pause for a moment before he interrupted. "Absolutely not. Make arrangements to come and get it today by noon. Keys are in it."

"Oh no! Liquid Ass baking in the scorching sun? Poor Dante. He's the actual victim here," Katie whispered. She made a mental note to give him a one-hundred-percent tip the next time he detailed her car.

Jeff was silent for a few long minutes. "Fine, I'll drive it down myself."

"See, there is a God, and he loves me!" Frankie cheered with a grin. "I've got to run to work. I'll text you later." She hugged Katie and then quickly left.

A few minutes later, Jeff entered the kitchen. His shoulders were tense and his expression pinched. He yanked open the refrigerator and searched for a solid five minutes before asking, "Where's the almond milk?"

"I don't drink it," Katie said sweetly. "Looks like that is something you are going to have to start getting on your own. Sorry." She wasn't sorry, not one little bit. His obvious irritation was filling her with satisfied glee.

She glanced down at her watch. Katie had a full day ahead. First a consultation at the Med Spa and then an appointment with Davina to go over the next steps. She walked to the door without another word, put on her shoes, and left.

———

Katie sat in the waiting room at the plastic surgeon's office, glancing over at the marketing cutouts for Botox and Cool Sculpting when a stunning woman waltzed in on a breeze of lavender. All the heads of the women in the waiting room swiveled to marvel at her. A fevered hum intensified as the women in the room whispered to each other. Katie could only make out bits and pieces of the conversation. "That looks like Ana Castanova!" and "No wonder she looks so good." and "Looks like I'm in the right place."

The name sounded familiar, but she couldn't place it. The other women's interest piqued her own, and she stole glances at the woman over the top of the issue of *Good Housekeeping* she was pretending to read. She was striking, her Marilyn Monroe curves poured into a body-conscious dress. Her long white hair gathered into a long plaited braid as thick as Katie's wrist and fell down to her curvy hips. Her complexion was porcelain, the perfect shade of ivory with a delicate blush on her cheeks. Where the other women in the waiting room (herself included) were sporting deep tans and age spots that came with decades of summers spent frying your teenaged skin slathered in baby oil, the woman in front of her was glowing. Her lips were full and thick. Her magnetic beauty transfixed Katie, and she was drawn to her. Katie's frequent glances escalated to unabashedly staring the woman down, unable to tear her eyes away. The woman winked, then put on chic sunglasses and was immediately whisked into a treatment room.

"Katie Beaumont?" A fresh-faced nurse called her name, breaking the spell.

"That's me." Katie stood and followed the nurse into the examining room. After taking her vitals and history, the doctor appeared within minutes.

"Tell me what you'd like to change about yourself."

"Everything," Katie joked with a self-deprecating chuckle.

He tipped his head, studying her quietly, his inquisitive eyes a pale shade of blue.

Katie shifted in the seat and felt her face flush. "A little freshening up, maybe?" she asked tentatively. "I just turned fifty. I'm getting a divorce, and gravity is killing me. I guess I'm looking for the whole midlife crisis starter kit."

He pretended to nod in agreement and used his feet to wheel his stool closer to Katie, where he examined her with a practiced eye. "We could do a little Botox here and here." His cool fingers traced the slight eleven that had taken up residence between her brows in her forties.

"Make a frown for me," he told her.

She did, and he continued to examine her forehead.

"Most women need their first facelift at fifty, but all I think you need is a chemical peel." He leaned closer and tugged at Katie's forehead while she clutched the mirror. "There isn't much movement. You've got great elasticity. Good genes."

The compliment prickled tears in her eyes, and she cleared her throat to distract him from seeing them. Compliments from Jeff had dwindled over the years, eventually coming to a halt when the kids were grown, so to hear a stranger give her one pulled at her heartstrings.

"If you wanted to do the treatment today, I can send one of my estheticians in right now." He gave her hand a gentle squeeze and Katie folded. In hindsight, she probably should have asked a few more questions about the procedure. But after she'd seen Ana Castanova's flawless skin in the waiting room, she was all in.

At the beginning of the treatment, the numbing gel had been cool and calming and she'd been instructed to relax with her eyes closed until her skin felt numb to the touch. The relaxing start did not prepare her for the full-on assault that came next from the laser that burned. For the next twenty minutes, a flawless esthetician was ruthless in her pursuit of treating Katie's entire face. Each electrical zap from her wand made Katie jump.

"I'm so sorry," the sweet twenty-something wielding the instrument of torture said. "I guess what they say is true. Beauty is pain."

"I'm not so sure it's worth it," Katie whimpered as she suffered a series of ten more zaps.

"Give it a week. Then you'll be singing my praises."

An hour and six hundred dollars on their joint credit card later, she walked out of the office and into the warm sunny day. Her face was on fire. Suffering a relentless burning sensation from forehead to chin, she heeded the advice to stay out of the Florida sun and put on a hat that was in the back of the car for her regular walks on the beach.

"Shoot," she said to herself, glancing at her watch. "I better hustle. I'm going to be late." Slamming her foot on the accelerator, she was relieved to arrive in record time and ran into the building without so much as a glance in the rear-view mirror. Her cheeks were still flaming and crying out for relief.

A few minutes later, she sat in Davina's office waiting for her lawyer to arrive, studying the framed diplomas on the wall to pass the time. Davina rushed in, all apologies, setting her briefcase on the ground.

"Sorry, I'm late. I was in court." She settled into the chair and finally glanced up at Katie. Her eyes widened. "Whoa. What did you do to yourself?"

Katie felt herself blush, but her cheeks were already so red she knew it was undetectable. "Just a little chemical peel. The esthetician said they call it a lunch break treatment. I'd be able to go back to the office right away with rosy skin."

"Rosy?" Davina laughed. "The verdict is in. You are dangerously deep into the lobster red category." A smile teased the corners of Davina's lips. "Why do women torture themselves to stay young?"

"I was just trying to spruce up the view a little… I mean, eventually, I'm going to have to put this fixer-upper back on the market." Really, she knew it would be a long time before she'd ever consider it.

"Men." Davina sighed. "They have it so easy. Why do they get to become distinguished and sexy when their hair turns gray, but we are supposed to stay smooth and supple like a co-ed until we die? That's the real injustice in this world."

She wasn't wrong.

"Okay. Let's get down to brass tacks." Davina plunged into the folder on her immaculate desk.

"They requested access to all the financial records going back seven years. That's typical. "

"I'll send them over."

"You must fill out this financial affidavit, and he will have to do the same. Do you have any reason to believe he has any undisclosed assets?"

The safe deposit image flashed in her mind. "I didn't think so, but I honestly wouldn't put anything past him now. I always thought I knew my husband, but I am learning I didn't really know him at all."

"I see this all the time." Davina shrugged.

"How do we find out if he's being truthful?" Katie asked, unaware of the ins and outs of divorce proceedings.

"A forensic accountant. They aren't cheap, but you can't hide anything from my guy."

Katie let out a long breath.

"Look," Davina said. "We have to prepare for war."

"I just want this all to be over."

"No. No. No." Davina leaned forward. "You need to change that mindset right now. We are fighting for the assets that are rightfully yours, so you can start over and rebuild your life."

"It's all so overwhelming." Katie sighed. "No wonder people stay in awful marriages."

"I know it is," Davina agreed. "But it's the only way to ensure he compensates you fairly. Trust me, you will regret not going hard core in a few years when the dust settles and you are stuffed into a tiny townhouse or apartment because that is all you can afford."

Katie shivered at the prospect. It wasn't that she couldn't do it, it just simply wasn't fair. She'd done her time in crappy apartments in her twenties and paid her dues. The idea of going backward made her skin crawl and anger roil up in her belly.

"Suck it up, buttercup. We are just getting started," Davina warned, then changed gears. "Where are you living?"

"At home."

"Where's Jeff?"

"At home."

"I would be remiss in my duties if I didn't advise you this sort of living arrangement is not recommended."

"I know, but I am not leaving my house and he's digging in and refusing to get an apartment. At least he's in the guest suite on the second floor of the house."

"Roommates?" Davina chuckled. "That never works out well."

Katie was quiet, scraping at the hole in her jeans,

fidgety and anxious. She fanned her hot cheeks with the documents Davina put in her hand.

"Do not discuss the case with him in any capacity," Davina said, leveling her eyes on Katie. Her gaze was relentless and unyielding. "He is going to manipulate you for information. Always remember this phrase. All further communication will be conducted through my attorney. If he starts in or tries to bait you, simply disengage and walk away. Stay as far away from him physically as you can."

"I'll do my best, but I think that's going to be a problem," Katie muttered. This conversation was exhausting her, and she was desperate to leave. She glanced at her watch. It had already cost her $250 of her precious retainer. "Is there anything else I need to know?"

"We'll be going to mediation after the financials are verified. I'll keep you in the loop."

Davina stood and Katie rushed out of the office to the privacy of her car and drove home. Tears cooled down her freshly lasered cheeks. Everything hurt.

TWELVE

Zoya watched Katie pull out of the driveway for her typical Thursday night shift at Kandied Karma, grateful her great, great granddaughter was such a creature of habit. She tugged down on the baseball cap that topped a blonde wig that she'd fitted tightly on her head. The rest of her outfit was shapeless and unflattering. A *Life's a Beach* t-shirt and some old sweat pants from Florida State. Just the way she wanted it.

Her eyes focused on a security camera at the corner of the roofline, and she spotted another on the eaves of the house next door. "Damn it," she muttered under her breath, annoyed at their presence.

Modern technological advances were the bane of Zoya's existence. There seemed to be a camera on every corner now, recording the day-to-day minutiae of life. It was tedious. What did all this incessant data gathering accomplish, anyway? Life was better in the 70s, before the wretched iPhone was invented and everyone began to photograph their food. It was easier to dispose of problems in the days before DNA technology and companies offering genetic breakdowns and ancestral links gave big businesses the ability to gather even more data points per individual. The ordins never saw the forest for the trees, but Zoya did.

She snapped her fingers to create static on all the security cameras within a city block. Then she slipped from the shadows, walked down the side of the house to the backyard, and went up the stairs to the deck. She opened the slider and Arlo ran out, nervous and jittery, a furry ball of spastic energy. While she waited for him to run down the steps to squat on the only green area below, she tugged a chair from the ones gathered around the table. She heard his tags jingling together as he raced back up the stairs and then sat down at her feet.

"So, how did it go?" she asked once he was settled.

"About as well as expected. He was an absolute douche until the end, though. Kicked me!"

"Don't worry, he'll get his comeuppance," Zoya offered. "But more importantly, Katia ate the truffles, correct? Did she have a reaction?"

"She did. I tested her, speaking using human words for the first time, and she got a little untethered."

"The first time is always the hardest to accept." Zoya knew from experience. Once you saw magic with your own eyes and heard the impossible with your own ears, other magical acts were easier to accept. Much like when men had affairs, the first one was always the hardest. After that, betrayal was a breeze. Zoya's full lips turned downward.

"Why she ever married that pretentious blow hard in the first place, I will never understand."

"She was young," Arlo reasoned.

"Your loyalty to your mistress is one of your most endearing qualities." Zoya gave the compliment, then patted him on the head to indicate that his line of reasoning was weak. "Do you have any idea how hard it was to sit back and watch her get used like that? Always at his beck and call? And the parade of mistresses?" She cried in frustration, "Sweet Jesus, the man is simply not that handsome. The only thing remotely attractive on his pompous, flabby body is his wallet."

Arlo fell on his back, offering a barking laugh that Zoya joined. When the moment was over, he recovered and sat at attention once again.

"You're in a good mood," Arlo observed.

"I am," Zoya confirmed. "The third in our bloodline has just been awakened, and as a result, all of our powers will become stronger. What's not to love about that?" She paused and then continued, "Back to the matter at hand. What other details do I need to know?"

"She's got a lawyer. A good one."

"Who is it?" Zoya asked.

"Davina Thorne. She's a real ball-buster, and I overheard a conversation Jeff had with his attorney. He's afraid."

"Good." Zoya licked her lips in anticipation. The news delighted her, and she felt an unfamiliar emotion bubble up in her core. One she hadn't felt in many years. Joy. She popped up, filled with energy, and paced on the deck. Zoya looked out at the strip of ocean in the distance, the same ocean that was visible from her estate. The waves rolled in and then receded, giving her a nostalgic sense of connectedness to Katia that was unexpected. She shook her head to clear it. There were so many plans to make and pawns to play. Zoya didn't have time for this diversion right now. She had to focus.

"Do you think she's going to be able to put together the puzzle from the flashes she received?"

"Yuli will…" He started to explain and then was interrupted.

Zoya scowled and then spat on the ground next to him. "You are never to utter that name in my presence. I thought I was clear."

"My apologies." He lowered his head, averted his eyes, and tucked his tail between his curly-haired legs.

She snapped her fingers impatiently. He barked once to clear his throat and then continued, "We might need to give her a few nudges here and there, but yes, I have faith that the strong female lineage she comes from courses through her veins. It may take a few more nibbles, but she'll figure it out. That I am sure of."

Zoya couldn't let it go. Her tone down-shifted as an angry sneer curled her lips. "Yuli has kept my Katia from me for too long. She will pay."

"This feud, it is getting in the way. Wouldn't you become more powerful if you worked together?"

"I will never join forces with that woman. Ever," Zoya spit out. "Careful," she warned. "Who do you think you are, questioning my motives?"

Arlo let out a distressed whine. "You don't need Yu— her," he stammered as he corrected himself. "You are the most powerful force in all the seven continents." He bowed deeply and backtracked, averting his eyes to the floor as he prostrated himself in her presence. "My apologies, again."

His compliment softened her rage. "Keep an eye on our girl."

"I will, My Queen."

"Flattery will get you everywhere with me. How many dog years are left on your sentence?"

"Seven."

"You will have paid your debt and secured your freedom next year, barring any further infractions."

Arlo's eyes sparkled at the thought of it. "You mean I only have to lick my arsehole for another year? You are too generous."

"I am." Zoya smiled as a soft sea breeze tickled her face. She opened the door and let Arlo back into the house, then left quickly. She had work to do.

THIRTEEN

A few days later, Katie was working the final minutes of her regular Saturday shift at Kandied Karma. The Aura Cove store was a jewel box of purposeful color that appealed to women. Yuli commissioned a well-sought-after interior designer whose proposed color palette of magenta, lime green, and gold leaf transformed the room into a posh boutique. Her success followed her from Chicago to Florida, and her chocolates were now receiving national attention. She'd also cultivated relationships with the five-star restaurants up and down the coast that drove the price of her truffles into the stratosphere.

"Never engage in a race to the bottom," Katie remembered Yuli telling her when she'd opened her store in Aura Cove and Katie had gasped at the prices on the menu. "Set the bar high. Give your customers an experience. Make them feel special. Then you can charge whatever you want and they will pay."

Compared to the brilliant businesswoman her grandmother was, Katie sometimes felt small, that her dreams of being a wife and a mother were not worthy pursuits, even though Yuli never voiced that opinion. The self-doubt popped up again and again like insecurity whack-a-mole. Because of an unplanned pregnancy, Katie didn't have the luxury of time to really consider the path her life was taking, but when the kids became more self-sufficient, the self-doubt and self-criticism returned with a vengeance. Now that the kids were adults and Jefferson would soon exit stage left, she could decide. It was a decadent idea that welled hope up in her center.

The bell on the door jingled as the last patron left with their gold package tucked under their arm, and Katie locked the door behind him. Needing a pick-me-up after eight hours on her feet, Katie added two scoops of coffee to the machine to brew a fresh pot to share with Yuli. The job was a simple one, but the reason she loved it was because of the quality time she got to spend with her grandmother. Jeff had made it known on more than one occasion that Yuli wasn't welcome in his home. Rather than fighting him, she increased her shifts at the store, offering to make deliveries and help customers choose chocolates for gifts. She loved working at Kandied Karma, where the scents of chocolate, vanilla bean, and browned butter hung heavy in the air. It was a joy to see the excitement on the faces of children who pressed their noses to the glass to be closer to the artisanal chocolates shaped like dinosaurs. She was often accompanied by Arlo, the most popular dog in Aura Cove, who became a bit of a celebrity due to her regular posting on Kandied Karma's Instagram account.

Katie hummed as she wiped down the chairs and cleaned a day's worth of fingerprints from the glass display case. She scrubbed the white marble countertops and tucked the chairs under the small bistro tables. Warm light cascaded through the plate glass wall at the front of the store, and in the back of the house was a fully functioning kitchen. It housed a commercial walk-in refrigerator, two sets of double ovens, four stovetops, and a chiller. In the center of the kitchen, four tables set in a square were covered in marble and offered workspace for cooling and packaging. There was an entire wall of gift wrapping paper on long spools fastened from the floor to the ceiling. Katie loved the wrapping station. It felt like Christmas every day in the store. Who could be mad at the world when you were busy placing magenta bows on top of neatly packaged treats wrapped in golden paper? It was impossible.

Finally, with the cleanliness of the shop passing her inspection, Katie poured two cups of strong coffee and added two dark chocolate truffles to a platter. She carried the tray to the back of the house where she was greeted by a smiling Yuli.

"What's got you in such a good mood?" Katie asked as Yuli pulled her in for a hug and then spun her around the kitchen. Katie laughed, intrigued by this outwardly joyful version of her grandmother, whose personality normally aligned more with the Queen of England. Stiff, unflappable, and even-keeled.

"Today is a great day," Yuli said, sitting on a hefty stool at one of the marble tables that could handle her large frame. She sipped on the coffee and waited while Katie settled on the stool across from her. "You are claiming your birthright."

Katie's forehead crinkled in confusion. "You're being cryptic and weird, even for you, Yuli."

"Untrue," she said with a secret smile as she gathered Katie's small hands in her own and squeezed. They were warm and soft. Her eyes locked on Katie's and she continued, "You do not know how long I have waited for this moment." She exhaled and then returned to her coffee, her thick fingers shaking as she stirred a tiny sugar cube into it. "I don't know where to start. There is much to tell you."

"You're speaking in riddles." Katie placed a dark chocolate truffle on Yuli's plate and slid it over to the older woman before serving herself.

"You know we share a birthday," Yuli began.

"Yep, July first," Katie confirmed; it was a fact that always made her smile. She loved celebrating with Yuli every year. It made the day even more special.

"But we share much more than that."

Katie leaned in closer, reaching out to squeeze the thick muscle of Yuli's forearm. "Yep, we share a lifetime of love."

"Ah. Yes. That is true." Yuli nodded. "But now that you are fifty, I am permitted to share our secrets. Many things you will not understand. You will need to suspend some of your limiting beliefs, but you will come to know our truth and step into your true form."

Soon you will know who you truly are. Katie heard the words again in her head. It had been easy to dismiss them the first time she'd heard them, but now they carried more weight. "This just keeps getting weirder and weirder,"

Katie said, feeling the first bubbles of nervousness release in her belly.

"We are alone, yes?" Yuli asked as her knowing eyes darted around the kitchen.

"Yes," Katie answered. "Unless you count Arlo." She pointed at the sleeping dog under her feet.

"What I am about to share with you will challenge everything you believe about life. I will answer all of your questions, but first, you must listen. Do you understand?"

Katie's eyes widened as she nodded. The urgency in Yuli's tone silenced Katie's questions, and her mouth felt dry.

"Our family has deep ties in history to the divine creation of the world. Our bloodline dates all the way back to Mesopotamia and the first civilizations. There was a division, an epic battle that was fought and won by the blood of your female ancestors that earned our freedom from the trappings of a male-dominated world." Yuli's eyes softened. "You are special, my sweet one. Your life has a greater destiny than your mother's. Since we won the war, it has given the women in our family lineage special privileges. We have extraordinary skills in an ordinary world."

"I don't understand."

"At the beginning of time, the first drop of blood was spilled from the pure soul of our first female ancestor, who was murdered by Cain. As recompense, angels endowed our female predecessors with special abilities of the supernatural. Generations later, our powers have only grown stronger."

"Wait," Katie interrupted. "What do you mean by supernatural?" Her tongue felt thick in her mouth.

"Magic," Yuli whispered with a knowing smile. Inside her head, Katie's heart hastened, and she felt it beat at her temples. "Women in our family with the gift have unusual abilities, live an exceptionally long time, and can only pass on to the afterlife when their gifts have been fully passed on to their successor," Yuli explained.

Accepting the answer, for now, Katie's curiosity got the best of her. "What can your powers do?" Katie asked, gazing at Yuli in awe. "What can mine do?" The prospect of discovering superhuman abilities was too heady to pass up.

Yuli continued, "We will get to that in due time." She took a sip of her coffee and continued. "The ordins have lost their connection to the source."

"The ordins?" Katie asked. "Who are the ordins?" she repeated, her brow wrinkled in confusion.

"Non-magical beings," Yuli explained. "Long ago, it was a level playing field. The difference was our bloodline kept the connection, the ordins did not, and each generation later was further removed. That is why, when you think of supernatural events or of the other realm, it seems ludicrous and impossible to believe. At one time, it was commonplace, but with each new generation, there has been further separation from our alternative reality."

Katie's head was swimming. Alternative realities? Yuli was the most levelheaded woman she'd ever known. It was hard to reconcile these two versions of her grandmother in her head.

Yuli continued, "The truffles I delivered to your door

on your birthday were an invitation to your awakening, to step into your birthright."

"Your note said, 'And then there were three. Taste and See.' What did you mean?" Katie asked.

"The truffles opened your third eye to enable you to see the true world and strengthen your intuition and insight," she explained. "Have you noticed anything unusual since you ate them? Or experienced a feeling you can't explain?"

Katie's eyes widened. "I *think* I did," she answered with uncertainty coating every syllable. "When Jeff touched me, I saw visions. They were flashes, mostly of scenes, like photographs in my mind."

"Retrocognition." Yuli looked at her with awe. "That's a very advanced power that isn't typically seen in a new Yaya."

"Retro-what?" Katie asked. "What's a Yaya?"

"Magical mother," she answered. "Retrocognition is the ability to see past events." Yuli nodded. "Your sight will develop. There are ways we can hasten its strength and clarity."

"But I thought it was all nonsense."

"Intuition is never nonsense. There are frequencies you can tap into and see actual events in the past. You are like a radio tuning into them, but instead of static, you are seeing and hearing messages," Yuli explained.

Katie nodded, remembering the message she'd heard.

Soon you will discover who you truly are.

The third time the message presented itself, goose-bumps broke out on Katie's forearms. She nodded but remained quiet. The information was hard to absorb and had turned everything she'd ever known on its head.

Yuli held up three fingers. "Now, there are three," she repeated from the note she'd written. "With your awakening, there are three generations of magical women and three others sandwiched in between. Our magic skips a generation and only awakens on your fiftieth birthday."

"Three generations?" Katie asked. "If what you say is true, and we count you and me, then who is the third?"

"Zoya. My grandmother," Yuli admitted, looking down. The mention of the other woman made her formidable form diminish. Arlo found his feet and howled, a forlorn cry that startled Katie.

"Shh, Buddy! Lie down." He whined, then circled her feet and plopped down in a huff.

"Wait a minute, are you telling me my great-great-grandmother is still alive?" Katie asked in astonishment. "Why have I never met her before?"

"I have protected you from her. Zoya is a selfish, hateful creature." Yuli's mouth pinched together and the lines on her forehead crisscrossed in concern. "You didn't matter to her for five decades, but with your awakening, you are the third in our bloodline. Three generations of witches complete the triad, which strengthens our power. It also is the beginning of the end for Zoya, and she will fight to remain."

"Wow." Katie was stunned, then started doing calculations in her mind. "She has to be over a hundred years old."

"She is one hundred and thirty-five."

Katie's eyebrows shot up, and she blinked several

times in long succession, trying to digest the words Yuli
was saying.

"Someone call Guinness because that is a record."
Katie tried to lighten the mood with a burst of levity.

"She's on her second identity. When you have unlim-
ited resources, you can shed your old life like a snake with
its skin," Yuli explained. "I've preferred to remain hidden
in plain sight. Zoya does not share that belief. It is the first
of many things we don't agree on."

There was another long pause as Katie tried to wrap
her head around the information that just kept coming.

"I believe magic should never be self-serving," Yuli
explained, "Do you know why I named the shop Kandied
Karma?"

"I never thought to ask," Katie admitted.

"Karma is simply energy. It is neither good nor bad; it
just is. For instance, if you plant apple seeds, you get an
apple tree. I decided long ago to use my powers to enable
good things, and to help right the wrongs of this world.
When I accepted this gift, people were drawn to me. I'd
touch them and see truths they were trying to hide. Over
the years, it's become very simple. I receive messages and
collaborate with Karma."

"What does that even mean?"

"The universe sends me people who deserve a rebalance, and I help Karma deliver it." Her eyes twinkled with
purpose.

"How do you know they need your help?"

"Touch. Skin-on-skin contact is like an electrical
circuit. When the circuit is complete, I receive messages.

Then it is up to me to interpret them. I believe we only receive messages from those who need our help."

Katie gulped. "It seems like a tremendous responsibility."

"It is," Yuli agreed. "But it is also incredibly rewarding. It's given my life a purpose, and I believe it will do the same for you."

Katie nodded, still stunned silent by the avalanche of information.

"What did you see?" Yuli asked. "You must always ask Karma, '*What are you trying to show me?*'"

"Okay." Katie nodded thoughtfully, reflecting on the flashes. She bit her thumbnail while concentrating. "I saw Jeff in a hotel room on top of a blonde woman. A bank statement and palm trees. A safe deposit box filled with stacks of cash. An ultra-modern kitchen with a million-dollar view. A pregnancy test and a water hut in Bali." Katie paused, then asked, "Wait, are you telling me I saw flashes of actual events that have already happened?"

"I am afraid so." Yuli reached out and squeezed Katie's forearm. "It seems Jeff has been a busy boy as of late. Maybe these are answers that will be useful to you as you begin your new life."

Katie felt the sting of shame, hoping there would be a purpose to her pain, but set it aside for now. "Tell me more."

"Don't despair, Katia. The answers will come to you." Yuli reached forward and smoothed her hand with her own. "Flashes are good. What else?"

Katie thought about the music box sitting on the curio cabinet shelf surrounding her fireplace. "I received a gift from Zoya a few days ago. It was an exquisite music box." Finally, understanding the gift was from her great-great-grandmother, the gesture bowled Katie over.

"Why didn't you tell me?" Yuli asked, clearly wounded.

"I didn't know." Katie tried to smooth over the hurt that registered on Yuli's face.

Yuli shivered. "She is the keeper of the archives."

"The archives?"

"Our ancestral history has been archived into music boxes. Zoya often wields them like weapons. She has subjected me to their harsh truths more than once." Yuli frowned. "What did you do with it?"

"I opened it, and inside was a miniature diorama of the day I took the kids to see the ocean for the first time. You're never going to believe this, but it pulled me inside it." She whispered the last few words. That sounded ridiculous when she said them out loud.

"I believe you," Yuli whispered. "Memory is a powerful tool. She is manipulating you for her own agenda." Her words were somber, and she was silent for a long moment. "You must never open the box again."

"I know, but it's been difficult. It's just so beautiful." Katie longed to relive the memory lodged deep in her mind.

"Magic requires sacrifice," Yuli said. "You have to give to get. If you re-open the box, it will be destroyed and you'll likely lose that memory forever."

"What? No way," Katie responded. "I'll never forget that day. It's one of my most cherished memories."

Yuli chuckled. "You will learn. There is a mystical

tradeoff, energy for energy. You must learn discernment, and Karma will ask you to do impossible things. To make sacrifices that could destroy you."

The weight of her sentiment filled the room with a dread Katie couldn't shake off. "Does Mom know?"

"Of course not. She is an ordin and can't handle our truth," Yuli answered. "It would sound like the insanity of an aging mind, and you know she has a tendency to hover."

"She does." Katie nodded. "Even at Northwestern, she still found an excuse to visit me every weekend."

"Her family is her heart. I raised her that way," Yuli said with pride.

"You're telling me you've been living a double life for decades?" Katie asked, shocked at the new information.

"It was the only way to keep the people I love safe."

Katie looked down at Arlo gathered at her feet, twisting and contorting his body to lick his undercarriage.

Yuli snapped her fingers at the dog, and he sprung up.

"Yes, Your Majesty." His voice was craggy from disuse.

"You can talk?" Katie flushed hot and began waving her hands in front of her face to cool down. Red hot heat rushed to her flushed chest and face. "I knew it!" Katie was thrilled with herself. "I thought I was losing my mind! Say something," she asked.

"Something," he repeated with a naughty grin on his furry face.

"You can think?"

"I'm not an imbecile!" Arlo explained. "I was a celebrated philosophy scholar when I crossed paths with Zoya."

Yuli snorted. "She believes all men are dogs, so when she is wronged by one, she casts a spell that forces him to become a dog, groveling and serving her until she feels he has learned his lesson and earned his freedom."

"I'm on my *fourth* lifetime in a furry body," he spat out, clearly frustrated.

"What?" Katie was stunned. "How could that be? I adopted you from the shelter."

"That is what Zoya has led you to believe, my dear."

Shocked to learn that a great-great-grandmother she'd never met had been behind the scenes orchestrating her life for years, Katie continued her line of questioning. "But dogs are love. They are everything that is right in this world. Why wouldn't she choose something more sinister, like a snake?"

"Snakes are sacred beings," Yuli answered, then an over-eager Arlo interrupted her, happy to offer an explanation.

"Most dogs are love, but there are a few of us that are trapped in servitude. If all goes swimmingly, she will free me to return to my human form in a year's time."

Katie leaned back, shaking her head to clear it. This was a lot of new information to take in.

"Unless, of course, your dear great-great-grandmother has been bread crumbing me." Arlo accused, his wariness evident.

"Careful!" Yuli warned him. "Do not speak ill of Zoya!"

"It's been eighty-two years, and you still tremble like a

scared child when you say her name." Arlo pushed his luck.

Irritated, Yuli snapped her fingers, and the dog whined, then collapsed back at Katie's feet in a huff.

"Eight-two? Since you've seen your grandmother?" Katie couldn't comprehend it. "I could never live that long without you. I cherish our relationship."

"I know, Katia," Yuli answered. "It's not what I wanted either, but now that you're awakening as the strongest female in our bloodline, she will know. Zoya will soon make an appearance. I'm sure of it. I must protect you from her."

"From my flesh and blood?"

"Especially from your own flesh and blood."

Fourteen

After her visit with Yuli, Katie struggled to make sense of everything. It was a heavy secret she carried, but she put it on the back burner in favor of a more important task. Katie glanced at the watch that ringed her wrist. Lauren was running late for their lunch date, a lesson she learned from her father, who always prioritized his precious time over everyone else's.

"Always show up five minutes late to any in-person meeting," he'd advised the kids when they were teenagers. "After all, the meeting can't start without you, and you'll gain the edge in any negotiation. It sends a message that you are the most important person in the room. It's how you become one percent better, and one percent compounded over time is significant." His life lessons went in one ear and out the other with Callie and Beckett, but Lauren blindly followed his advice to the letter. It had served her well as she climbed the ranks at her own law firm, making a name for herself in patent law.

To fill the time, Katie pulled out her Kindle and dove into her latest download. Ten minutes later, a wary Lauren breezed in. Her long dark hair was flat-ironed straight, so it fell like a curtain down her back. Wearing a demure pink suit and nude heels, she looked like she stepped off a runway.

"Hey, honey, you look beautiful," Katie offered as she stood and opened her arms tentatively, an olive branch attempt Lauren ignored, sitting down quickly. The dis made Katie's cheeks flush pink with embarrassment. Katie cleared her throat and hastily sat back down.

Across the expanse of the Formica table, Lauren's eyes locked on hers and Katie was the first to break the gaze and look away. This would not be easy. Katie picked at a chip on the edge of the table, a tiny speck compared to the enormous chip currently resting on her daughter's shoulder. She glanced up with a tight smile, registering the stiff set of Lauren's jaw. "You obviously have something on your mind, so let's talk about it."

"Why are you doing this to Daddy?" Lauren started right in, like a dog with a bone. "You're a fifty-year-old woman. It sounds more like you are having a midlife crisis to me."

The cruelty in her oldest daughter's assessment was a stab to her heart. "Wow," Katie said aloud, gathering the courage to continue one of the toughest conversations she'd ever had with Lauren. "I don't *have* to give you an explanation, but I will. Sweetheart, there are things that happen inside a marriage that no one outside it will understand."

"What's to understand? Dad told me he wants you to

stay together. Why would you destroy your family like this? It's selfish."

Katie grabbed her water glass to cool the fire in her belly. Hearing the word selfish, an ice cube in the water dislodged and the deluge of water sent her into a choking fit. After five agonizing minutes of hacking and sputtering so loud most of the heads in the restaurant swung toward her to see if she'd survive, she finally called out in a hoarse voice, "Nothing to see here, folks. Go about your business." The event left her red-faced and breathless as she continued to clear her throat.

"It went down the wrong pipe." She coughed again, making a fist and beating on her chest as Lauren fidgeted in her seat.

Lauren's eyes darted around the crowded dining room as Katie repeatedly coughed and sipped the water, fighting to get herself under control. "Mom. Jesus, you are so embarrassing."

"What?" Katie asked, oblivious.

"Nothing," Lauren muttered, then continued, "Dad said he wants to go to couples counseling. Isn't that great news?"

Katie choked again on the water. "Warn me next time before you say something that ludicrous! Seriously, girl, you are killing me." Two short coughs later, she finally rasped out, "Your father? In therapy? By choice? Come on, Lauren, you know as well as I do that would never happen." Katie dared to take one more long sip of cool water before she continued. "I know you love your father, and I don't want to speak ill of him behind his back, but our marriage is over."

"But why?"

"It's been dead between us for a very long time."

"That's just an excuse."

Katie's anger was rising in the face of her daughter's absolute loyalty, and she fought the desire to spell it out for her. She wanted to shout, *'Your father is a cheating pig who's been banging his legal assistant for over a year,'* but she stilled her heart. Katie was smart enough to know that, eventually, the truth would come out, and when it did, then Lauren would understand. Katie didn't want to be the one to destroy the façade of the perfect father Lauren idolized. Jeff would destroy it on his own, and when he did, Katie would be there to pick up the pieces.

"What are you going to do?" Lauren asked. "You're going to have to get an actual job, you know. Starting all over at fifty is not easy. Or you could just apologize to Dad and go back to the life you love."

"You sound just like your father," Katie accused, but Lauren took it as a compliment. "Right now, I'm looking at all my options."

"Options?" Lauren's tone was snarky. "What options? You have no degree, no marketable skills. What are you going to do? Wither away in that house, slinging candy on the weekends for Grandma?"

Katie recoiled. She'd underestimated how deep Jeff's programming ran in this one. "Respectfully, darling, I disagree. I put my children first and was the CEO of our home for almost two decades. Apparently it was a *thankless* job, but I excelled at it, and I'll *never* regret the time I spent raising you, Callie, and Beckett. Not for one minute."

The word thankless jolted Lauren from her judgmental mission. With a sigh, she leaned back in the booth and hugged her arms to her chest, then a fat tear gathered at her lashes and she turned away to dab at it with her napkin. "I'm sorry, Mom," she finally whispered. After a long moment, she continued, "We were a happy family, weren't we? I don't understand why you would want to walk away from us. I'm so conflicted because I love you both."

"Listen to me. I'm not walking away from you. I'll always be here whenever you need me. And, of course, you love us both! No one is asking you to pick sides," Katie offered, her tone soothing. "You don't have to worry about me. I'll figure it out. I always do." Lauren sniffed and swiped at the tears at her lash line. Katie offered her napkin to her daughter and continued, "You're right, I *am* fifty, and starting over is daunting at my age, but I would never let that stop me. This time, I get to do it on my own terms. Honestly, it's thrilling to get a do-over this late in life."

Lauren's head cocked to the side. "Do you regret having us?"

"Don't be silly! Of course not!" Katie protested with a teary smile. "On the resume of my life, my kids are my greatest accomplishment. You know, family has always been the most important to me."

Lauren nodded, the sentiment putting her fears to rest. "I don't know how to do this," she admitted, teary-eyed. "How do I walk this line between you and Dad?"

"I am not asking you to do that," Katie offered. "This will be difficult for all of us. We are all going to have to transition to a new normal."

"God, I hate that term." Lauren turned up her nose at it. "New normal. There is no such thing as normal."

"You have no idea how right you are," Katie said, thinking about Yuli and Zoya. "No idea." She reached out to squeeze her daughter's hand. "I love you, Lauren. Nothing is ever going to change that. I promise." Pointedly, she looked down at the menu. "Now, can we go back to just being a mother and a daughter out for a pleasant lunch, enjoying each other's company? It's not your job to fight our battles."

Lauren let out a sigh of relief and offered her mother a smile and a nod.

"Good. Why don't you order for us?"

Lauren chose the fried pork belly with micro greens, miso soup, and a spinach and raspberry salad. They chit-chatted about everything under the sun, except for the divorce. When Katie drove home, she put the top down, enjoying the last rays of the Florida sun warming her shoulders. Making the last turn onto her street, her heart rejoiced when she saw Callie's car parked in the circular driveway.

Katie pulled into the garage and opened the door, lured inside by the musical quality of her children's voices. "Hello, my loves." She pulled Beckett and Callie into her arms. "This is a wonderful surprise."

Beckett was filling out and becoming more handsome by the day. The dark wavy hair on his head was rocking a pompadour cut that made him devilishly handsome. Callie's long bohemian skirt and white linen tank were effortlessly beautiful. Her glowing skin never needed makeup to enhance her gorgeous features. Now she saw them both with fresh eyes. Yuli's admission that their supernatural powers skipped a generation meant her children would be spared. They would live normal, average lives like her parents. At first, the thought brought her comfort and peace.

She studied their youthful features with a smile as they teased each other. Beckett hip-checked Callie, who playfully shoved him back and then reached down to give Arlo's splayed belly a long rub that made his tongue lallygag outside his mouth. She laughed, initially, but then the simple everyday moment made a lump form in Katie's throat.

All at once, an undeniable truth hit her like a lightning bolt as she watched an interaction unfold she'd witnessed a million times before, and she gripped the countertop to keep herself from reeling. She gasped as the painful truth was revealed, recognizing its heart-wrenching accuracy immediately. Katie would outlive her children, without a doubt. One day, she would have to let them go. As vibrant and youthful as they appeared at this moment, they were aging. One day, their short lives would end and she would be forced to continue to live in a world without them. It was a stab to her fragile heart.

It was the first brutal truth of her new life she would have to hide from the people she loved most in the world, and it made her wonder how Zoya had done it for almost a century.

FIFTEEN

The next month sped by as strategy meetings with Davina consumed most of Katie's time. At the end of the month, a thick white envelope arrived holding an itemized, seven-page statement of her legal fees. As she watched her retainer dwindling, she was flooded with anxiety. She was so consumed by the impending mediation she had little time to consider or even accept the information Yuli shared. Her shifts at Kandied Karma were peppered in-between, but Yuli understood Katie was distracted, and neither of them broached the subject of their last discussion. There is only so much bandwidth a woman has in a day, and Katie's was currently consumed with her own survival.

Katie drove to her first mediation appointment, arriving five minutes early, and used the extra time to calm her nerves. Her mind cataloged all the foreseeable outcomes, scurrying thoughts around her head in a frenzy that wasn't helpful. She gathered up her handbag and entered the revolving door. On autopilot, the door forced her through, swiftly depositing her into an expansive lobby where Davina waited, holding her leather attaché case.

The lobby of the mediator was inside a slick glass skyscraper that stood sentinel at the shore with sprawling penthouse views of the Gulf. "Are you ready for this?" Davina asked when Katie was within earshot.

"I'm ready for this to be *over*," Katie admitted with a tight smile, a joke that Davina ignored.

"Let me handle all the negotiations. Your job is to keep calm and take your emotions out of it. Think of this as a business transaction. Best case, we walk out of here in agreement and can write the final divorce decree. Worst case, it's the first battle of a very lengthy war."

Katie nodded. She knew the likelihood of them coming to an agreement today was nil, but she was paying Davina a small fortune and was going to take her advice. Wearing blood-red, a perfectly pressed Davina cut an impressive figure, striding through the modern lobby toward the elevator. Her red-soled Christian Louboutin heels clicked out a threatening morse code on the marble floors. Katie skipped closely behind, hoping some of the woman's confidence would spill onto her in Davina's wake.

The young receptionist greeted then seated them in a mahogany conference room with a wall of windows on one end. A Waterford crystal pitcher of water sweated in the center of a massive conference table as they sank into the leather chairs that ringed it. Katie eyed a pyramid of bagels stacked high on a serving dish, but nixed the idea, acknowledging her dry mouth and the nervousness swirling in her belly.

"Davina," Harvey Waldinger said as he swept into the

room carrying his ebony briefcase, with Jeff in tow. He exuded the slick cockiness all successful attorneys did. It hung heavy on them both. The Rolex on Harvey's wrist was visual evidence of his exceptional skills in negotiation. A small smile crept onto Katie's face as she registered Jeff's suit, knowing it was his second choice since his lucky charm was now deep in the bowels of the landfill, stained with coffee grounds and bacon grease. She'd heard him chastising their dry cleaner yesterday, his anger seeping down from the guest suite through the vents, demanding to know what they had done with it. The exasperation in his voice was a minor victory she celebrated.

Jeff's silver hair was slicked back from his tanned forehead as he licked his lips in anticipation. The pair of lawyers were parasites cut from the same cloth, and it was like the blinders she'd worn her whole life lifted. She regarded Jeff as if seeing him for the first time. His eyes bore into hers, and for once, she didn't flinch and break the gaze. He was smug and self-satisfied, and there was no remnant left of the man she'd married. Sitting in her chair at the conference table, she realized the man in front of her now was a stranger.

At the head of the table was another man, a balding mediator named Gene, dressed in a cardigan sweater and corduroy pants, who was tasked to work through the details of their assets and find an amicable settlement. He gave off a Mister Rogers vibe that eased Katie's jumpy heart. After exchanging pleasantries, he rifled through the thick folder in front of him. Inside, it housed pages filled with the findings from Davina's forensic accountant, who was still digging but had already unearthed several discrepancies in Jeff's initial reporting on the affidavit. It was a card Davina planned on playing if they couldn't agree in mediation and their case had to go before a judge.

"Mrs. Beaumont is asking for spousal support in the amount of five thousand dollars a month," the mediator began.

The words were barely out of his mouth when Jeff bellowed, "That's preposterous!" Then, with one withering glance from Harvey, Jeff stopped speaking.

Davina interjected, "My client has sacrificed for her family her entire life and now is simply looking to maintain her standard of living."

"And can she explain why she has never pursued a viable career?"

"My client is employed, Mr. Waldinger, at Kandied Karma, her grandmother's luxury chocolate shop."

"That's an entry-level job fit for a sixteen-year-old," Harvey criticized. "There are no small children to care for in the home and haven't been for years. It looks to me like Mrs. Beaumont has coasted on the coattails of my client's hard work for the last decade when she could have better used the time to complete her education and enter the workforce. Instead of contributing to the family financially, she chose under-employment. It's despicable behavior."

Katie's blood boiled as she studied Jeff seated across from her, refusing to make eye contact. He stared down at the paper in front of him. His lips pressed together, his expression grim.

"My client agreed to maintain the household and care for the children," Davina began. She was unshakeable.

"Mrs. Beaumont dropped out of college when *your* client impregnated her. They decided *together* to divide their responsibilities, and it was an arrangement that worked for the better part of three decades. Why should my client be asked to sacrifice now and change her standard of living? The marriage was a long-term commitment my client made, and we believe the court will take her sacrifices into consideration."

"Mrs. Beaumont is able-bodied. There is simply no reason for her not to take the necessary steps in order to provide for herself," Harvey continued. Katie fixated on the ascot tight at his throat, wanting to cross the table and adjust it tighter until his lips turned blue. His direct gaze shook her from her daydream. "Is Mrs. Beaumont refusing to do so? The judge can have her professional skills evaluated to determine her level of potential compensation. My client will not continue to pay to maintain her lifestyle when Mrs. Beaumont is a fully capable woman. She cannot refuse to find viable employment."

"I am aware," Davina said.

"My client is simply asking that she participate in earning the family income and be responsible for some bills."

"You've got to be kidding me." Katie fumed and could not keep her mouth shut any longer. "You're making me sound like a deadbeat. I could have been anything when he met me, but I put my dreams aside to support his. It was the worst mistake of my entire life, chaining myself to this selfish bastard. It's always been about Jeff's goals and what Jeff wants. And now that he's got everything he's ever wanted, he wants to upgrade his wife now, too?"

"Katie," Davina warned, but Katie was just getting started. She stood and leaned in closer to Jeff, locking eyes with him.

"I hate that I wasted my best years on you! A secret credit card? A handful of mistresses that I turned a blind eye toward, not wanting to disrupt the kids' lives? Your behavior was deplorable, and I deserved better! The kids are grown now, and a judge will finally hold you accountable for the mess you've made. I am done making excuses for you."

Davina shot her a cutting glare.

"I'm not finished," Katie continued. "I sacrificed everything, and it was never enough. You always wanted more, and now that you're successful, *you* get to enjoy the finer things of the life we both strived to create and *I* get left behind? No way! I worked just as hard as you did, and there is no way I will sit here and let you minimize my contributions."

"You heard my client, Harvey. We're seeking five thousand a month in spousal support," Davina said.

A vein pulsed in Jeff's forehead. "That's ridiculous."

"You know what? I agree with you. That number *is* pretty paltry, but we will compromise if we can wrap this up today," Katie declared.

"No way," Jeff interjected.

"Okay. Let's take a beat. Emotions are running high now," Gene finally said, his voice meant to be soothing, trying to coax the genie back into the bottle. "Maybe we should pivot to the shared property and circle back?"

Jefferson leaned in and whispered to Harvey words Katie strained to hear, but couldn't make out.

"If we go to court, I'm advising my client to ask for ten thousand a month in perpetuity, half the equity of the house, and half of Jefferson's retirement assets," Davina stated without batting an eyelash.

"You've lost your mind," Jeff muttered. "There's no way any judge will agree to that."

"I'm willing to take my chances," Davina shot back. "Are you?"

A thick silence hung in the room, and neither woman flinched. Katie's head was throbbing.

Harvey stood. "Gene, looks like we're at an impasse here. We don't want to waste any more of your valuable time. Looks like we're headed to court where cooler heads will prevail. We'll be in touch."

"Can't wait," Davina said and marched out of the office as Katie struggled to keep up with her long legs. Davina was a woman in constant motion.

"I can't help you if you don't listen to me," Davina called out over her shoulder. At the elevator, she waited for Katie to catch up, pressing the button repeatedly with one red stiletto nail. "What was that in there? I thought we agreed to keep the emotion out of it."

"I can't just sit there and be spoon-fed his bullshit anymore." Katie paced, getting more heated as she remembered his words. "Get a job? Finish my degree? He acts like I was a squatter taking advantage of his generosity. I put aside my aspirations to chase his, and now I'm just supposed to pick up where I left off nearly three decades later? I have to start all over from the beginning. Go sit in a classroom at the University of South Florida with people Callie's age and claw my way back up the ladder, but this time with wrinkles and gray hair."

"Look, I understand your frustration. They fed women in our generation a big bag of lies. It's bullshit all the constant sacrifice the patriarchy has shoved down our throats for a hundred years. It's probably the reason I never got married. I never loved someone enough to walk away from my own dreams."

"You made a brilliant decision," Katie admitted bitterly. "And as a result, you won't find yourself in court someday trying to attach a dollar figure to your worth. Begging for money that is rightfully yours from a husband who thinks he can lord it over you. I wish I'd been half as smart."

Katie followed her out of the elevator to her car parked in front.

Davina turned toward her and exhaled a long sigh. "Katie, you are in the fight of your life. Jefferson is going to drag this out as long as possible. I can already tell he's digging in and will contest every motion we try to file. I don't know if you're strong enough to see it through." Her criticism stunned Katie silent, and her cheeks burned in shame. When she finally found her voice, she said, "Then you don't know me at all. When we first met, I might have agreed with you, but I can assure you after what he tried to pull in there that I am in this for the long haul. There is no way in hell I will let that snake get away with paying a penny less than what I deserve."

"I'm going to remember you said that." Davina shot her a smile as she tossed her briefcase in the front seat of her gleaming Aston Martin. "I've got to get back to the office for a client meeting, but we'll be in touch." Katie watched her pull away, then walked to her Beetle. She backed out of the parking spot and flew down the streets with the top down. The wind whipped her hair around, making her wish she had a hair tie. She cranked her 80s playlist up and laughed at the irony when Def Leppard's *Love Bites* blasted through her speakers. It was true. Love did bite.

Sixteen

While she waited for her court date, the next six weeks passed in a blur. August in Florida was riddled with thunderstorms and oppressive humidity that punched you in the face at ten o'clock in the morning, limiting her regular beach walks with Arlo to the early mornings. The rest of the day Katie holed up at home and kept to herself, coming to grips with Yuli's revelations. It was strange how the idea of magic at first seemed outlandish, but with the passage of time, she moved to a place of gradual acceptance. Now understanding the flashes she'd received were actual events, Katie fed this information to Davina, encouraging her attorney to hire a private investigator to search for a safe deposit box and property records for a penthouse condo with an ocean view.

Katie stayed in her bedroom suite when Jeff was home, eating what she wanted, when she wanted, and spent many evenings relaxing poolside with Arlo. She read books on intuition and manifestation. She listened to podcasts and obsessively binged the Netflix phenomenon, *Life after Death with Tyler Henry,* feeling a kinship with the famous medium who was also adept at seeing events of the past. Her curiosity had no bounds and kept her occupied racing down magical rabbit holes.

The kids popped by for visits, and on more than one occasion, she'd been compelled to clear her search history. They would really think Mama was losing it if they saw her deep dive into the Wikipedia pages on supernatural powers, retrocognition, and her newest fascination with the Salem witch trials.

Katie pulled away from everyone as she alternated between the agony of loss and the temptation of hope while she processed the end of her marriage. It had to happen, but that didn't mean it didn't hurt like hell. When you're engrossed in the Monday morning armchair quarterback analysis of your life, it was easy to see the pitfalls that, in retrospect, could have been easily avoided. Some days, she beat herself up for being too trusting and took to her bed with a tube of cookie dough. Other days, she worked through simple yoga poses on the beach, letting the wind whip her hair and the ocean heal her soul.

For the first time in her life, she only had herself to take care of, an unsettling feeling so foreign it took her weeks to recognize it. Looking in the mirror at a woman she felt she hardly knew, she burst into tears. Feeling bold, Katie apologized to herself. "I am sorry. You deserved better. From now on, I will take better care of you." Arlo was her only constant. His warm body snuggled up next to hers gave her solace and comfort. He followed her closely from room to room and listened as she broke plans with

Frankie and asked for space. Even Frankie couldn't argue against her desire for self-care.

At the end of September, she was finally feeling up to visitors again and reached out to Frankie. Within twenty minutes, Frankie was seated at her island with a Margherita pizza and a bottle of wine.

"I missed you," Frankie admitted as she poured the contents of the bottle of red wine into two glasses and handed one to Katie.

"I missed you, too. I just needed to take a breath."

"I get that." Frankie looked around the kitchen for something. "Is asshat around?"

Katie laughed. "I don't know. I don't even pay attention anymore."

As if on cue, Jeff entered the kitchen, dragging luggage behind him. Seeing Frankie, he didn't bother to hide his scowl. His presence sucked all the air out of the room.

"Where are *you* headed?" Frankie asked, perpetually nosy, as Katie nibbled on a slice.

"If you must know, I got an invitation to the Autumnal Equinox Party at the Castanova Compound."

"Wow." Even Frankie was impressed. The name he dropped sounded familiar. At first, Katie couldn't place it. Then it hit her—the woman in her dermatologist's office. The information was oddly unsettling. There was still a frustrating intersection of her life with Jeff's even after all her efforts to dead-end it.

"I'll be damned, you actually made it happen," Katie said, shocked that his prediction had come true.

"I did," he confirmed.

"You're the man," Frankie said, her sarcasm so thick Katie almost choked on it.

After running into her at the dermatologist's office, Katie's curiosity was piqued enough to do some research. Ana Castanova was a bit of an enigma, a fixture in the social scene of Tampa and St. Petersburg's elite. Secretive about her origins, she had the kind of wealth people only dreamed of and the power that dismissed any questions and curiosity about her past. She was the president of a club that Jeff could never join. He'd stood outside the locked gate for years looking for a way to weasel in, and it appeared he'd finally found it.

"It's a long weekend event at her estate, so I won't be back until Monday." He filled her in on his plans with a kind of pretentious glee Katie usually found nauseating. But today, a rush of joy bubbled up in Katie. She was going to have the entire house to herself for the weekend without Jeff dragging down her energy, and it seemed like a dream come true.

"Enjoy yourself."

"Oh, I plan to." He was smug. "Ana Castanova sent her private jet for me and insisted I come alone."

Katie snorted, listening to him brag. His machismo was sickening.

"Wow. Cheating on Brittany already?" Frankie smiled. "That's got to be some kind of record, even for you." She held up her glass of wine in a mock toast.

"Brittany knows we aren't exclusive. I need to be free to step into a relationship of significant importance. I can't tie myself down and limit my options to just one woman."

"I wish you'd filled me in on that twenty-eight years

ago," Katie jabbed with an awkward chuckle, unable to resist.

"Good one." Frankie held up her glass, and Katie chimed it with hers as Jeff rolled his eyes and then focused on his phone.

"Looks like my driver is here," Jeff announced and then rolled down the driveway. When he left, he took the lion's share of the tension with him and Katie's shoulders finally relaxed.

"So what do you want me to do, put Nair in his shampoo bottles? Text his mother his dick pics? Or… this will take a bit longer, but I could set up a fake social profile and we can catfish the hell out of him."

Katie laughed. "While all of those options sound endlessly entertaining, I'm going to stay in my own lane."

"You're taking all the fun out of this," Frankie whined, pouting a little, then her shrewd eyes narrowed on her friend, assessing her. "I have to admit, traveling the high road looks good on you." She studied her best friend, squinting her eyes to suss out the source of the change. "You're glowing, and your skin is flawless. Are you using something different on your face?"

"I guess that chemical peel did make a difference."

"It did. You look great!" Frankie pulled back the skin on her forehead to erase the firm elevens that were bookends to the bridge of her nose. Then she let go and they snapped back down into place. "I hate this stage of womanhood we're trapped in. We're not allowed to get wrinkles or crow's feet or, God forbid, have a forehead that actually moves. Why are we struggling to remain desirable in a world that worships at the fountain of youth?

I wish we could just fast forward to our late sixties, where we can just give up. Eat what we want, when we want, and let our hair go white. Pull out the stretchy pants and the New Balance tennis shoes and spend our days playing canasta."

Katie laughed. "You stop. You've still got cheekbones for days, and the kind of icy blue eyes that made me fall in love with Brian Bloom in the eighties. You still turn heads." Long and lanky, even after the early onset of menopause, Frankie could still eat whatever she wanted and burn it right off.

"You know I do!" she agreed with a grin. "That's why this works." She waved a hand between them. "You pump me back up when I deflate. And girl, everything has been deflating lately." She cupped her breasts, and they jiggled up and down. "Especially these sad sacks. I remember when they were perky and riding high. Now, when I take off my bra, they unroll to the floor and I trip over my nipples."

"You do not," Katie said, laughing.

"True story. Scout's honor." She held up her three fingers with a goofy grin.

"*You* were a girl scout?" Katie asked.

"It's not my fault they'll take any warm body with a vagina. It's all about the cookies, man. Did you know those suckers are five bucks a box now? It's highway robbery and illegal child labor all rolled into one!"

Katie chuckled at her almost accurate assessment. "You're ridiculous!"

"And that's why you love me!" Frankie glanced over at Katie with an appraising eye. "But let's talk about you.

The divorce diet looks good on you!" She smacked Katie's behind, and Katie jumped with a giggle. That was what she loved about Frankie. You just never knew what would come out of her mouth. "Seriously." She reached out and squeezed Katie's tighter cleavage, batting the sides of her breasts with her hands. "The girls look fantastic. Practically perky! Wait! Did you take some of Jeffy's money and get a mommy makeover while you were MIA, too? Spill it, you sly minx!"

"Not exactly," Katie said, thinking it over. "It's all the hot flashes. I think they are speeding up my metabolism."

"Girl! You are single-handedly putting the H-A-W-T in hot flashes," Frankie encouraged. "Your skin is flawless. It's like you're aging backward."

She was dying to tell her friend the truth. It had been burning inside her since Yuli revealed the flashes she'd seen were true events. Frankie would figure it out, eventually. She was like a bloodhound when it came to finding secrets. Katie carried the knowledge Yuli shared like a burden, unsure who could help her shoulder it. "What if we have a good old-fashioned sleepover tonight since Jeff's out of town for the weekend?" Katie asked.

"Will we need to have a pillow fight in our underwear?"

"Well, even though I was really looking forward to it," Katie deadpanned. "I was thinking we could grill some skirt steak for tacos and mix up a pitcher of margaritas."

"You had me at skirt steak," Frankie said. "Count me in!"

SEVENTEEN

Zoya grew up a spoiled only child in Ukraine and was the apple of her aristocratic father's eye. He encouraged her shrewd and unconventional thinking during an age when women's opinions were discounted and ignored. When she was fourteen, she jumped at the chance to serve the men their brandy and cigars in the parlor after the lavish society dinner parties her father threw. While she tended to the men, she absorbed the nuggets of information they shared with each other. Away from the women who gathered to talk about tedious topics like child rearing, needlepoint, and piano lessons, she learned about business and investing.

The most devastating, yet useful lesson she'd learned was the hands-on education of male desire and domination. At first, she was shocked when their meaty hands squeezed her bottom, boldly just out of her father's view, when she'd barely turned sixteen. Their unwanted pursuit only intensified as she grew more beautiful. One night, her father's closest advisor trapped her in the wine cellar, yanked up her skirt, and forced himself deep inside her. Ashamed and terrified, Zoya pretended nothing had happened. She learned to let her mind float away when others began to take what they wanted from her with their demanding tongues and fervent manhood. Often returning to find herself disoriented and her cheeks wet with tears. The frequency of their violation was so constant she couldn't accurately identify Nadia's father amongst her father's royal friends. As a beautiful young woman in the presence of powerful men, there was a high price they forced her to pay, and she'd paid it.

When his private physician found her virginity had been compromised and Zoya was with child, her father banished her. The look of absolute disgust on his face was seared into her soul and had scarred her heart, but it was the words she'd never forget. "You little whore, allowing yourself to be used and degraded like trash. You've brought dishonor to my door. I will not allow you to sully my good name."

Putting the blame squarely on her young shoulders without so much as a whisper of it awarded to his friends, he secured passage on an immigrant ship headed to America. Six days before her seventeenth birthday, he thrust a tin box filled with cash into her hand. Her mother watched the interaction, compliant and obedient, but presented her with a secret lifeline. A petticoat filled with gold coins and gems she'd hand-sewn into the liner. In America, Ukrainian money was nothing more than useless paper, but the gold coins and jewels had kept her out of brothels in the New World and had secured a modest country house deep in the woods. Fueled by rage and feeling powerless, she gave birth there to her daughter, Nadia, utterly alone. Engaged in a daily struggle for survival, Zoya's bitterness grew. Eventually, even the little bits of happiness she'd been able to find with her daughter were ripped away too.

Decades later, thanks to her female ancestors, Zoya rose like a phoenix from the ashes. She'd been given keys to the Castanova Compound the day of her awakening. It sprawled out over a hundred acres on a remote island. It was a palatial, remote estate in the Gulf of Mexico, and when Zoya stepped off the plane onto the island soil for the first time, she'd wept. The timing of the universe was impeccable. At the very moment that all hope had been destroyed, and she accepted her life was over, her second chance appeared.

Her good fortune came with a literal one. When you take into consideration the power of compound interest spread over ninety years as opposed to a mere fifty, the Castanova fortune was now reaching into the hundreds of millions. The financial windfall was secured inside impenetrable shell companies that employed clever accountants and brilliant female venture capitalists who'd exploited every tax loophole they could find.

Since taking possession of the estate, she had spearheaded many renovations. Now, the magnificent main house was over ten thousand square feet, and every window framed a postcard view of the sea. Lush vegetation covered the island with sweeping palm trees and blooming bromeliads and bougainvillea. Under Zoya's tight control, the island thrived and became a verdant oasis filled with tropical flora and fauna. It was a vibrant ecosys-

tem, flourishing without the manmade threat of defor-
estation.

The main house was three stories tall, with a rooftop
terrace that offered panoramic three-hundred-sixty-degree
views of the sea and sugary sand. It was a view that many
former U.S. Presidents confirmed was the best in the
world. Overall, they were a pathetic lot, except for one. He
was a hunk of a man with questionable morals she easily
coaxed into doing her bidding. Her only regret was they
had assassinated him before she could punish him appropriately for desecrating her favorite blonde waif of an
actress. Someone had to hold these powerful men accountable, and Zoya wholeheartedly believed that someone was
her. She'd learned the hard way the biggest weakness of
powerful men hung between their legs.

She filled the estate with artworks and antiquities from
all the prominent male artists and sculptors since
Michelangelo. Bathed in the glaring natural light that
washed in from the unobstructed windows, it exposed the
priceless canvases to an onslaught of harmful UV rays.
Massive gold leaf frames covered the walls, housing origi-
nals from Degas, Picasso, and Rembrandt. Zoya took
perverse pleasure in the fact they were fading, their colors
less vibrant and dulling under the oppressive Florida sun.
She relished their cracking and desecration, savoring the
steep loss of value as the powerful brushstrokes deterio-
rated year after year.

She tucked her most prized art collection away from
view, deep in a climate-controlled wing of the estate.
There, precious works of art from her favorite female
painters, Frida Kahlo, Georgia O'Keeffe, and Mary

Cassatt, were meticulously preserved from the elements. The paintings were hung and lit with special archival lights that did not degrade the artwork. She had a docent on retainer, scouring the world and international auctions for pieces to add to her vast collection of female painters.

Her home was sumptuous and awe-inducing. Zoya enjoyed the reactions from guests who wandered the halls, mouths agape, elbowing and whispering to each other. The estate had a modern kitchen staffed with a rotating collection of Michelin chefs, all of them male, not because women weren't capable, but because she relished the servitude of men. Often, they would fall over themselves to tempt her with gastronomic combinations they were sure would woo her. Through trial and error, she'd discovered that chefs could be equally arousing in the bedroom. Their exacting ways, attention to detail, and incredible finger dexterity led to many enjoyable nights, indeed.

She'd erected a ring of cabanas around the coastline on a whim, and it had been an incredibly profitable endeavor. The false sense of privacy gave her the ability to monitor the financial moves of the powerful men that inhabited them without detection. More than once, she'd profited on a real estate deal or hot stock tip her security eagles had overheard. It was a lucrative investment that amassed her further wealth. Men really were insufferable blowhards, and to Zoya, there was nothing better than reducing them to blubbering fools by swooping in and undermining their more lucrative deals at the eleventh hour. Their pure astonishment in the boardroom was delicious, and she ate it up with a golden caviar spoon.

Part of the joy of having her own money was the

luxury she could buy with it. The two-thousand-count silk sheets that her staff of house boys changed every day. Fresh flowers flown in weekly from Ecuador and Columbia emitted the dewy scent of rose hips and gardenias. Her garage was full of toys, including a 4x4 Jeep and other all-terrain vehicles perfect for traversing the primitive roads on the island. She docked her yacht further out in the sea, and it was only accessible by boat. It was a fully-staffed getaway that could be ready to set to sea in an hour with a single phone call. In the hangar, near a private airstrip, was a small fleet of aircraft she could utilize herself or use to transport guests to the island. The best feature of owning a private island was the fact no one got to her sanctuary without her express invitation and knowledge. There were no 'wrong turns' yielding annoying interruptions by curious travelers or passersby. The only way onto the island was through Zoya.

It was a magnificent life, but the surrounding silence was deafening. To fill it, she threw lavish parties, inviting the crème de la crème of the international elite. Surrounded by ordins—non-magical idiots—Zoya always felt a rush of superiority. Part of the fun was seeing the lengths men were willing to go to indulge their selfish desires, and for her own entertainment, she often pitted them against each other. Zoya was an all-seeing puppet master, but even that enjoyment had worn off in recent years. As the decades passed while she awaited Katia's awakening, she grew bored and restless.

An invitation to her estate was the equivalent of getting an invitation to a certain pin-up mogul's mansion without the quaaludes. Her Autumnal Equinox Ball was the event of the year. Sultans from Dubai and the most powerful men and women from the East and West Coasts angled for their invitation all year. They courted her with outrageous acts of outright begging that made Zoya's hardened heart thrum in her chest. She loved to be loved in safe ways. Being put on a pedestal, protected from danger, yet awash in their adoration. It meant never having to risk opening her heart.

She walked to her expansive closet that took up an entire wing of the estate. Inside were the precious works of art from all the eras of fashion. She was an obsessive collector, investing in estate sales and holding the largest privately owned haute couture collection in the entire world. The worst decision she'd recently made was loaning a 1950 bombshell's dress to a museum, which conspired to loan it to that dreadful Carmichael pseudo-celebrity girl. Zoya tried to intervene, snapping her fingers and adding ten pounds to the dark-haired beauty's ample bottom to prevent her from pulling it on, but it only made the starlet starve herself more. Three more snaps added another twenty, but the troll had the balls to force it on anyway, dramatically draping a fur coat behind her waist to hide the fact she couldn't fully zip it up. Celebrities used to be ultra-glamorous with standards. Not anymore. It was a pity.

The closet was arranged by decade. She tapped on the switch nearest it, and the mechanical closet bars sprung to life. Whirling the garments in their see-through archival bags to the front, they traversed an oval track. Halston, Dior, and Dolce and Gabbana whirred by on metal hangers, making a scraping sound against the bar. She pressed another button to pause the track when a sequined green vintage Versace gown caught her eye. She swiped her hand up, and it floated to the wall of high hangers while she considered it. Maybe. Johnny Versace had been such a bright light in the fashion industry, and he knew how to dress a woman. She continued perusing her choices and selected a slinky Chanel mermaid gown and a beaded Donna Karan wrap dress. Four more dresses landed on the hangers, awaiting their time to shine.

She strode over to the wall of windows and observed the crew constructing the tent below. It was like watching worker bees in a hive. They dressed tall tables in dark navy blue velvet that draped to the ground. A team of florists was making last-minute tweaks to vases of flowers in fuchsia and lime green. The DJ was setting up on one stage, and sound checks were happening on the other two. She was pleased to see the entertainment schedule hit every high note. Pitbull and Marshmello for the kids. Miley Cyrus because she was ballsy. And Lizzo, her favorite full-figured chocolate queen. Delicious. This party would rage for a full forty-eight hours and require at least seven outfit changes. She flew in a team of doctors to administer IVs to help the guests recover from hangovers and increase their stamina. A forty-eight-hour wicked rager was hard on the ordins. While Zoya could hold her own against the likes of Keith Richards, the ordins were weak and needed more caretaking.

This year, she was particularly looking forward to seeing a special guest who had RSVP'd to the event, Jefferson Beaumont. He'd accepted immediately like she knew he would. A small fish in the big pond of the East

Coast elite would never turn down the opportunity to level up his social status. The invitation would be irresistible even with the one caveat she'd insisted on. He had to come alone. Zoya encouraged all the other guests to bring a plus one. She'd learned that lesson the hard way in the seventies during her stint as a swinger. Single men at her parties could become predatory, preying on the women in attendance, which created more headaches than they were worth.

She was particular about security, enlisting twenty teams of eagles who flew in pairs around the estate. Zoya's parties were decadent and dangerous, allowing the ultra-rich to luxuriate in any fantasy consenting adults could indulge in, but she had a zero-tolerance policy for sexual assault. Her highly-trained teams swept the island continuously with their eagle eyes and hyper-vigilant hearing. They separated offenders from the partygoers, then held them on the other side of the island with primitive lodging and only the necessities for several hours as punishment. Eventually, they were escorted off the island and flown home, never to return. She'd been elated when the worst offender self-inflicted his early demise in prison. Her only regret was it hadn't been more painful.

She walked to the luxurious bathroom and cast one longing glance at the porcelain tub in the center of the room. A crystal chandelier dripping in baubles cast rainbow prisms all over the Carrera marble walls from where it hung from the ceiling. She'd spent many evenings in it soaking and plotting her next move. Sometimes she'd share it with a lover who relaxed her in alternative ways as the bubbles tickled her skin. It beckoned, but it would have to wait.

The warm lights from crystal sconces on either side of the beveled mirrors illuminated her face in a soft glow. She lightly brushed her fingers under her eyes. A small smile darted up the corners of her lips as she felt the skin tighten. She smiled wider and swiped her fingers at her temples, watching the crow's feet smooth away. Then her fingers swiped across her brows and eyelashes, darkening them and shaping them into beautiful arches. She rubbed her fingers in a circle on her forehead, and the skin tugged up into her hairline before disappearing. She was flawless, a fact confirmed by the dermatologist who was quick to take credit for her hard work when she was photographed leaving his office, but it had been worth it to see Katia.

Her hands moved down her curves to her breasts. Cupping her hands around her cleavage, she felt them rise higher and stand at attention. Her fingers wrapped around her waist next, smoothing all her internal muscles in one soft caress, forever banishing her need to wear the insufferable corsets that had been part of her wardrobe as a teenager. The act of putting it on registered in her brain as the first act of submission she'd cataloged as a young girl. It tightened her ribcage until her breaths were stunted and left her lightheaded and in a state where it was impossible to put more than two thoughts together. Keeping her compliant, diminished, and reliant on men, three qualities she'd freed herself from fully and never looked back.

"Pigs," she said out loud. The stench of their control left a bitter aftertaste in her nose, even after all these years. With the tables turned, teaching Jefferson a lesson was going to be a delight. She'd hated him since the moment Katia had brought him home from college. Zoya was a powerful witch, and her magic only grew stronger, but she was never powerful enough to overcome free will. Katia had chosen to love and be faithful to him, and there was nothing she could do but wait.

Twenty-seven years of putting up with his bullshit! It had been like watching one of those melodramatic soap operas or a car wreck you couldn't look away from. Now that Katia had chosen to walk away, finally, Zoya could help.

She opened a drawer and pulled a dagger out, then walked to an ornamental tree sitting in a granite planter near the window. Zoya dragged the point of the knife against her skin and watched as a crimson line appeared. She squeezed her wound tightly to encourage the flow of blood to hasten. Dark red drops dripped onto the ebony soil at the base of the tree. It had thick glossy leaves supported by a strong leathery trunk and emitted a soft glow that waned then flickered. A single curvaceous pear was maturing in the exact center, nested in a tangle of thick branches. When her drops of blood hit the soil, the entire tree brightened, stealing energy from her life force. The branches and leaves stretched to grow to new heights. Then the glow intensified, and the pear became larger and more engorged. It was coming along nicely, but her impatience won out. She dared to squeeze a few too many drops before collapsing to the ground drained by the magic required to infuse the pear with her power.

"Madam." Her Great Dane butler, Magnum, arrived at her side. He was a gorgeous, gray canine who was nearing the end of his servitude. From a pouch around his neck, he produced a bell and rang it. A few moments later, a maid appeared with a tray of porridge and Goji berries and a steaming mug of chamomile tea. She turned down the bed and helped Zoya into it before placing the tray over her lap and leaving the room. Zoya weakly sipped at the tea and munched on the berries as her strength slowly returned. Feeding the pear was taxing, but her sacrifice would soon be worth it.

She snapped her fingers, and the dog stood taller, delivering a report. "As requested, Beaumont will arrive on the next flight. I have arranged everything that you have specified."

"Thank you, Magnum. If all goes as planned, you will have earned your release after this party. But it must go off without a hitch."

His tail wagged furiously, but then he dribbled pee on the rug in his excitement. "Oh, dear." He hunkered down and averted his eyes from Zoya's watchful glare. His tail now lowered between his legs and he trembled.

"Just like a man." Zoya's nose wrinkled in disgust. "Can't control yourselves. Do you need me to add another year to your sentence so you can learn your lessons?"

"No, My Queen, please." He lay down on the floor, prostrating himself in her presence. "It was simply a momentary lapse. I'll get housekeeping to rectify it immediately."

Zoya stood and stretched, then opened the door to her supernatural glam chamber that blocked all sound and light interferences. It was an isolated, soundproof meditation room she'd constructed inside her suite. After her awakening, her body didn't require sleep anymore, but she found being around ordins mentally taxing and emotionally draining. She recharged her batteries and recuperated there.

Shutting the door behind her, she padded slowly into the center of the room, while plush memory foam on the floor cradled her toes. Sitting down, she folded her legs into a yoga pose and rested her hands on her knees, breathing deeply to release the ever-present anger that had been simmering within her since she was a young girl.

She clapped once, and darkness enveloped her as she calmed her mind. She felt the flutter of butterfly wings caress her face as they transported her to a peaceful meadow. There was a gentle tug on her scalp as her hair was pulled into an elaborate braid and intertwined with soft purple flowers and a lavender crown. She felt the sweet scent of it calm and clear her mind. Keeping her eyes closed in the dark, she felt a brush against her eyelids, and then a kiss of dew that set her freshly made-up face. The fleet of butterflies shimmered as they danced around her, infusing her skin with effervescence and a glow that starlets paid hundreds of thousands of dollars on Rodeo Drive to achieve. They floated in a current of glitter that encircled Zoya, spiraling higher and higher, leaving nothing but beauty and peace in their wake.

She stepped out of the glam chamber as the sun set lower on the horizon. Below, the staff stood at attention, welcoming the first few guests who were open-mouthed and wide-eyed as they took in the gold-leafed dancers she'd placed on pedestals. They were living statues hired from the cast of off-season circus performers she'd found at Ringling. Every twenty minutes, they would morph their bodies into a new pose, the abstract paint on their bodies shifting to reveal the next creature they would form. First an elaborate flamingo, then a sleek jaguar with golden spots. It was a little magical treat the ordins believed was a simple optical illusion. Their tiny pea brains always accepted the most logical solution. It gave Zoya a cheap thrill to get away with using her powers in public undetected.

Magnum entered the room again. "Jefferson Beaumont has arrived. I have shown him to his quarters."

"The suite directly adjacent to mine?"

"Yes, My Queen," he answered. "We've settled everyone else in the guest house, private cabanas, and the pool house, as you instructed."

"Very good."

Magnum sat next to her, and she tugged on the velvet softness of one ear as he sighed and partially closed his eyes. "Have I pleased you?"

"Very much."

Cloaked in a brilliant white Versace dress that hugged every curve, she glanced once more in the mirror. The slit in her gown shot from the ground to her upper thigh, and her creamy décolletage was alluring with a cluster of diamonds resting on her ample breasts. She pulled her white gloves up to the elbows. Wickedness glinted in her eyes, and she licked her lips in anticipation of the delicious snack that destroying Jefferson Beaumont would be.

Pleased with her reflection, she stepped out of her suite and made the descent down the twisting double staircase guided by the sound of faraway laughter. She stopped to grab a flute of champagne and drained it in one long guzzle before setting it down and grabbing another. The only way to endure being around this many ordins at once was to welcome the warm buzz of champagne. Without it, they were difficult to withstand.

Twenty minutes later, as she was attending to her first guests, Magnum appeared at her side. With one bark, he announced the arrival of Jefferson. Zoya glanced over at the man preening in the hallway mirror just inside the estate. He buttoned the top button of his jacket, exposed his teeth like a baboon at the zoo, then whirled around with a fake smile as they opened the doors for him. As he descended the staircase into the courtyard, their eyes locked for one long moment. Zoya tipped her chin down, then beckoned him with one finger as she pulled off her glove.

Smiling broadly, he held out a hand and Zoya took it palm-to-palm as an icy jolt hit her core. 11,922. Deep in her center, she felt a twinge of disappointment he would live so many days.

"Pleased to make your acquaintance, Ms. Ana Castanova." He pulled her closer and brushed kisses on both her cheeks. It pleased her in a perverse way that he would never utter her given name because he would never matter enough for her to share it.

"Likewise," she answered and dropped her chin slightly, looking up at him through her eyelashes. A pandering move she detested, but learned men were powerless to defend against.

He offered a smug smile. "Your estate is magnificent," he remarked as he took in the waning moon and the soundtrack of endless waves kissing the shore. He stood at a table and accepted the drink the waitstaff offered him. "And *you* are a vision. Is that Versace?"

A small smile twisted at her lips. "Yes, it is. You have a brilliant eye."

"Can't help it. I'm always drawn to the most beautiful woman in the room."

She had to fight the urge to vomit. He was laying it on thick, and while she enjoyed watching him work hard to win her favor, his bold pursuit was nauseating. She pulled her glove back on to avoid further direct contact with his skin.

Zoya sized him up, wondering what Katia saw in him. He blurred the line between masculine and feminine. His hand was too soft, his oval nails manicured and buffed to a shine. This was the hand of a man who had never completed a day of hard work in his life. The ends of his silver hair brushed the shoulders of his tuxedo. He was softening in the middle, the result of too many rich client dinners and not enough time in the gym.

"Would you like a private tour?" she asked, knowing he would not resist her.

"Very much." He offered his arm to Zoya, and she took it, lacing her gloved hand through the crook of his elbow. She led him up the marble staircase and into her wing of the mansion. At the door to her expansive library, she paused and then opened it for him. Inside, light from three carefully placed Tiffany lamps illuminated the space. From the floor to the fifteen-foot ceiling, books in every color and size filled the room. A rolling ladder waited in the corner to help navigate the top shelves, and moonlight flooded in from the expanse of windows that lined one wall. Zoya snapped her fingers, and the first sultry notes of a melancholy ballad strummed into the room.

"That's quite a parlor trick," Jefferson admitted. "I didn't know you could enable Alexa with a snap."

"It's a feature that's still in Beta. Jeff and I go way back."

"Jeff Bezos?"

Zoya nodded. "The very same."

Jefferson was falling over himself.

So he's a fame monger. She made a mental note.

Zoya walked to the window. "Ariana Grande is taking the stage next. Did you want to see her performance?"

"She doesn't hold a candle to you," Jeff lied, then slid over to the bar cart that was tucked into the corner. He pulled a crystal decanter of whiskey from it, tipped a generous pour into two Waterford glasses, and then offered one to her.

"What are we drinking to?"

"To new beginnings and the company of an exceptional woman." His snake eyes slid from hers to scan around the room, taking it in, precious item by precious item.

Zoya concentrated, focusing on her breathing and stilling her heartbeat. A few moments later, she heard his first muffled thoughts deep in her psyche.

That Degas in the stairway, I need to call Sotheby's and get an estimate of its value at auction.

He wandered down the shelf that held all her first editions, using his fingers to walk down the spines.

"Do not touch! Those are priceless tomes," she snapped as anger zipped up her spine and out to her limbs.

She's a control freak. Noted.

He stepped back and offered her his open palms with a grin. Then he tucked his hands behind his back and bent closer to examine them.

Alice in Wonderland? The Wizard of OZ? A Christmas Carol? That's got to be worth half a million alone. Play your cards right and half of this could all be yours. This is the life you deserve.

Zoya's eyes widened in shock at the speed with which he assessed her wealth and his entitlement to it.

How do I get her into bed?

Zoya shuddered at the thought, but it was the only way. Men were stupid, thinking the way to a woman's heart was through her legs. It never was, but they still went that route, anyway.

"You are an exceptional woman of discriminating tastes," he said, thrusting his shoulders back as he took steps closer to her.

"That is true." Zoya sipped at the whiskey and tugged off her glove again. She needed the intel, and since she was already nauseated, she stepped closer.

"It is an honor to be in your presence." He continued to kowtow to her. He picked up her hand and kissed the back of it. Zoya fought off the repulsion as she saw flashes of him in the Caymans with a much younger blonde. A distorted close-up of him laughing hysterically.

"My ex-wife is so unrefined and simple. To be in the presence of a sophisticated and refined woman is a treat."

"Ex-wife? Your divorce is final?" Zoya asked, already

knowing the answer to her own question, but enjoying watching him squirm when she caught him in a lie.

"Almost," he clarified. "We're just working out the finer details."

Still holding his hand, she saw large sums of cash and precious metals inside a bank vault. Untraceable transfers of Bitcoin. Zoya frowned and yanked her hand back with a tight smile.

She quickly pulled her glove back on, then walked her fingers down his torso, letting them linger down the front of his pants. A powerful surge of feminine strength welled up in her when he hardened on contact.

He was going to pay for his sins against her great-great-granddaughter. This was going to be easy, and she was going to enjoy the hell out of it.

EIGHTEEN

Much later that evening, Zoya snapped her fingers, and the lighting transformed from cool blues and purples into sultry reds and fuchsias. Surveying the thinning crowd as the night wore on past two am, it was almost time to begin. She'd been studying Jefferson from afar for a few hours, biding her time, making sure he was over-served and partaking in all the pleasures that her opulent life afforded. She'd changed into a skintight black dress with ostrich feathers at the bust line and a plunging low back.

Magnum appeared at her side. "I have readied your chambers as requested, My Queen."

"Very good." Zoya eyed the tall, delicious ebony foot-baller surrounded by a harem of leggy blondes that looked like blow-up dolls. If she wasn't so preoccupied with the task at hand, she would have taken him up to her bedroom instead.

"Ah, the sacrifices you must make for the ones you love," she mumbled aloud, then changed her mind. She *could* have her cake and eat it too. There was no need to sacrifice. "Magnum, please show Mr. Robinson to the red room at four am for a nightcap."

"As you wish."

She sipped at an elixir of soda water and gin. An edible flower sat perched on the rim of the glass. Setting it down on the table, she picked her way toward Jefferson, who had moved to a sectional and was leaning back into a deep pit of cushions, carrying on a one-sided conversation with four women who reeked of boredom. Zoya purposefully stood just out of sight, listening to him. He was a braggart and exactly what she'd expected. Powerful men were often cloaked in insecurity. They overcompensated, desperate for female approval to confirm their manhood. It was rare to find a man in a place of power that was comfortable and well-adjusted. Often, they needed an audience to acknowledge their greatness, especially reveling in the attention of beautiful women. It was exhausting.

"You know, I like to bend the letter of the law as far as I can without breaking it. That's what they taught me at Columbia," he waxed on prophetically, never missing an opportunity to drop the name of his Ivy League school in conversation. "Johnnie Cochran practically wrote the defense attorneys' bible during the OJ Simpson trial."

"Who's Johnny Cochran?" a dense blonde asked.

Her youthful ignorance made Zoya smile like a Cheshire cat. She enjoyed watching Jefferson bumbling for their attention and knew his poorly chosen reference aged him immediately. It would chip away at his confidence and make him more amenable to her plans.

"Never mind." Jefferson casually draped a hand over

the dim-witted blonde's knee and squeezed her upper thigh as he continued with his mind-numbing diatribe. "As the top defense attorney in the Bay Area, I get to cherry-pick my cases. One little seed of doubt, that's the difference between death row and an acquittal."

Top defense attorney? Looks like someone is embellishing the truth.

Jefferson was capable, but not the star he claimed to be. His big wins during the last few years were cases that fell into his lap, thanks to a little push from Zoya. She'd been pulling the strings to ensure her great-great-granddaughter's comfort for years.

Zoya rolled her eyes and grabbed a martini from a tray, downing it in two gulps, hoping it would make Jefferson Beaumont more palatable. It didn't.

A few moments later, she felt his eyes searing into her, and she watched him stand. "If you'll excuse me, I'd like to confer with our gracious host." She forced on a tempting smile and beckoned him closer.

He buttoned the top button on his tuxedo and took Zoya's extended gloved hand. She tugged him away from the crowds and down a softly illuminated path toward one of her favorite areas on the estate—a meticulously maintained formal garden with exquisite, sculpted topiaries. The heady scent of jasmine and gardenias was thick in the air.

"Someone is eager to get me to herself," Jeff quipped.

"Of course, darling, I don't like to share." She glanced over her shoulder with a secret smirk and led him deeper into the darkened corner of the garden maze. It featured immaculately trimmed boxwoods standing seven feet high, creating a wall of privacy as the verdant garden engulfed them. The concert in the background provided a soft, sensual soundtrack as the late night wore into the early morning hours. Taking the change of scenery as a sign he was being waved in for a landing, Jeff pressed her into the hedge and closed in on her.

It was a predictable alpha male tactic that made bile rise in her throat.

"Careful," she warned. Above her head, two eagles circled, and she heard one cry out.

"Don't be coy with me, Ms. Castanova. You've been telegraphing your intentions all night." He tucked a wayward strand of hair behind her ear, another act of blatant brown-nosing that made a tide of rage swell in her gut.

"I would disagree with that assessment."

"Playing hard to get, are you?" he asked with a chuckle. "Okay, I'll chase. Jefferson Beaumont never backs down from a challenge."

"Darling, never refer to yourself in the third person again in front of me. It's positively dreadful."

His cheeks pinked up, and she saw a flash of barely concealed rage flicker behind his eyes.

I'll make her pretty mouth pay for that comment tonight.

His intrusive thought rankled her.

No, sir, you'll be the one paying tonight.

He held her steely gaze for the briefest moment before she took a different tactic and ducked under his arm and away, hoping Jeff interpreted the move as playful. She shivered in repulsion and forced herself to giggle—another useful tool of the weak woman in her coquettish tool belt. It was effective in keeping men engaged and thinking she was a dim-witted debutante. Stepping lively down the cobblestones, she headed to the private play areas and cabanas in a hidden enclave near the oceanside. Waves crashed to the shore, drowning out the crooning from the musicians on the stages. Above, in the cloudy sky, the moon ducked and hid, playing peek-a-boo in a sea of stars.

Jeff pursued her down the path that led to the first of seven cabanas draped in heavy navy velvet. Men loved a chase, and Zoya was giving Jeff the chase of his life. She turned to him and pressed a finger to her lips to shush him. Then she pulled back the curtain, exposing a sea of bodies, moaning and writhing against each other, their sensual display outlined in the moonlight. His eyes widened, taking in the erotic scene kissed by the glow of moonlight that grazed down the circle of ample breasts and illuminated long, tight legs.

Well, well, well, what do we have here?

He reached out a hand to stroke her breast, and she leaned back just out of his grasp, giving him a playful wink.

This is the kind of life I deserve. I'll play this stupid game as long as it takes.

Ah, the pity. If she wasn't otherwise engaged in this critical cat-and-mouse game with Jeff, she might have found herself in the thick of it, fully engaged in the throes of passion. Lit by moonlight, she couldn't help but recognize Thor, whose real hammer was found between his legs. Such fond memories she had of the once-over he'd given her in her private chambers last year. Playing on Jeff's insecurities, Zoya pointed at Thor. The lusty sight of his swollen member at full staff rendered Jeff speechless.

Look at the trouser snake on that one! Bet he calls that thing the almighty bitch splitter.

Zoya snorted at the shared thought. He was juvenile. "You're a voyeur?"

"It's a powerful aphrodisiac, isn't it? Seeing others engaged in the pursuit of pleasure without limits or hangups," Jeff whispered urgently as he leaned closer, angling for a kiss.

"I can see it has a powerful effect on you," she breathed out into the sultry air between them, his lips inches away as she boldly stroked Jeff below. Zoya relished the jolt of power she had in her pinky to turn him into a panting tumescent teenager. Looking up at him doe-eyed and with forced longing, she bit her bottom lip and leaned a breath closer. He took the hint and pressed his lips to hers. Over eager for the contact, his lips were too moist. She fought the urge to vomit and continued on her way, stopping at various cabanas to offer Jeff more eyefuls of salacious acts. His hunger for her increased with each sexy view. His obvious interest tented in his tuxedo trousers as he painfully trailed behind her, nursing his blue balls.

"How about a nightcap?" she purred, knowing he would take the bait.

"How about we go somewhere a little more private?" he suggested as if it was his idea. Zoya let him believe it was and nodded eagerly.

"You've read my mind. Hurry."

She can't get enough. Putty in my hands. Now it's time to seal the deal.

She navigated the maze back to the main house with Jeff following closely behind. They made quick work of climbing the marble steps that led to the suite adjacent to her quarters, where she poured two drinks. Handing Jeff one, she sipped at hers as she pulled off her gloves, her eyes locked on his dark ones. She bit her full bottom lip, then asked, "Do you mind helping me out of this dress?"

"Of course." He rushed to her side and then deftly unzipped her gown. He tugged it down, freeing her from it and helping himself to her ample breasts. She closed her eyes, imagining they were Salvatore's rough hands. Her body ached for him always. A loss so profound, even almost a century of scar tissue couldn't conceal it. She turned away and swiped a hidden tear, letting out a deep breath.

Focus on the task at hand.

Stepping out of the garment, she unbraided her hair, letting it cover her nakedness that was outlined by the moonlight. "You're magnificent," Jeff whispered, unbuckling his own belt. His tanned chest was smooth and his hardness was evident through his boxers.

Zoya swiped her index finger to the floor and had a hard time concealing the grin on her face as he softened. Panicked, he looked down.

Dude. Get it together.

"Looks like someone is a grow-er, not a show-er," Zoya offered, unable to stop herself from the insult.

Trying to recover, he took her in his arms and kissed her. His thick tongue darted into her mouth, and she felt him harden again. At her hip, she swiped her index finger down again and then reached out to verify. His groin was a soft pile of lumpy manhood.

What the hell is happening?

The panic in his racing thoughts filled her with glee. She fought to keep it from spreading to her face. "It seems you dislike what you see?" she said with a sad smile as she stepped back from his embrace. She stood tall, every curve traced by the moonlight pouring in from the windows behind her. A magnificent specimen resplendent with feminine energy in the prime of her life.

His skin pinked, and he stammered. "No... No, that is not it at all. I've never been more attracted to a woman in my entire life."

What the hell? I'm going to sue Cialis.

His eyes walked down her body, and she relished the power of seeing him rise again. She stepped forward to kiss him and felt him relax as relief flooded back in. She continued to kiss him, stroking his desire to a fevered pitch before swiping down again and demolishing his passion as fast as it had gathered. He pulled back and adjusted himself, stroking his manhood that had essentially turtled up. Hiding. A wad of unattractive skin dissolved into a useless floppy appendage.

"This never happens to me," he claimed, clearly distressed. "Maybe it's the whiskey?"

"Maybe," Zoya agreed. "How about we just have a cuddle, then?"

"Yes, let's," he offered and pulled the down comforter from the bed and climbed in. Resting on the soft pillow, he beckoned her close.

Zoya climbed between the sheets, bracing for the

torture of the skin-to-skin contact and the revelations that would come with it.

Tomorrow morning, you have one chance to bed her. This is it. It's go-time.

Out of eye-shot, as she lay across his chest, she let the repulsion play across her features. It had been draining to hold it in all night.

How old is this broad, anyway? She's not exactly a Playboy bunny, but she looks damn good for her age. She must use the same plastic surgeon as Cher!

Another barge of insulting thoughts rushed by Zoya.

Women are simple-minded and easy to manipulate. All I have to do is turn on the old Jefferson Beaumont charm that had all the co-eds panting for me in law school. Focus, champ, and this magnificent world is your oyster.

He glanced around the room, taking in the gold-leafed ceiling with elaborate plasterwork and the four-poster bed fit for a queen that had been purchased from the estate of Louis the XVI.

All of this could be mine.

Zoya's head lay on his hairless chest, waiting for her chance to escape. Bathing in his toxic masculinity had been like dying a thousand deaths, and she barely survived it. She listened to every scattered selfish thought that drifted into his head as he became drowsy, and she was most grateful when the thoughts slowed down and then stopped coming altogether. As he snored, she gently pulled back the comforter and slipped out of the suite. Stopping at her closet to pull on a long lace robe that left nothing to the imagination, she then walked into another bedroom where the ebony football player awaited. With a warm smile, she forced herself to blush, knowing the pink tinge of blood rushing to her cheeks would make her even more attractive.

"Come with me," she whispered as she took his hand, pulling him to bed, where he made her thighs quiver after release. She cried when she came. He was an exquisite 7, destined to be destroyed in the very prime of his life in just seven days by an undiagnosed heart defect.

Only the good die young.

She already knew he'd leave behind a legacy from the years he'd returned to his hometown every Thanksgiving to serve thousands of meals to the homeless. When he went pro three years ago, he adopted a high-risk class of seventeen freshmen and promised to give them all a free ride to the college of their choice. It wasn't the way she chose to distribute her wealth, but it was admirable. He didn't even know that in the year following his death, they would name a street in Detroit after him.

Spent, she lay across his chest. His dark skin glistened in the moonlight as he drifted off to sleep with her arms wrapped snugly around his massive shoulders. It was then the emptiness that lurked in the shadows overtook her. It was always the quiet moments where it found its opportunity.

NINETEEN

The next morning, in the clear light of day, Zoya slipped back into the bedroom where Jefferson was snoring. She eyed him sleeping from afar. His mouth was wide open as he snored. With a heavy sigh, she disrobed, slipped back into the warm bed next to him, and closed her eyes. A few minutes later, Jefferson shifted on the mattress and she heard the first few thoughts cue up in his mind.

Morning wood. Check. It's time to seal the deal.

Repulsed, Zoya stretched like a cat and swung her feet to stand when Jeff pulled her back to bed. He nibbled at her neck and whispered, "Not so fast. I was thinking you had a place where I could put this." With a proud smile, he swept the sheet off his naked body where his manhood stood tall in all its glory. Zoya allowed herself to be pulled back into his embrace, and then straddled his thighs. She pressed her index finger down again and looked down to watch him soften. A bewildered expression was painted on his face.

Not again. What in the hell is happening? Get it together, man!

"Jefferson, physical intimacy isn't as important to me as complete trust and honesty," Zoya offered as she dismounted his legs. "I'm looking for a companion, a partner who can be on my arm when I meet important people. Heads of state, senators, and celebrities. I am looking for someone who can handle themselves among elite society and not reflect poorly on me."

Jeff sat up, unable to physically please her, he had to lean harder on his bravado and charisma. "Look no further, you can trust me."

Zoya snorted in response. "Trust *you*? You've made your living twisting and distorting the truth to set rapists and murderers free. Aren't you counsel for the Gabriano Family?" Saying the Gabriano name aloud made a storm of fury and hate thrum in her chest. They were responsible for the death of her Salvatore—the only man she'd ever loved.

"Look at you following my career! I'm flattered." He smiled, then continued, "It's true, I've been handling their east coast business dealings."

"How do you reconcile being an integral part of a system that sets the guilty free?"

"Every man has a right to a defense," Jefferson argued. "Like it or not, I play a crucial role in the justice system."

"*In*justice system seems a touch more accurate," Zoya proclaimed. "High-profile attorneys with silver tongues will say anything to get their clients off."

"How about I use *my* silver tongue to get you off right

now?" He grinned in a way that made Zoya's stomach turn.

"That needs to stop."

"What?" he asked, oblivious.

"The innuendo, the crass talk. It's deplorable behavior, and I do not appreciate it." He was a child, and she was baiting him by running hot and cold. A tactic she'd discovered worked nearly one hundred percent of the time with self-proclaimed alpha males. Being accommodating wasn't the way to their heart; they had to go to battle to win your affections. If you made it too easy and gave in too quickly, they were onto the next pretty thing.

Dial it back, you're losing her.

"You might want to dial it back. You're losing me." Jeff jumped like he'd been shocked with a cattle prod, and Zoya's defiant eyes leveled on his narrowed ones. She didn't normally quote ordins back to themselves, because it was off-putting to their tiny minds and dangerous. But there was just something so irritating about Jefferson Beaumont that made her throw all her rules out the window. She couldn't help herself.

There was a soft rap on the door, and a butler rolled a tray into the room with tangy oranges and bright green kiwis. A thermos of coffee and a dish of sunny eggs whipped into omelets sat in cloches. Zoya popped up, served two plates, and placed one in front of Jeff. It was an act of subservience she often used to confuse and manipulate men. They loved to be waited on, doted on, and taken care of. She made a minor concession to carry out this act of servitude for the greater good.

"Thank you," he said as he speared a kiwi with his fork and brought it to his mouth.

That's more like it. This one needs to be broken down, to understand her place, and I'm just the man for the job.

Zoya pursed her lips together to prevent the litany of insults she wanted to rain down on him.

Stay the course. You will have your chance. Katia. Katia. Katia.

She took a deep breath to settle her frustration and then continued. "How long will it take to negotiate the finer points of your divorce?"

A smug smile lit up his features. "So you can have me all to yourself?" he asked with a grin that was meant to be disarming, but it fell flat. Zoya noticed with disdain a green chive lodged in his canine as he scooped eggs into his open mouth.

"As I said, I'm looking for a companion, but I don't like to wait." She carefully buttered her toast and took a bite before continuing. "I know how long and drawn out messy divorces can be, and they are even more ghastly if they are public." She planted the seed and then waited. "But I don't have to tell you that. You're a brilliant attorney." She buttered him up like she had the toast, and she would feast on him the same way. One only had to allow the seed to take root. She sipped at her coffee. Waiting.

This is the payday I have been waiting for. Don't look over-eager. Play your cards right and you'll have this siren eating out of the palm of your hand.

At the word siren, Zoya brightened up, but what dear Jefferson didn't know was that he was going to be the one eating out of her hand.

She stood. "I must get dressed and check on my guests. Take your time here and enjoy breakfast. I'll see you downstairs."

He scrambled to stand up as she left, feigning chivalry. Closing the door behind her, she strode back to her suite and to her master bathroom. She opened the drawer beside her bed and pulled out the gold dagger she kept there and walked over to the pear tree. It was barely aglow, and on the branch pregnant with her prized pear, the fruit lacked its usual luster. A dried leaf dropped from the top of the tree and floated down to the ground.

"I'm sorry, my darling," she said to the tree as she dragged the blade of the dagger across her skin. "I've been busy as of late." She poked the end of each one of her fingers and let the crimson blood gather into a drop, then gently massaged her hands to hasten the flow of blood. Each drop that landed on the blackened earth brightened the tree until it sparkled and showered the rest of the room with a soft, bright light. Her pear responded by perking right up and filling out even more. She felt the weight of it in her hand.

"You're almost ready," she said, kissing the fruit and nestling it back into the nest of branches to ripen. "Rest now. We'll have important work to do soon."

The release of her blood left her lightheaded, and she rang for Magnum, who brought her dark chocolate, mandarin oranges, and macadamia nuts to nibble on as she lay on her opulent velvet coverlet. After a short rest in her bed, she spent the next thirty minutes standing under the rain shower head, washing the scent of Jeff off her skin. She emerged from the shower, reddened by the hot water, and strutted nude to the wall of windows. From her perch above, she watched her staff turn the pavilion into a decadent brunch display. Carafes of champagne and freshly squeezed grapefruit and pineapple juice for mimosas stood in buckets of ice. They set up a raclette station next, where a chef melted a two-foot-wide wheel of cheese with a torch and then ceremoniously dragged a sword across it, covering potatoes in succulent cheese sauce, then added caramelized onions and crispy bacon. At another station, a chef was sawing off large slabs of prime rib and offering drawn butter for fresh lobster tails.

Guests stumbled into the brunch, still drunk. They dropped into cushy seats where nurses started them on an IV of fluids and B vitamins. Her staff rallied the hungover ordins for round two, as shirtless butlers passed Bloody Marys on silver trays. Their bodies were tanned and tight from hours in the gym.

Zoya pulled on a lilac sequined romper that clung to her cleavage and exposed her creamy, long legs. Six-inch stilettos were added to give her the height she needed to be slightly taller than Jefferson. It would subtly shift the balance of power to undermine him and throw him off, but he'd never be able to single out the reason. Her thick white hair was braided loosely and intertwined with orchids and freesia and draped over one shoulder. Every inch of her radiant skin was polished smooth, the sun giving her shoulders a tawny glow.

She walked down to the pavilion to greet her guests. Plucking one mimosa flute up, she drained it, letting the bubbles tickle her tongue that had been overworked in the early morning hours with Mr. Robinson. Across the distance, she raised her glass to the gorgeous creature who'd shared her bed. She didn't even ask his first name. It was easier that way.

A few minutes later, a refreshed Jefferson made his way down the marble staircase, where he took up residence at her side. He placed his hand at her waist, claiming ownership, as he guided her around the room. It was a gesture she abhorred since she'd first felt it in her early teens. Irritated, Zoya forced her rage through her nostrils when she wanted to shake his sweaty paw off her back and make her own way. Women didn't need to be guided and controlled. They weren't the weaker sex, unable to be trusted to navigate an appropriate path through a crowd. Her jaw clenched as she forced herself to remain calm.

"Ready for your first test?" She looked down at him, her eyes shining.

"Of course," he answered, and she laced her fingers through his.

"I've got to put in an appearance at the press pit. The step and repeat has been reset, and I have promised the paparazzi I've flown in they'll get their way with me once each day."

"Absolutely," he said with a smile as she led him to a golf cart and they traveled to the main gate.

"Page Six," here I come.

Once outside the heavy wrought-iron gate, she pulled him closer and smiled broadly at the sea of paparazzi that lingered there. Over fifty cameras with long-range telephoto lenses focused on them. She turned on the charm and was positively glowing standing next to Jefferson.

"Ana, who are you with?" More shouts as they clamored for her attention, "Ana, Ana! ANA!"

"A new friend," she said with a tiny smirk. Turning to Jeff, she whispered, "It's better to let them do the hunting. Don't worry, they'll chase you down. Figure out your name before it goes to print."

He leaned closer and kissed her cheek as a wave of white flashes blinded her. *Click. Click. Click.* It was a ballsy move. She had to give him that. He waggled his eyebrows at her, trying to be charming.

What did Katia ever see in this jackleg?

She studied him from head to toe. He was decently dressed and moderately attractive. On a scale of one to ten, he was a solid six. So where did the cockiness and over-confidence come from? He wasn't attractive or powerful enough to command it.

After teasing the paparazzi a little more with a tiny peck on Jeff's lips, she saw the opportunity to pull away. She wiped her mouth with the back of her hand and rushed away to her sanctuary, mentally exhausted by the level of fakery required to carry out her plan. Pulling off her clothing, she let it fall to the floor and then lowered herself into the freestanding tub, letting the hot water work on the tension in her shoulders.

A few moments later, Magnum appeared at her side.

"What is it?" she snapped. "Can't you see I'm busy?"

"Yes. Of course, My Queen. I simply wanted to report Jefferson Beaumont has taken the bait. He found the key you left out in your study and helped himself to your financial records. I saw him scanning them with his phone."

"That's the best news I've gotten all day," Zoya said, delighted with the report. "He'll be positively dripping with greed now." She rippled the bubbly water with her fingers, considering her next steps. "See that he is on the first charter out of here in the morning and make sure you give him my most profound apologies for not seeing him on the plane, but I was needed elsewhere. He'll also need a phone so I can be in contact to carry out the rest of my plan."

"As you wish." He bent into downward-facing-dog for a long moment then yawned.

"You're dismissed," she said.

He whined, then tucked his tail and ran out of the room.

TWENTY

Katie's weekend unfurled luxurious and lazy without the heavy pall Jeff's presence cast on the house. After a blissful Sunday of brunching and relaxing on the patio, knowing Jeff was going to return to the house in less than twenty-four hours filled her with dread. She'd invited Yuli to join her and Frankie for dinner and was delighted when Yuli accepted the invitation. Katie was scraping the remnants of their blackened sea bass and mushroom risotto dinner into the trash can before rinsing the plates and stacking them in the dishwasher. Yuli sat on a stool next to Frankie, sipping at a small shot of Horilka, a Ukrainian spirit usually served at weddings that Katie kept in her liquor cabinet solely for her grandmother's visits.

Finished loading the dishes, Katie sank onto the stool next to Yuli with a heavy sigh.

"It's been nice having the house to ourselves, hasn't it? I didn't know how much I needed a break from Jeff."

Next to her, Yuli murmured in agreement as she bit into a dark chocolate truffle and offered the crystal plate to

Frankie, who popped a truffle in her mouth, moaning in delight when the chocolate began to melt on her tongue.

"Yuli! That's some next-level truffle action, better than an orgasm any day," she praised, still blissed out. Coming back to earth, she stole a glance at Katie. Seeing her pinched expression, she said, "No! I refuse to let that man ruin our last night of freedom. I have a better idea." Frankie ran to the liquor cabinet and returned with a bottle of Patron, three crystal shot glasses, a shaker of salt, and a lime she cut into wedges. She poured three, licked the space between her thumb and forefinger, sprinkled the salt on it, and hoisted her glass toward Katie's then Yuli's where they clinked when they met.

"May we be in heaven half an hour before the devil knows we're dead." With a wink, Frankie downed the shot with a smile and promptly poured herself another. Yuli tossed hers back and held a hand over the glass to prevent Frankie from filling it. Katie wasn't as quick on the draw and was poured another shot.

"Girl, my liver hasn't had this much action since I was twenty. You're a bad influence."

"And *you're* a lightweight."

"This will have to be the last one for me, Frank. The world is starting to spin," Katie admitted. She found her feet, then crossed the kitchen to flop back on the sofa and grabbed the remote, trying to signal to Frankie she wanted to wind the party down. Frankie usually wasn't very good at reading the room, but when she saw Yuli walk to her favorite chair in Katie's living room and sit down, she got the hint.

"Should we watch a movie or something before bed?"

"Sure," Frankie answered.

Katie flipped through the channels one by one and stopped cold at a story on *Extra! News*. In the background, Frankie was chattering about something, but Katie tuned her out, transfixed on the screen. Stunned, she leaned forward as Frankie stopped laughing, and a familiar face flashed across the television.

"Is that…" Frankie asked in shock. "No way… it can't be."

"Shh." Katie waved her hand at Frankie, trying to focus her attention on the story. She cranked up the volume and leaned in closer to the screen.

"We're giving you a front-row seat to the most exclusive party of the year. *Extra! News* has an inside look at the Castanova Compound where the Autumnal Equinox Ball is underway. It celebrates the official end of summer and spans three days and nights where the famous, ultra-wealthy, and beautiful people gather." The camera panned to a wide shot of the oceanfront estate, showcasing the stunning aqua water and white sand, and then it transformed into the musical stage where Billie Eilish and Adele had cameos. Katie leaned forward, squinting at the screen, and recognized Jeff, who was gyrating on the dance floor next to a very attractive white-haired woman. A glint of recognition tickled her subconscious, and Katie searched her fuzzy, imbibed brain for where she'd seen her. She felt déjà vu again. This time, the answer lingered just outside her reach as she strained to come up with a name.

Next, the screen filled with a close-up of the stunning curvaceous woman whose age was difficult to gauge due to the combination of her long white hair and her glowing smooth skin with the pores of a teenager. It was an unsettling ageless beauty standard that only the uber-wealthy could maintain.

Yuli's eyes were locked on the screen, and the glass in her hand fell to the ground with a crash, but Katie couldn't tear her eyes away.

Katie jumped to her feet with the answer. "I've seen her before!"

On the screen, the host asked, "Ana, scoring an invitation to your Autumnal Equinox Ball is the coup of the year. How long does it take to put together an event like this?"

"Well, Landon, if I answered your question, it would take all the magic out of it." Ana laughed and squeezed his arm playfully. "It's a secret."

"That's Ana Castanova!" Katie exclaimed as she focused on her face. "She was in the waiting room at the dermatologist's office the day I got my chemical peel."

"No way," Frankie discounted. "Girl, you're drunk. Castanova money means the doctor comes to you. She wouldn't waste one moment of her precious time sitting in a dermatologist's office."

"But she was there!" Katie cried. "I know it was her!"

"Why would she be there?" Frankie continued to question.

Katie struggled to put the pieces together in her inebriated state. On the screen, more footage of Jeff with his arm slung across the shoulders of Ana hit a nerve, and the unexpected jolt of jealousy stung. It was one thing to know he was out there pursuing women, but it was another to be visually assaulted with the proof. She shook her head, trying to find the answers that lingered just out of her grasp.

"She was looking for you," Yuli answered matter-of-factly, her face white.

Katie's face scrunched up in confusion. Her eyes were glued to the television and to Jeff's shock of silver hair.

"What? Why?" Frankie was determined to stop this crazy train. "Yuli, you aren't making any sense right now."

"She might call herself Ana Castanova now, but the woman on the screen is Zoya," Yuli said stoically. Her eyes landed on Frankie, filling with fear, and she cleared her throat.

Katie finally understood. The revelation stunned her and propelled her back onto the sofa.

"Who's Zoya?" Frankie asked.

"She's my... we're related," Katie tried to explain in as few words as possible.

"Related? Psssh! Now I *know* you've been over-served." Frankie laughed, dismissing her. "I blame the bartender." A fresh peal of her laughter rang out into the room. "Man, this is a tough crowd."

Back on the screen, the dark footage panned across a group of dancers while fire-eaters began their elaborate show. Flames illuminated the packed dance floor. The next shot zeroed in on a drunk Jeff pawing at Zoya, his hands running up and down her hips while she laughed and carried on.

"I can't believe she's letting Jeff manhandle her like that. Ana Castanova is a freaking female supremacist. Why would she waste her time with that asshat?" Frankie made a grimace. "It's like seeing your hero for the first time and watching them pick their nose." Her face wrinkled up in disgust. "I gotta admit, I expected more."

Katie's mind swirled like a merry-go-round. Thoughts bobbed up and down as she tried to piece it together. "I have no idea," Katie said as she wandered into the kitchen absentmindedly to grab paper towels and a broom to clean up Yuli's spill.

When she returned, she was surprised to see the fear on Yuli's face. "Frankie, there are some family secrets that could put Katie in danger, and I need to know you can be discreet."

"Discreet is my middle name." Frankie offered Yuli a drunken salute with her fingers, her other hand over her heart.

"This is no time for jokes. I need you to take me seriously," Yuli said, her tone harsh. Normally unflappable, Yuli was clearly distressed, and it unnerved Katie.

"We can trust Frankie." Katie vouched for her friend, who seemed to sober up upon hearing those words. Yuli pressed her lips together, looking Frankie up and down as if deciding for herself.

Awkwardly, Frankie sat up taller and reached out. "Katie is my best friend. I would never do anything to hurt her."

Resigned, Yuli let out a hot breath between her lips and started to explain, "Zoya is Katia's great-great-grandmother. She is obviously inserting herself into Katia's life for a reason. Zoya always has a motive, but I'm just not entirely sure what it is right now."

Frankie's jaw dropped. "Are you serious?" The last

syllable shot up an octave along with her eyebrows. "How come this is the first time I am hearing this? You've been holding out on us." She wagged her finger at a sobered Yuli.

Katie's head was heavy, and she leaned back and closed her eyes.

"Mind blown!" Frankie cried, and flopped back on the sofa next to Katie with a tremendous sigh. "I don't know what to say."

"That isn't all," Katie admitted, the tequila becoming a truth serum.

Frankie bolted up in shock. "What else is there? You're related to Ana Freaking Castanova! Or Zoya Castanova? Or whatever the hell she wants to call herself! Do you think she'll put you in her will? More importantly, do you think she'd put *me* in her will?"

"Frankie, focus. I think I will only be able to get this out one time."

"Okay." Frankie stilled herself.

"Katia," Yuli warned. "This is a terrible idea. She's not ready. She'll put us all in danger."

Frankie's face blanched, and her gaze darted from Katie to Yuli and back again. Yuli stood, clearly conflicted. "I must go."

Katie hugged her grandmother, and Yuli muttered softly, "It's free will. Your choices are always your own, but the more people that know your secret, the more dangerous it is for you. For all of us."

"She's my best friend. I can't keep this secret from her anymore. It's killing me," Katie whispered, clinging to her.

"Then do what you must. But I cannot bear witness to

it." She walked away, shutting the door quietly behind her. Katie was silent.

The room held a pregnant pause now that the older woman was gone.

"What is happening?" Frankie asked.

Katie began slowly, "At fifty, the women in our family go through a change."

"Honey, we all do. It's called menopause," Frankie cut in. "It's when we put the men on pause and focus on ourselves." Her infectious cackle filled the air.

"Good one." Katie smiled weakly.

"Come on! That was some of my best work."

Katie shook her head with a low chuckle. Internally, she was conflicted about opening up. The truth was stuck in her mouth at the tip of her tongue, longing for freedom. The secret weighed on her, and she yearned to share it with someone she trusted to take away some of the intense fear that accompanied it. "If I tell you this secret, you're going to think I'm crazy."

"Girl, I already think you're crazy. You might as well prove me right."

Katie laughed. "You have to take this to the grave."

Frankie crossed her index finger over her heart, kissed it, then held it up solemnly. Katie paused for a long moment, knowing how monumental and dangerous it was to share what she'd learned.

"Women in our family have special powers. Supernatural powers."

"What? Are you high?"

"No, it's the truth."

Stunned, Frankie's eyes bugged, and she gulped. Then she popped up from the sofa and paced.

"I think this is the first time I have ever seen you rendered speechless." Katie offered a joke to diffuse the tension.

"Are you saying what I think you're saying?" Frankie asked, struggling to understand. "I'm going to need you to use your words."

"We have magical abilities."

"Magical abilities? No way!" Frankie asked. "What can you do?"

"I don't know yet. Yuli says it takes time to develop. So far, I've figured out that I receive flashes of events from people that need my help... and..." She paused, knowing this was going to be one of the most outrageous statements she'd ever made. "...Arlo speaks."

"Did you just say Arlo talks?" Frankie staggered back to the chair, her eyes glued to a bored Arlo that huffed before plopping down on the area rug.

"You know if you repeat everything I say, this explanation is going to take forever."

"I'm sorry, but this is some Twilight Zone heeby-jeeby stuff." She took a sip of her tequila shot that had been abandoned in the excitement. "Okay. I'm ready. Go on."

"I'm just figuring it out myself. There isn't very much to tell yet. It skips a generation and awakens on our fiftieth birthday. That's all I know right now, I promise."

"What did you see?"

"Flashes and bits of things. Jeff screwing a blonde. A safe deposit box packed with cash. Bitcoin transfers. Luxury real estate. It was a mash-up of flashes. Nothing concrete, but together, they raise suspicions. Yuli calls it retrocognition, the ability to see past events."

"Are you serious? Holy shit, most divorcees would kill to have this kind of intel on their spouse."

Katie laughed sadly. "I guess. I never thought of it that way."

"You have to show me how it works."

"It's all so new." Katie's words slurred as she walked to the freezer where she'd hidden the remainder of her birthday truffles wrapped in plastic. She pulled them out and set them on the kitchen counter.

Eyeing them, Frankie reached out. "Yum. Even partially eaten, chocolate is never a bad idea."

Katie slapped at her hand playfully. "You can't have those."

"Girl, never get in between me and my chocolate."

"They are a sort of gateway."

"To what?"

"I'm not totally sure. I took a bite, and everything intensified—the colors, the smells, and then when Jeff touched me, I got flashes of scenes in my mind," Katie answered as she looked at the little half-eaten truffles that held such a power over her.

"Whoa." Frankie's chin dropped to her forearms as they both studied the candy with a new reverence. "Do it."

"It's physically draining. Last time, Jeff had to carry me to bed."

"Then we'll start you there! See, there is a solution for every problem." Frankie picked up the plate and set it on a tray with a full glass of water.

"I don't know." Katie was reluctant. "Yuli said magic

is not without sacrifice. It's not a parlor trick. It needs to have a purpose." Across the room, Arlo barked, a sharp warning sound. "See! That's his way of agreeing with me."

"Fine." Frankie pouted. "If you want to make your very best friend in the whole wide world wait, then I guess that is okay."

Relieved she'd placated Frankie for the time being, she put the truffles back in the freezer while Frankie walked over to the fireplace where the music box was displayed. "What's this? It's so beautiful." She pulled it down from the shelf it was resting on and turned the tiny crank on the side.

"It was a birthday gift from Zoya."

"Wow." Frankie turned the box over in her hands, admiring the craftsmanship of the instrument. She stroked the smooth wood, angling it into the light so she could see it better.

"Inside is a living diorama of me and the kids from the vacation I took to show them the ocean for the first time. It's truly exquisite," Katie offered, her words infused with wistful longing. "I can't explain how it works, but when you open the lid, it's like going back in time," she gushed. "I was miniaturized and pulled into it. It's the most remarkable, astonishing gift to be transported to your past to relive one of the happiest days of your life."

"The detail…" Frankie said in awe, transfixed by the golden box that emitted a soft glow.

"Don't open it."

"Why not?" Frankie lifted it closer to appreciate all the intricate carvings that made up the face of it. In a trance, she tipped the box to the side, inspecting it closer, then tugged on the lid. Mesmerized by it and tuning Katie out completely, she became obsessed with seeing inside and tugged again.

"Wait! You can't…" Katie warned, but it was too late.

Her words were interrupted by a flash of yellow light that razored the walls of the kitchen when Frankie lifted the lid. Dread filled Katie's belly with lead a split second before she was transported back into it.

A miniaturized Katie walked through the memory again, savoring the feeling of the warm sun on her shoulders, basking in the absolute joy on her children's faces. She let out a whoop at their shared triumph when the kite staggered into the air, then took flight. Katie watched her family from a distance, looking up at the stars that filled the night sky. She closed her eyes, letting the sound of the pounding surf lull her into a drowsy state of relaxed bliss when she felt the first glitch.

A subtle tremor from the center of the ground she stood on unnerved her. Looking up, she saw a single star fall from the sky and burst into flames. Burning, it ripped down, threatening to land on the younger version of herself seated by the campfire with two children on her lap. Then another flaming star slammed down to earth, this time hitting the sand next to her family before it fizzled out. Unaware, they remained still. Katie's lungs started to fill with smoke, and she raced toward her family. She opened her mouth to scream a warning to them as a huge fireball erupted in the sky, but no sound came out. She ran toward her miniaturized family, ducking the toxic rain as flames raged down, struggling to breathe as smoke filled her lungs. The cabanas on the beach were next. Two exploded as Katie raced closer. A young Beckett stood and looked at her with his enormous soulful eyes. Katie's heart ached to pull his tiny form to her and she reached out, desperate to shield him from the firestorm. Just before her fingertips wrapped around his warm chubby hand, he disintegrated into dust in front of her eyes.

The loss ripped through her core, shattering her heart into a million pieces that scattered into the smoky air. Katie coughed and sputtered, yanking her shirt over her mouth and eyes. She shook a sleepy Lauren and then a wide-eyed Callie, and one by one, they dissolved into a mash of burning ash and dust that floated away and joined the swirling funnel of smoke. Her younger self opened her mouth to scream, and a sound came out. Piercing and excruciating, the wail cut through the crackling and burning of the pitch-black night. The flames danced around her and her frightened younger self stood, then exploded on contact.

Katie bent her elbow and sucked air from the crook of it. The acrid scent of burning flesh and hair seared into her nostrils. Her eyes burned as the smoke overcame her. Then her skin tingled and caught flame, the agony of the pain too much to bear. She tried to run, but the hell-storm followed her relentlessly, swirling like a tornado around her. It was inescapable. "Beckett! Callie! Lauren!" She screamed their names into the smoky void. Sorrow cut through her core like a machete. Again and again, she shouted into the engulfing blackness, unable to accept the truth. Her babies were gone. Tears coursed down her sooty face, making tracks and providing little relief to her seared cheeks. There was no escape. Finally, understanding this, she submitted to the raging fire and walked into it, wanting to end the suffering. She dropped her arm, closed her eyes, and gave into the wave as the excruciating pain howled for release.

———

Back on her bed, Katie coughed and gagged. Disoriented, her eyes darted around the room. Her cheeks were stained with tears and flushed red, and her forehead knitted in concern.

"Katie!" Frankie was distraught and shaking her. Katie continued to cough. Bile rose in her throat, her taste buds charred and acrid. She gagged again, then bolted into the bathroom and vomited. Black, sooty liquid spewed from her nose and throat. Katie clung to the cold porcelain of the toilet and retched into the bowl over and over again. Frankie held her hair back from her face, placing a comforting hand on her shoulder. She reached over and pressed her cool palm to Katie's forehead, then in shock, she pulled back her hand.

"Oh my God, honey! You're burning up. We have to break this fever. Let's get you in the shower." Frankie turned on the water and let it run, then returned to Katie's side, helping her to her feet.

"They're all gone. My babies," Katie cried inconsolably, the devastating sorrow etched on her face. She clung to Frankie, blubbering.

"What?"

"They're dead," she cried out as fresh pain hit her square in the jaw.

"Who's dead?"

"My Beckett, Callie, and Lauren." Katie cried out their names, wailing as the cold water from the shower rained down on her fully clothed body. She didn't have the strength to sit up, much less stand. Her flesh was on fire and her heart was destroyed.

"Honey, the kids are fine."

"No. I saw them," Katie wailed. "I tried to help."

"Shhh." Frankie pressed the back of her hand to Katie's forehead. "The fever made you delusional. It's coming down now."

In the tub, Katie's teeth chattered, making her jaw quiver.

"Let's get you out of the shower and into some paja-mas. You need rest." Katie leaned on Frankie, who covered her in a warm towel.

She let Frankie dress her. Meekly following her to the closet and then to the bedroom, Katie leaned on her best friend for support.

"My arms and legs are so heavy; they aren't moving right."

"You'll feel better after some rest." Frankie pulled back the covers and tucked Katie into the bed. Leaning down, she pressed her palm to her friend's troubled face. She was much cooler, though still feverish. "Shh," she whispered. "You're safe now. The kids are okay, I promise you. I'm so sorry." Her voice cracked. Seeing Katie wallowing in the agony she'd unleashed crushed Frankie.

"You're lying. Stop lying to me. I saw them with my own eyes. They burst into flames in front of me." Another tortured sob left her lips, and she shivered. After ten long minutes, she quieted to a whimper.

"Shh. Go to sleep, honey. Everything will make sense in the morning," Frankie consoled.

Katie was drowsy and had a hard time opening her heavy eyes. There was a weight on her chest that filled her limbs with lead. "My babies," she whispered one more time as sleep overtook her. She curled up into the fetal position and slept for seventeen hours.

TWENTY-ONE

Around noon the next day, Katie's eyes flickered open. A raging headache pressed at her temples and made her head throb. Her mouth was ashy and dry, and the lingering scent of smoke hugged her nostrils. Her arms and legs felt thick and unwieldy, and she glanced around her bedroom, trying to piece the events of the previous night back together. With a heavy sigh, she swung her feet off the bed and onto the cool floor and then glanced over her shoulder to where Frankie lay snoring. Her mouth was open, taking long snorty inhales of breath, then barking them back out. Curled up between them, Arlo lay immobile, his thick chest rising and falling in tandem with Frankie's.

Katie rubbed her face with her hands to spread the tension from her temples to her forehead and back again as she tried to remember. She stood and walked to the kitchen in search of caffeine, rousing a drowsy Arlo that jumped off the bed. His dog tags jingled as he lumbered at her heels. Softly, she closed the door behind her and started making a cup of coffee when he spoke up.

"I hope you're proud of yourself."

She jumped, and a dribble of coffee stained her t-shirt. "Jesus, I forget you can do that." Katie replied as she let the coffee work its magic. "I have no idea what happened last night. Maybe you can fill me in?"

"Yuli is not happy. Frankie knows your secret."

Katie gasped. "She does?"

"Seems like tequila is your truth serum," he offered. Katie closed her eyes. His voice was warm and rich, and he spoke with authority. It was comforting and grounding, and Katie felt herself open up to it. "She opened the box."

"What box?" Katie asked.

"The music box."

"No!" Katie rushed to the fireplace mantle to see the music box was gone. In its place was a pile of ash and the remnants of the metal hinges that had held it together. "I don't know…" She started crying, feeling a deep sense of loss at seeing the pile of ash, but disoriented as to why she was having such a reaction. She walked back to the easy chair, sat down, and leaned back on it as the well of sadness deepened inside her. "It hurts. My heart physically hurts," she cried.

Arlo jumped up into her lap and put his paws around her neck. Katie hugged him, squeezing into his fur, stroking his coat as sobs wracked her body. "Everything hurts."

"I know," he consoled. "You suffered a substantial loss. It will take some time to heal."

"What was inside?" Katie dared to ask.

"The most precious of memories," Arlo answered.

"What do you mean?" She was confused and continued to cry. Arlo licked her tears away and snuggled into the crook of her neck. For several long moments, they remained that way, lost in thought. Eventually, he jumped down and delivered some tough love.

"Yuli will not like this recent development."

Katie gulped, and a chill passed through her. She thought about his statement for a long time before coming to the right conclusion. "We have to tell her."

"No. *You* have to tell her. *I* want nothing to do with this." He tucked his tail and scampered away, looking for a place to hide.

"Are you a dog or a chicken?" Katie asked.

"I guess I'm technically considered a dicken or a chog. And I'm completely okay with that," he tried to inject some humor, but it fell flat. "You know, Yuli can get angry, but you really feel the wrath of Zoya."

"What can you tell me about her?"

"Nothing if I want to live to see a day where I can walk down streets on two legs."

"What does that even mean?"

"Never mind. I've said too much already."

"Dude, who buys the grass-fed beef kibble and organic bully sticks around here?"

Arlo chuckled. "You do, and I deeply appreciate it."

Frankie stumbled out of the bedroom, her eyes half-closed. "Who are you talking to?"

"Myself," Katie answered, and Arlo lay back down at her feet. She didn't have the energy for a demonstration of Arlo's more human qualities.

"Coffee, I need coffee," Frankie begged as she padded into the kitchen barefoot and took up residence on a stool at the island.

"Of course." Katie got up and started brewing another cup.

"Last night was a trip." Frankie stared down at her hands, holding up her chin with a dazed look in her eyes. Her curly mop was frizzy from a night spent rubbing her head back and forth against the pillow. Black mascara smudged under her eyes, and her t-shirt and shorts were rumpled. "You were so wasted last night." Frankie explained, "When I opened the music box, you went full-out zombie on me. Your body was here, but your mind was gone. I snapped my fingers in your face and shook your arm, and you didn't respond at all. You have no idea how close I was to calling an ambulance for you."

The knowledge of the events didn't make the dread any easier to shake. Hearing her recount them didn't bring the night suddenly into focus like a vision test, where a new lens of clarity made everything in the world sharper and more vivid. There was just the all-encompassing heaviness of it. The overwhelming weight that felt impossible to shoulder.

"How about some carbs?" Katie offered, eager to have a task to do to take her focus off the agony she felt. The fuzziness of her memory niggled at her as she diced an onion and her biggest fears cued up.

Do I have a brain tumor? Should I get screened for early-onset dementia?

"Carbs are always the right answer," Frankie joked, pulling her out of her worries. "I'll cut some veggies up for a frittata if you want to get the loaded hash browns started."

They worked silently for a few minutes when the doorbell rang. Glancing over at the iPad, she saw her grandmother's stocky figure waiting at the door, Katie announced, "Yuli's here."

"Don't worry, I'll finish this up," Frankie said as she cracked eggs into a mixing bowl.

Katie wiped her hands on a dish towel she slung over her shoulder and walked down the long hallway to open the front door. She felt Yuli's arms surround her, grounding her with a sweetness that made the ache in her heart lessen. The confusion remained, muddling her mind with anxiety. "I don't know what's wrong with me. I'm so weepy lately." She wiped her tears away. "Frankie is here, and we were just about to sit down for brunch. Are you hungry?"

"I can always eat." Yuli followed her down the hallway, her footsteps heavy on the floors. Yuli paused at the fireplace, where she noticed a pile of ash in the display cubby along with melted mechanical pieces. "You opened the box." She sighed, her eyes locking on Katie's confused ones.

"No, it was me," Frankie admitted, raising her hand. "It was bananas. Katie zoned out, then it spontaneously combusted, and when she came back she was delusional, saying all kinds of crazy things."

"I did?" Katie had no recollection of it at all.

"Free will," Yuli said. "It complicates everything. I tried to warn you."

"I know, I'm sorry." Katie frowned. "I'm so confused." Yuli reached out to squeeze her granddaughter's forearm with one liver-spotted hand. Yuli's eyes locked on Arlo, who was still under the table. Rising to stand on his legs, he barked several staccato beats, then he whined and barked again. After a long moment, Yuli waved him down.

"What's done is done," Yuli muttered.

Frankie dished out wedges of the frittata studded with bright red chunks of tomato and a delicate chiffonade of basil and chives sprinkled on top. The hash browns were oozing with melted gouda and caramelized onions.

"This looks great, Frankie. Thank you." Katie offered a sad smile of approval to her best friend. They took bites and chatted under the discerning gaze of Yuli, who left nothing unnoticed. Her scrutiny made Katie antsy as she scrambled to fill the awkwardness with words and chattered on about the kids coming by, and that she was thinking about making ham this Thanksgiving instead of the turkey that Jeff always insisted on.

Yuli reached out and squeezed her arm.

"Katia, please stop." Yuli finally spoke. "We have important matters to discuss."

Katie nodded. Her mouth felt filled with cotton balls.

Yuli turned to Frankie. "Katia's powers leave her vulnerable. She's like an infant in the supernatural world, and she is defenseless to our enemies. It's my job to protect her until she is strong enough to survive on her own."

Frankie's eyebrows shot up as she tried to digest Yuli's words.

"Now that you know her secret, that burden also rests on you."

Frankie gulped and her index finger latched onto one

of her curls at the base of her neck, twirling it tightly around her finger. Katie watched her twirl and twirl it and felt responsible for her friend's anxiety.

"I should have never told you," Katie said. "It's too big of a burden."

"No, it's not," Frankie replied, then turned back to Yuli. "Tell me what I need to do to keep her safe."

Yuli's voice dropped lower. The tone was more ominous. "Our survival depends on the ability to keep secrets, and Katia failed." Katie jerked back as if slapped. Yuli's accurate assessment stung. Yuli muttered to herself, stirring her coffee with a spoon. Her thick white hair was pulled tight at the base of her neck into a bun.

"I'm sorry, Yuli," Katie apologized. "But I think she would have figured it out, eventually. She's my best friend."

Yuli nodded, then turned to Frankie. "You must never speak of this. Ever."

Frankie crossed her heart with her index finger. "Cross my heart and hope to die."

"Be careful what you wish for," Yuli warned, and her fervent tone silenced even Frankie.

Yuli's brow furrowed, and she laced her knobby fingers together on the table, deep in thought. After a long minute, she sighed and made the sign of the cross on her chest. "We can't trust Zoya."

"Why?" Katie asked. "I don't understand." She felt a shiver cut through her and hugged her body with her arms.

"What's most disturbing is Zoya is removing obstacles so she can get closer to you," Yuli offered, looking into her cup as if the answers she was seeking were in the bottom. She straightened the napkin in her lap.

"Why would she want to do that?" Katie asked.

"She is a selfish, hateful woman. Rest assured, her plans are always self-serving. She's been the most powerful entity in our family for decades, and your awakening threatens her power."

"Me?" Katie was in shock. "How?"

"As you get stronger in your superpowers, she will become weaker until, eventually, she will die," Yuli explained. "Energy cannot be created nor destroyed. The same laws of nature apply to supernatural energy. You are the only one capable of hastening her demise. Zoya is not the type to go softly into the good night. She is going to fight like hell."

TWENTY-TWO

Katie braced for impact when Jeff returned from the Castanova Compound, but instead, he withdrew, spending even longer hours at the office. He was preoccupied when he *was* around, glued to a cell phone Katie had never seen before, and there was an ever-encroaching distance between them now. It had reduced them to roommates, and Katie welcomed the shift.

She felt stuck, however, with one foot still inside her marriage and the other clearly out, surviving the long middle ground of any high-profile divorce. Katie wanted to move on and was ready to embrace her newly single status, even though the idea of dating again made her stomach turn. She had absolutely no desire to do it and doubted she ever would.

"All a girl really needs is a good dog," she said to Arlo late one night and his tail wagged. Wriggling with praise, he snuggled his body closer to hers, putting one paw protectively over her heart. The warmth of his body was welcomed, as well as the comforting weight of him pressed against her legs.

Going through their mail a few days after Jeff got home, Katie was opening a brown padded envelope absentmindedly when she pulled out a dark bottle labeled "Horny Goat Weed." After a quick Google search, she discovered it was a natural supplement for male impotence. At Frankie's urging, she displayed it proudly on the entry table, where she usually left his mail, and waited for a reaction. The next day, it disappeared up into the guest suite without a word.

The following weekend, she was cleaning the guest bathroom and found a copy of *The New York Post*, folded open to the gossip column, *"Page Six."* A photo with a caption read, "Having a Ball with Ana Castanova." Katie studied her face. Finding the resemblance between them was easy. They shared a curvy figure and matching widow peaks. Zoya was a remarkably beautiful woman, but her smile never reached her eyes. There was a deep sadness there that tugged at Katie's heartstrings. She yearned to know more about her and, at the same time, was conflicted by her loyalty to Yuli. It was as if she was the rope in their tug of war.

During her shifts at the store, Yuli had been preoccupied, and Katie was afraid to keep asking questions about her great-great-grandmother. Whenever she got the courage to say Zoya's name, Yuli clammed up and changed the subject. Katie knew Yuli was hiding something, but couldn't get her to open up. When she asked point blank, "What happened between you two?" Yuli's eyes darkened and she just shook her head. Katie knew Yuli would eventually answer her questions and so she simply waited.

Twenty-Three

B
ack at the Castanova Compound, it had taken Zoya the better part of a week to clear the taste of Jeff out of her mouth and to stomach the idea of seeing him again. Every day, she checked her pear. Impatiently, she cut deeper and released more blood into the blackened soil, wanting to fast-track its development. Zoya was stubborn enough to think she could hasten its growth with a stronger sacrifice. She lost the better part of two days by draining half of her blood volume into the soil, willing it to mature.

You could not rush magic. It was a universal principle, and even though Zoya knew it to be true, she was hardheaded enough to continue to try to speed it up to no avail.

After a long two weeks of keeping Jeff waiting, it was time for a grand gesture.

She sent a text to the private phone Jeff had been given before boarding his flight home.

Zoya: *I've sent you a treat. Please be available for delivery at noon today.*

She made one fifteen-minute phone call, and an hour later, a shiny, yellow Ferrari was delivered to Jeff's home with a huge red ribbon on the hood. Being wealthy was as close to magic as the ordins ever got, and she wanted Jeff to have a taste of the opulent life she lived, knowing his insatiable greed would drive his desire to gorge on it.

An hour later, flashing a wicked grin, she picked up his phone call.

"Thank you doesn't seem like a strong enough word," he gushed. "It's beautiful."

"Oh, it is just a little token of my affection," Zoya answered. "I'm glad you like it. Spoiling the man in my life is one of my greatest pleasures." Her voice was all velvety sweetness, precisely the tone she knew would tantalize Jeff the most.

"Like it? I love it!" he cried.

"There is also a small matter I need to discuss with you."

"Anything." The eagerness dripping from his words made her shiver with power.

"I am a woman who is used to getting what she wants," she began.

"And what do *you* want, Ms. Castanova?" Even though his delivery was smooth like butter, it had a corny quality that grated on her nerves. His pitiful attempt at flirting was nauseating and transparent.

"I am concerned." Zoya waxed dramatically with a

forced sigh, executing a stellar damsel in distress performance for his benefit, and he ate it up with a spoon.

"Well, we can't have that." He chuckled. "Let me put every single one of your concerns to bed right now."

"I am aware of your current living arrangement, and it doesn't afford us the level of privacy my lifestyle requires," she admitted and then waited for him to do what all men did in this situation—problem solve.

"That's easy to rectify," he offered. "I have options I can exercise."

"Then I would encourage you to do so," she purred into the phone. Having set the hook, she hung up. It really was too easy. A few shiny toys and he was eating out of the palm of her hand.

With a satisfied smile, she walked back to the pear tree. The fruit was plump and luscious and the perfect shade of lime green, almost ripe for the picking. On the stem, it glowed and showered the room with warm light.

"Soon," she said, and the light flickered.

A few weeks ago, right after the ball, an unexpected event occurred that still confused her. She'd driven to the archives with the golf cart as she often did. But once inside, she sniffed the air, smelling the acrid scent of burning flesh. Trying to suss out the source, she cleared her mind and chanted under her breath. Holding her hands in the air, she began to draw figure eights as the shelves of the archives shifted and moved, screeching by on metal rails as the smell of smoke intensified. She stilled her hands, and they roared to a stop. When she opened her eyes, she saw the box she'd sent Katia for her birthday was now a pile of ash and melted metal on the shelf.

She gasped at the discovery. From Arlo's detailed reports, Katia was by all accounts a rule follower. Zoya was instantly intrigued by this new development and wondered if she had more in common with Katia than she originally thought. A smile spread out over her features. Maybe there was hope for Katia yet, but there was still the problem of the ever-present and hovering Yuli. Luckily, she had just the tool to divide and conquer.

————

Later that evening, when Katie arrived home, she almost tripped over the stack of suitcases by the door. Jeff was whistling as he dragged two more behind him.

"What the hell is that in the driveway? I thought our assets were frozen until the divorce was finalized."

"If you must know, it was a gift."

"From who?"

"A friend." He smirked. The self-righteous glee on his face formed a lump in her throat. A sear of unexpected jealousy hit her heart, and she hated herself for it. She walked to the freezer and pulled out a pint of Ben and Jerry's then grabbed a spoon, digging into the hard-packed Phish Food ice cream with it. She scraped along the frozen edges and popped the spoon into her mouth, letting it dissolve on her tongue along with most of her rage.

"What's with all the suitcases? Are you going on a big trip?"

Finally, he stopped, taking a second to acknowledge her. "Katie, this living arrangement is toxic, and I think it's time we lived apart." He stood, hands balled at his hips, legs spread wide, the white cuffs of his blue French dress shirt contrasting deeply against his tanned wrists. It was so ludicrous she burst out laughing.

"Really? You're pulling out the Superman pose for me?" Katie called him out on it, rolling her eyes.

"You never were on my level," Jeff said. "You can take the girl out of the trailer park, but you can never take the trailer park out of the girl."

"My parents had a *manufactured* home on a private…" she started to explain. "You know what? Forget it! I'm not wasting one more precious breath on you!"

She pinched the bridge of her nose to dispel the tension that was stuck there as a sea of emotion churned in her belly. She knew this day was a long time coming, but it was the end of an era. At first, she felt a sense of loss, but then immediately realized this was *exactly* what she needed. There would be no more tiptoeing around each other—the house was hers. Secure in that knowledge, the first burst of hope rushed to the surface like bubbles in a flute of champagne, and she bit back the grin that tried to escape. "I'm confused. Why the sudden change of heart? Does this have anything to do with the time you spent with Ana Castanova?"

His eyes locked on hers, looking like the cat who swallowed the canary. The corners of his mouth quirked up in a smug grin and he replied, "I'm not at liberty to say."

She was dying to reveal he was hot for her great-great-grandmother. The look on his face would have been priceless, but instead, she forced herself to keep silent.

"We both know this relationship is over. It's time for us to start our new lives and to be open to new experiences."

"Oddly, I agree with you," Katie said truthfully.

"I'll send Brittany over for the rest of my things."

Stunned at his audacity, she said, "Wow. That was quick. She's already outlived her usefulness in your bed and has been demoted to schlepping your dirty underwear to your new digs?" She let the vicious words leave her tongue, thinking they would impact him, forgetting temporarily Jeff was heartless. Refusing to acknowledge her criticism, he spun his impatient finger in a circle, prompting Katie to wrap up the conversation.

"Fine, have her coordinate with me over text then."

He nodded, then pressed the key fob that beeped before opening the trunk of the new car in the driveway. Then he made his dramatic exit, scooping up two suitcases and walking them to the Ferrari. She watched him through the window, trying to cram his fat suitcases into the tiny trunk of the sexy sports car. A few futile moments later, he was forced to regroup and load them into the backseat of the Beamer. Without another word, he dragged the final two suitcases outside and shut the door behind him. In a daze, she watched him load the remaining luggage and then pull out of the circular driveway.

Katie eyed the slick yellow sports car that remained, waiting for Frankie to arrive. Its obnoxious red bow bobbed up and down in the twilight breeze. She balled her fists, waiting for the rage to pass, the desire to pull out her keys and cut through the glass factory finish welling up with the anger. It would be so satisfying to slice through it. Instead, she walked to the wine refrigerator and pulled out a bottle of pinot noir she'd been saving for Christmas dinner. She yanked the cork out and let it glug into a glass before draining it, not even pausing to let it breathe.

She refilled her glass and was back at the window when Frankie tapped in the code to unlock the door and slipped inside. "What the hell is that?"

Her words startled Katie out of her reverie, and a dribble of wine stained her white t-shirt. "Apparently, some gift from an anonymous benefactor? My guess is Zoya." Putting the pieces together, a suppressed laugh escaped her lips. "My great-great-grandmother appears to be dating my ex-husband. It's insanity! Too bad Maury Povich is off the air. This is bizarre even by his train wreck TV standards."

She took another sip, letting the emotions course through her. "She nailed him, though. I have to give her that. The neon yellow is almost as obnoxious as he is."

"It's perfect for an attention whore like Jeff. Don't you think?" Frankie commiserated.

Katie turned to face her friend, tears in her eyes.

"Those better be tears of joy," Frankie scolded.

Katie laughed and swiped at her lash line. "Mostly, they are. I knew this day was coming, but to admit that my marriage failed is a bitter pill to swallow."

"Honey, no woman would be successful in a marriage with that man," Frankie reasoned. "Come here." Frankie awkwardly opened her arms and gave Katie a quick, clumsy hug with a series of four pats on the back. A gesture that said, "I'm done now." Katie burst into tears and laughed at the same time.

"*Now* I know you're worried about me if you're offering voluntary hugs."

"This is not your fault," Frankie said, pulling back to look her friend in the eyes. "Understand?"

"In my head, I do. The hard part is convincing my heart."

Frankie nodded. "I get that. You deserved better."

"I did. And now I'm going to get it."

"That's my girl," Frankie cheered.

Katie smoothed her wrinkled shirt and pulled out her phone. She Googled locksmiths and made an appointment to have the locks changed the next day. The new and improved Katie was a woman of action.

TWENTY-FOUR

The next evening, Beckett walked in the front door carrying a pizza box. "Hey, Ma!" he bellowed, always the loudest of her three children. Katie ran out from the kitchen to the front door to greet him with open arms and squeezed him tight, refusing to let go. She still struggled to shake the genuine feeling of loss that hovered in the air around him. Confused, she told herself that it was just a side effect of the divorce and her sentimental heart. The truth was, she was having a recurring nightmare where she rushed into a burning building, knowing her children were inside. Each time, it ended the same, and when she reached out, they burst into flames and disintegrated before her eyes. In the morning, she woke up shaking, her heart pounding, with tears on her cheeks.

"Woman, you need to learn to let go." He extracted himself carefully with a chuckle and walked into the house. Katie pulled Callie into her arms next, squeezing her tight.

"I missed you so much," Katie gushed into her hair, breathing in the scent of her daughter with her eyes shut tight.

"Mom, we talk on the phone every day. What is going on with you? You're acting weird."

"Nothing," Katie said, releasing her hold, and Callie walked into the kitchen.

Lauren was her next victim. "Hey, sweetheart." Katie pulled her in tight and squeezed, then pulled back, clutching Lauren's hands tight in her own and refusing to let go.

"My babies. All gathered together under one roof," Katie exclaimed, swinging their intertwined hands out and back in for emphasis. "I love having you home, safe and sound."

Lauren's eyes widened, and she side-eyed her siblings. "Guys, we have a stage-four clinger here! I'm going to need an extraction."

Katie laughed at herself, finally dropping Lauren's hands. "Okay, fine, mock your mother's love. But some-day, when I'm dead and gone...."

"...we'll all be wishing we'd said I love you one more time," the kids chorused in a strong unison, singsong voice that made Katie laugh.

"Alright, fine, I get it."

In the kitchen, she pulled out a stack of four plates and opened the refrigerator where she pulled out a six-pack of root beer from the glass-encased beverage station at the end of the marble island. From the freezer, she retrieved four frosty mugs, setting them on the island with a grin. "And the best part is, I didn't even have to cook!"

"We thought since your birthday dinner was such a bust, we owed you one." Callie reminded her. Becket flipped open the lid and pulled out two huge slices, depositing one on his plate and the other on a plate for his mother.

"Thanks, buddy." Katie folded the thin crust in half and dunked it in the side of marinara Beckett handed her. Her teeth bit through the chewy, golden-brown crust and she closed her eyes. "Pizza is the world's perfect food." She took another bite, then studied the kids' tense faces one by one. "Okay, weirdos, you all need to relax. I am fine. Better than fine, really."

Their faces were uneasy. They had been consumed with their own lives at work and school. During their last few visits, they collectively ignored the elephant in the room, but it was time to finally address it.

"Tough talk time," Katie said, and they collectively groaned. "I want to know where you are at emotionally with the divorce. I've purposefully kept things light during your last few visits to give you some time to process your feelings. But I need to know where you are now that you've sat with it for a few months."

They offered her tight smiles, and Katie knew she was going to have to nudge them more. "Callie?"

"I don't know. I guess part of me was hoping no news was good news and that you'd get back together."

Shocked at her revelation, Katie's eyebrows shot up. "Well, I can confirm that is definitely not happening."

The silence in the room was sobering, and Katie could hear the seconds tick by on the clock on the wall of the kitchen.

Lauren broke it first. "Things are going to change around here, but I think we all ultimately want to see you happy."

Beckett grunted in approval, nodding with his full mouth. His fingers compressed the slice of pizza in his hand before he devoured it in three huge bites.

"And Dad," she added quietly.

"Of course, you do. I know you love us both, and that will never change, no matter what transpired between your dad and me. That's a promise."

"I still don't understand. Why?" Callie was intent on putting the scattered pieces of her life back together, unable to accept the truth. "I'll admit, I've been going over my memories with a fine-tooth comb looking for cracks in the foundation, and I never found any. Were we that oblivious to what was happening? Were you ever happy?"

Katie laughed. "Of course, I was. We had a wonderful life together. Filled with so many happy memories."

"Remember that time you took us to Florida to see the ocean for the first time and we flew those kites?" Beckett asked with an infectious grin. A red dot of pizza sauce on his stubble-covered chin reverted him back to the mischievous little boy he'd been.

A puzzled look knit Katie's brow as she strained to recall it, but her mind was blank and unyielding. The smile waned on her face. "What are you talking about? We never went to Florida when you were little. I always *wanted* to, but your dad said we could never afford it. "

Callie and Lauren exchanged tight glances, taken aback by her questioning of the event. "Come on, Mom, you have to remember. You tell us that story every Christmas. About how we all fell asleep in the back of the car, and you told Beckett to just unload the essentials and he grabbed the kites."

The words didn't stir up a familiar feeling. Instead, they tugged at her memory, refusing to surface, filling her with confusion and doubt. She rifled through her subconscious, coming up empty, and the presence of a possible gap in her memory was terrifying to admit. Seeing the fear lighting up on her children's faces, she lied, "Of course. How could I forget that day?"

Wanting to ease their concern, Katie quickly changed the subject. "More pizza? Or how about some ice cream?" She pulled the Rocky Road out of the fridge, the flavor that summed up the last few months of their lives perfectly, and dished up four bowls with gleaming spoons.

"Mom?' Lauren asked between bites. Her lips pursed together, and Katie suspected what was coming next.

"Yes, honey?"

"Did you happen to see Dad on *Extra! News* a few weeks ago?" Lauren asked. Beckett's fervent glance silenced the rest of her words. His jaw clenched in anger. "What? I'm just making sure she doesn't get blindsided when she's…" Lauren's words trailed off, silenced by Beckett's glare.

Katie reached out to touch his cheek. "It's okay, sweet boy. He is entitled to live his life."

Beckett shrugged. "He could have at least waited until you were officially divorced. It was a slap in the face."

"These things take time. If he thinks he's emotionally ready to move onto bachelorhood, then it really isn't up to us to tell him different."

"How can you be so calm and collected about this?" Beckett wondered.

"Well, I've had a lot more time to accept it's happening. You guys will get there." She walked over to the drawer to pull out the bottle of Liquid Ass to lighten the conversation. "And I may have given Frankie the go-ahead to engage in a little petty revenge a time or two to help soften the blow." She grinned and handed it over to Beckett. "You might find this useful to get your deadbeat roommate to move out."

He twisted open the bottle and gagged. Screwing it shut, he ran to the sink, dry heaving as Lauren plugged her nose.

Katie smiled and cupped a hand to her mouth. "A tiny word of caution. Do not, under any circumstances, use it in small enclosed spaces." Beckett started laughing, and she continued, "Especially in the air vents of a fine piece of German automotive engineering."

"Dad's Beamer!? You didn't!"

With a grimace, Katie muttered out of the side of her mouth, "*I* didn't, but *Frankie* might have."

"Frankie's the best," Beckett said with a grin. Not having kids of her own, Frankie had adopted Katie's immediately. She was like a second, more wacky mother without all the rules.

Waving her hand in front of her face to dispel the stench, Callie burst into a fit of giggles. "He might have deserved that."

"He did," Katie muttered under her breath.

Beckett grinned and held up his hand for a high-five,

but Katie couldn't bring herself to give him one. "Come on, Mama, don't leave me hanging."

"I can't," Katie said with an embarrassed smile. "I'm not proud of my actions, but Lord, it *was* satisfying." Even Lauren started to giggle. "I'm only human." Changing tactics, she stood and put the dishes into the dishwasher. "But seriously, I don't want you to worry, and speaking of things changing around here, your dad moved out."

"He did?" Callie was stunned.

"It's probably for the best," Lauren admitted.

"How can you say that? You're just like him!" Beckett cried.

"Guys!" Katie interrupted. "Let's take a beat. It was time. Living here together was an untenable situation and unhealthy for everyone. It just made sense."

The kids nodded and drank their root beers quietly. A sad pall hung over the room.

"Kids!" She ringed arms around Beckett and Lauren and brought them in closer. "We've all been sad pandas for far too long. It's time to believe in the magic of new beginnings." She felt them coming around. They nodded and tried to take this new information in stride.

"To new beginnings." Lauren hoisted up her frosty mug, and they all followed suit. Katie looked into the faces of her children, the ones she loved most in the world.

"I love you guys," Katie said, her voice cracking.

"Hurry!" Beckett teased. "The waterworks are about to start, and do I need to remind you, dear sisters, that we barely escaped from the prison of her embrace just mere moments ago?"

Katie ruffled his hair and smirked at his accurate assessment.

"Who's up for Kings on the Corners?" Callie asked, pulling their worn deck of cards from the junk drawer in the kitchen and waving it in the air. It was a game they'd played together for years. Beckett and Lauren groaned but gave in and dealt the cards, their competitive streaks on full display. It was one simple moment they shared that proved to Katie her new life was going to be filled with laughter and joy and moments of authentic connection with her children. It was the beautiful calm before a storm none of them saw coming.

TWENTY-FIVE

A week later, Katie sat in Davina's office waiting for her next appointment when a young woman rushed in, clearly in a panic. She burst into tears and took the seat next to Katie, even though there were four open seats across from her. A wave of anxiety ushered in with her as she sat on the edge of the chair, her knees bobbing up and down.

Surrounding the woman were bursts of frenetic red energy that surged in a halo around her. Confused, Katie's head cocked to the side as she studied the woman, blinking rapidly a few times to clear the red aura that created a fogginess around her. There was a magnetic pull Katie felt from her center she couldn't deny.

"Are you okay?" Katie asked as she reached into her handbag to pull out a package of tissues. Through the red haze, and even in her distressed, tear-stained state, Katie could see the woman was gorgeous. "Here." She handed the package to her, and Katie's hand brushed against her skin.

Images rocketed forward and a flash of photographs invaded her mind. She shivered as seething hatred seeped into her. The room started to close in around Katie, and phantom fingers circled her throat. Katie clawed at the tightness she felt around her neck, and a lightning flash illuminated a man's face. Dark-haired and brooding, he hovered inches from her. His chokehold on her throat was unrelenting as she struggled to breathe. He gritted his teeth, forcing his fingers tighter and tighter together. Gasping for air, she began to slip away when, faintly, she heard the ambient sounds of the office. She focused on the ringing of the telephone to ground herself and was relieved when she heard the woman speak.

"Thank you." The woman accepted the packet of tissues and dabbed at her eyes. The words pulled Katie the rest of the way free from his grip, and she shook the oppressive energy off like a wet dog. She felt an unmistakeable tug toward the young woman she couldn't deny. Confused at first, she'd seen what appeared to be an emotional aura, and it was the first time she'd received flashes from touching a stranger. Katie remembered Yuli's words. "The universe sends me people who deserve a rebalance, and I help Karma deliver it." Freshly emboldened with purpose, she felt a distinct shift in her own energy, and her senses were flooded with adrenaline—hyper-focused and alert.

Katie studied her, energized by the idea of helping this woman. Her platinum blonde hair was pulled back from her face with huge soft spirals that cascaded down her back. She wasn't much older than Callie, but where Callie walked through life with child-like innocence, this woman had a harder edge. She oozed sexuality, even while wearing a hoodie and yoga pants. Her full wide mouth was painted red, and her bright white teeth contrasted sharply against it. Hourglass-shaped, her creamy skin peeked out of the top of a camisole where a gold M dangled from a chain between her cleavage.

Her voice was barely a whisper when she asked, "Do you ever wish you could have a do-over? That you could go back in time and never cross paths with the one person who was destined to destroy you?"

"I think you've summed up the dream of every woman who has ever sat in this waiting room." Katie tried to introduce levity to the conversation to cast away the fear that lingered after the vision dissipated. "I'm Katie, by the way."

"Marisa."

Katie extended her hand, and Marisa reached one manicured hand out to shake it. On contact, lightning flashed again, illuminating a figure in the rain digging a hole. A gun on a nightstand. Marisa was tied up and on her knees as a muscled man dragged the muzzle of a gun up her body, using it to caress the underside of her chin before jamming it against her forehead. Katie shuddered as fingers of fear traced down her spine, sending chills down her arms. She was terrified. It required focused effort to pull her hand back from Marisa's, the same sensation of pulling powerful magnets apart.

Marisa exhaled a long sigh and tried to catch her breath. "Every bad thing that has happened in my life can be traced back to Rocco."

"They say the person you choose to share your life

with has the most impact on it. He's the one you'll share twenty thousand meals with, the one whose day you'll hear about eighteen thousand times, and he'll be your travel companion for a hundred vacations."

"I wish that was all we shared." She picked at the acrylic at the base of her thumbnail absentmindedly. Clawing and scratching as fresh tears rolled down her face.

"He's also the one person who will deeply influence your children," Katie offered. "As someone who made a terrible choice, that ultimately landed me here, choosing a father for your future children is one of the most important decisions you will make in your entire life. Do you have any kids?"

"Not yet." Marisa pressed her left palm against her belly like Katie used to love to do when she was pregnant, and Katie's heart dropped. The diamond on her fourth finger was an enormous status symbol that caught the sunlight and refracted a prism on the wall behind the secretary.

"Then this is your chance to undo your decision before it bleeds into your children. Do you have any friends, family, or a support system? You need to find a safe place."

"I can't. He controls every aspect of my life. He systematically destroyed all my relationships with my family and friends until he isolated me completely. I had to squirrel away money in a secret account for two years in order to get here, in front of Davina Thorne. I'm desperate. She's my only hope."

"Marisa, I know we just met, but I have a very important message for you. You must leave." Katie said, "You are in real danger if you stay with him."

Marisa's already pale face whitened in fear. She trembled and her legs bounced up and down, nervously dispelling the tension gathered there. The red energy intensified and pulsed around her, overpowering all of Katie's thoughts.

"I know." Marisa looked down at her feet. Her hands were tucked between her knees as she quivered in fear. "But it's not that simple," Marisa said. "He's never going to let me go."

"It's not up to him," Katie said, emboldened by the truth. "It's your life. You make your own decisions."

"I used to think that was true." Marisa's shoulders dropped. "When we met, I thought he was my ticket out of survival mode. Rocco pursued me, and I found his intensity charming. It reminded me of all those stupid Harlequin romance books I stole from my grandma's bookshelves when I was a teenager. You know, the tortured dark hero who will burn everything to the ground to rescue the beautiful heroine? What a crock of shit!"

Katie nodded. "You're not alone. I might have subscribed to that theory when I was younger myself."

"Power is an aphrodisiac for me. My whole life, men took advantage of me and used me. My mom's flavor of the month, even teachers at school, and I felt powerless. And then I met Rocco. When he gives an order, men jump up to carry it out. Being with a man who commanded that kind of respect, who'd destroy anyone who wronged you? It was hot." She laughed through her tears. "God, I must sound like an idiot."

"No. You were naïve and vulnerable."

"So naïve," she admitted with a long pause before she continued. "He spoiled me with clothing, lavish vacations, and romantic carriage rides through Central Park. It seemed like a fairytale." Marisa shuddered. "Turns out I traded one battle of survival for another. This one comes with a better closet and travel perks." She exhaled a hot breath. "I feel so stupid. By the time I noticed what was really happening, it was too late. Why does love blind us to reality?"

"It's a tale as old as time," Katie said. "Women are taught to wait for our Prince Charming to ride in on his white horse to rescue us."

"Instead of the white horse, mine rode in on a private plane." She shrugged her shoulders, her face turning into a scowl. "It's criminal teaching young girls to be so helpless." She rubbed her flat belly absentmindedly.

"It took me half my life to wise up," Katie said with an engaging smile. "You're waking up to the truth early. It's a gift you are here."

"Maybe," Marisa mumbled under her breath.

"I know this feels like an unsurmountable mountain you have to climb, but one day, maybe a few years from now, you'll look back at this moment and see how far you've come. One day, he will just be an annoying blip on your radar."

"I hope you're right." Marisa hugged her arms tight around her abdomen. Katie pulled out a pen and wrote her phone number on a card and handed it to Marisa.

"Memorize my number, but do not put it in your phone," Katie directed. "I have a daughter your age, and I know this is going to sound crazy, but you are not safe with him. Make a plan and get yourself to safety. Let Davina do all the heavy lifting. He may have isolated you, but he doesn't know I exist. If you need help, any time, any day, you call me."

At the gesture, Marisa burst into fresh tears and jumped up to hug her, brushing her hands across Katie's. When they connected, she felt two heartbeats. One strong and steady, the other fainter and faster, skipping and intensifying the tighter the woman hugged Katie. Yep. She was right. Marisa was pregnant.

"Marisa Gabriano, Davina Thorne will see you now."

Katie's heart dropped. Her last name was iconic. An Italian family whose lineage could be traced for a century all the way back to Sicily. Running moonshine, then guns, meth, and coke. She'd heard Jeff mention that name over the years. The Gabriano family had Jeff on speed dial. He'd been navigating their skirmishes with the law for the better part of a decade. Before she could put any more thoughts together, Davina's fresh-faced assistant breezed through the door.

"Ready?"

"Thank you," Marisa murmured and squeezed her hand, then followed the woman down the hallway. Goosebumps broke out on Katie's forearms, and the metallic taste of fear coated her throat.

Twenty minutes later, when she sat in front of Davina, she mentioned, "I met Marisa Gabriano in the waiting room."

"As the almost ex-wife of an attorney, you know I cannot discuss her case with you. It's privileged."

"I know," Katie answered, "but she's in real danger. *And* she's pregnant."

The last few words got Davina's attention. She sat up and leaned toward Katie, her eyes betraying nothing. A blank look covered her poker face that had been honed from years of being in the courtroom.

Katie continued, "He's going to hurt her."

"How do you know this?"

"I just do."

Still sizing her up, Katie wilted under Davina's direct gaze. "We're here to discuss *your* case, Katie." Davina insisted, snapping Katie's focus back, but not before scribbling a note.

"There's been a recent development. Jeff moved out of the house."

Davina smiled. "That is fantastic news. Voluntarily giving up an asset, especially a primary residence, is detrimental to his demand to keep it."

"That *is* good news," Katie repeated, brightening at the prospect.

"We've got a court date set up at the end of December."

"Well, Merry Christmas to me," Katie mumbled sarcastically under her breath, annoyed it was going to take that long and taint her enjoyment of the holidays.

"The wheels of justice move slowly," Davina said. "I told you to buckle up and settle in."

"You did," Katie confirmed. "There are a few more things your forensic accountant needs to check on. I think he might have a safe deposit box somewhere tropical, or possible tax haven accounts offshore. How do we uncover those types of assets? I also remember him blabbering on about bitcoin. He was obsessed with it. If I know Jeff, he's got to have a wallet he's hiding somewhere."

"Crypto is hard to trace in the system," Davina admitted. "That's part of its allure. I'll have my guy do some more digging, but I can't promise you he'll get anywhere."

"At this point, if I can keep my home and enough assets for the upkeep, I'll consider it a win." Katie stood to leave.

"I think we can do better than that," Davina said, rising. "I'll keep you posted on what we find."

Katie nodded and walked toward the door, then stopped to deliver a cryptic message. "He's going to kill her," Katie said under her breath, just loud enough for Davina, engrossed in making notes on her file, to hear.

Davina's eyes widened and locked on hers. "What did you say?"

"Rocco Gabriano. He's going to kill her. Don't ask me how I know, I just do."

TWENTY-SIX

The next day, Katie was anxiously waiting for Yuli to arrive. The questions she was desperate to ask churned through her mind on repeat. Right on time, the older woman rang the doorbell and let herself in. Katie watched her beloved grandmother walk across the wood floors, and she swore she was stepping lighter and more limber.

"Jeff moved out," Katie admitted once they were in the kitchen, eager to share her good news.

"Hmm. Now that's interesting." Yuli mumbled as she pulled out a chair and set her massive black handbag on the table next to her. It resembled an old-fashioned doctor's bag with its sturdy plastic handles and twist-bar fastener.

"Interesting how?"

"I'm not quite sure yet. We are all pawns in Zoya's game."

"I've been trying to be patient because I know there is bad blood between you two, but I can't help my curiosity.

And now that she's inserted herself into my life, don't you think I deserve an explanation?" Katie begged as she served Yuli a slice of coffee cake at the table. It had swirls of deep orange pumpkin and sprinkles of cinnamon and was studded with chunks of walnuts.

"Please, Yuli. I need to know," she whispered. The older woman was quiet, and Katie could feel a tug-of-war going on inside her. Unwilling to push her further, Katie poured Yuli a cup of coffee. In the stillness, she watched her pluck two sugar cubes from the pile on the tea plate with silver tongs before stirring to dissolve them fully. They sat in silence for a few more moments when the doorbell rang. Arlo sprang to life, barking like he was trying to save Timmy from the well.

Frustrated she was getting nowhere with Yuli, Katie popped up to answer the door and returned to the table with a plain cardboard box. Taking a knife from the block, she sliced through the packing tape to find black tissue paper inside. She pushed it aside and pulled out an exquisite music box. This one was stained a deep crimson and black, with delicate webbing that covered the entirety of the box. Katie immediately felt the oppressive weight of it. Heavy in her hands, she shivered as a chill raced through her, and tears welled at her lashes. Katie set down the box and felt the heaviness dissipate, finally able to exhale a hot and heavy breath.

"I'm sorry. I don't know what's come over me," Katie apologized.

Yuli gasped when finally she saw it. She stood and walked over to the crimson box, mesmerized by the tinkle that came from it as Katie cranked it up. "You feel its power," Yuli said as her own eyes welled up. "I haven't laid eyes on this since the day I turned sixteen." Yuli's lips turned down, and pain crossed her features.

"What is it?"

"It's from our family archives," Yuli whispered.

Yuli's reaction was filling Katie with unease, but she couldn't stop herself from asking, "What's inside?"

"It's the worst day of my life." Stunned, Yuli couldn't tear her eyes away from the music box. For several long minutes, she was deep in thought, then finally spoke. "I don't remember my mother." Her words were barely a whisper, and Katie had to strain to hear them as a tear cascaded down Yuli's soft, wrinkled cheek. "I never felt her arms around me. Never heard her laugh, or her voice. I never felt the warmth of her love."

Katie's heart broke open. She remembered asking her mom about her own grandmother when she was ten. Kristina shut down the conversation with such ferocity, it stunned Katie silent and she'd been forbidden to ask again.

"What happened?"

Yuli choked on a strangled sob, and Katie rushed to grab a box of Kleenex. After wiping her cheeks, she continued in a hushed whisper. "I killed her."

"What? I don't understand."

Yuli turned toward the box. "You must go inside to see it, but I have to warn you. This box is full of despair and contains decades of pain and suffering."

"Do I have to?" Katie's words were meant to be a joke, but they fell flat.

"It's the only way for you to understand."

"Can you come with me?" Katie asked and was disappointed when Yuli shook her head no.

"This is a journey only you can undertake. It will explain so much. You must go."

"I'm afraid. If this memory brings you so much pain, how will I be able to endure it?"

"You can and you will." Yuli reached up and stroked Katie's cheek. "Knowledge is power. You cannot know yourself when you do not know where you come from. I love you, Katia. It is time to see." She pushed the box toward Katie with two solid fingers. "I'll be waiting for you when you return."

Katie swallowed hard and took the box in her hands. It felt weighty and oppressive. A trickle of dread snaked around her, looking for an entrance. She gulped and struggled with the lid, prying it apart with her fingernails. The effort made her break out in beads of sweat near her hairline. Finally, a crack of red light ran around the edge of the black box, and with one more burst of concentrated effort, she finally yanked it open wide. An army of thousands of cockroaches and spiders raced out and over Katie's fingers, up her forearms, and down her back to the floor. Her skin began to twitch and burn. She clamped her lips together and fought the urge to scream.

Ominous music tumbled out, violins swooned, and a melancholy cello pushed her deeper. It was a symphony of woeful strings that filled her with dread. She felt her entire being constrict and tighten together as she was tugged into the box. Her heartbeat thrummed in her ears as she felt her human form fall away, enduring a terrifying long second of weightlessness before she landed hard in the middle of a grassy field. Katie glanced around to get her bearings as blue light from the full moon cascaded onto every patch of tall switch grass and outlined every tree. She stood still for a long breath and looked down. Her bare feet were on a dirt path, and she felt the sensation of being tugged along as she walked slowly toward a little cottage tucked into the forest. When she got within earshot, the first shrieks sent a bolt of terror through her. Panting in fear, she pressed her body against the rough trunk of a tree. She waited as another blood-curdling cry ripped through the silence of the night.

Katie gripped the tree, struggling to hang on as the force of the wind breezed past, yanking her closer to the cottage. At the door she hesitated, hearing comforting murmuring on the other side of it. A shrill yelping sound followed by sobbing pressed her into action. She pried open the heavy wooden door and entered a crude dwelling with stucco walls and a dirt floor. Katie's eyes adjusted to the dim light coming from candles placed around the room, illuminating a figure lying on a bed made of logs and covered with animal hides. Another terrifying scream pierced her soul.

"Nadia, my sweet. It is almost time." Nadia was drenched in sweat and lying in a pool of blood that colored her dressing gown. The other woman was stoking a fire, adding chunks of wood underneath a kettle. "I'm warming water for your bath when this is over. It will feel so good."

"I can't, Mama." Nadia's voice was weak and breathy. "I'm so tired."

As she watched them interact, she put the pieces

together. Zoya was tending to her daughter Nadia, who was pregnant with Yuli.

"You must," Zoya demanded, clearly concerned. Katie slipped into the darkness against the wall at the foot of the bed, unnoticed by both women. Nadia's legs were spread open, and she saw something tiny and impossible between them. A foot.

Katie gasped. A breech birth. Zoya sat on a wooden stool at Nadia's feet, singing a sweet song to calm a frightened Nadia who writhed and shook on the bed as another round of contractions gripped her belly. She emitted raw, animalistic howls that tore through the cabin, clearly in agony, and Katie's heart ached immediately, in tune with the gravity of the situation. There was no hospital in sight, no medical equipment to assist a delivery, and no doctor available.

Zoya, consumed with worry, stroked Nadia's arm. "My darling, I need to turn the baby. It cannot come this way."

"No, Mama, please," she begged, her long black hair knotted and sweaty. "I cannot bear it."

"You must. I'm sorry, my sweet." Zoya pushed on her belly, forcibly turning the unborn infant wedged inside.

Nadia shrieked in agony, her cries making her mother scream out in unison. Loud, guttural wails reverberated in the enclosed area, making Katie tremble.

In horror, Katie watched helplessly as the older woman cupped her hand and inserted it inside while she pushed her daughter's burgeoning belly down, muttering words that were obliterated by her daughter's shrieking. Zoya sobbed as she pushed and tugged the baby into position. After ten long minutes, she stopped. Nadia's pale skin was damp with sweat, and she moaned, unable to summon the energy to scream anymore. Spent and exhausted, she quieted and became still, her legs quivering.

Grasping her daughter's slack hand, Zoya brought it to her lips.

"We are almost there, my darling. The end is near. You've been so brave." Zoya wiped away her tears with the back of her bloodied hands. "Bear down now and push your baby out!"

"I can't, Mama," Nadia said weakly.

"Now! You must push now!" Zoya shouted, shaking her forearm to rouse the exhausted woman.

Guttural noises came from deep in Nadia's throat as she summoned the last bit of strength she had left and bore down. A vein surfaced on her forehead from the effort. After four long, agonizing pushes, the infant arrived, her first wail filling the humble home from floor to rafters. Zoya cheered with relief and finally smiled. Humming, she cleaned the infant's face and wrapped the bloody baby in a cotton flour sack before handing her to Nadia.

"You did it, my love. She's a strong one and twice the size you were," Zoya said, wringing out a cloth from the warmed water and wiping the sweat from her daughter's brow. Nadia smiled sweetly, looking down at her daughter.

"She needs to be strong, Mama, as she will move mountains." Nadia looked into her face. She reached out her pinky, and the baby squeezed her delicate fingers around it. "My little angel. My sweet Yuli."

"Yuli?" Zoya asked as she handed Nadia a wet washcloth.

"Yes." Nadia brushed the soft cotton across the crown

of her head to clean the infant and kissed her forehead. She sobbed with relief and utter joy, exactly as Katie had done during the births of her own three children. "We have been blessed today with three generations of strong women," Nadia said with a content smile.

Zoya nodded, watching her daughter transform before her eyes from a daughter to a mother. It was a bittersweet rite of passage. "I am so proud of you." She bent and kissed her daughter's cheek. The tenderness of the moment swelled as Zoya wrapped her arms around them both and sobbed in relief. "I don't know what I would have done if I'd lost you," Zoya admitted as she clung to her daughter and granddaughter.

"God is good," Nadia answered.

"He is, indeed." Zoya pressed a cup to her daughter's lips. "Drink, my love. We have one more task, and then you can eat and rebuild your strength. You need to push once more to expel the afterbirth."

"No, Mama. No," Nadia cried, her eyes glued to the little girl swaddled in her arms.

"The hard part is over, my sweet. I just need one little push."

"Okay." Nadia nodded and gave the little infant a kiss on the tip of her nose before surrendering her. Zoya bundled up the newborn and tucked her back into her mother's arms to keep her warm.

"Are you ready?" Zoya asked.

Nadia nodded and bore down one more time. There was an unexpected gush as a pool of red rushed between her legs and out onto the white cotton bedding. The deluge covered the fabric as Zoya pressed fresh cotton rags to stop the flow of blood. Every few seconds, she'd peel them off and press fresh chunks of clean cloth to the wound, only to have them turn red in seconds.

Katie gasped. Too much blood. It was too much blood.

Nadia sighed once, and the baby in her arms rolled onto the bed next to her and screamed. Nadia's body went limp, and her face was a ghastly white. The infant hiccuped and jutted her tiny fists in the air before letting out another bloodcurdling wail.

"No. No. No!" Zoya continued to press cotton cloths down to stop the overwhelming flow of blood. Unable to stop herself, she continued the task in vain, shrieking in pain in tandem with the plump, inconsolable baby on the bed. She didn't stop until the cotton was gone. Panicked, she held a hand in front of her daughter's mouth, desperate to feel the passage of breath. On the bed, her daughter lay there unmoving. Still. Silent. Katie focused on Nadia's chest, willing the bleeding to stop and her chest to rise. A long minute passed while they both stood paralyzed, united by the sanctity of the moment. When the veil between life and death was but a single breath followed by an eternal silence that was devastating.

"Nadia!" Zoya shouted, shaking her daughter, refusing to concede. "Wake up!" She shook the woman, whose body was slack and lifeless. "Please, God. No!" She buried her head in her daughter's chest, willing her heart to beat, but it was deathly silent. Gone. Her beautiful Nadia was gone. Around her, the world grayed, and the baby screamed, desperate for her mother. Cries that would go forever unanswered.

In shock, Zoya stood covered in her daughter's blood,

her fists balled in rage, and let out a terrifying primal scream that reverberated through the cottage. It ebbed and flowed, piercing Katie's heart with a pain so unimaginable it took her breath away. Zoya's agony ripped through Katie's core in waves as time stood still.

Ignoring the wailing infant, Zoya was sobbing and hysterical, cursing God in a language Katie didn't understand. Tears coursed down Katie's cheeks, and she pressed a hand to her mouth to stop the pain from escaping as she felt a force yank her back, pull her out of the cottage, down the dirt path, and out of the forest lit by the full moon. She was yanked back to the safety of her familiar kitchen, where she sat next to Yuli.

Katie struggled to catch her breath, exhausted by the journey, and she wailed. Crushed under the weight of three generations of grief, it ripped her apart. Katie was inconsolable. She clung to Yuli, and after several long moments, the pain subsided. Katie's breath was jagged. Through her own tears, Yuli led her to her bedroom, tucking her into the bed like a small child, and the act broke Katie's heart.

"Oh, Yuli." Katie tried to bring a shaky hand to her grandmother's face. "Your mama. I saw her. I saw you."

"I know, sweet one, and now, so do you."

Katie's voice cracked, and she sobbed with exhaustion and generations of pain. The trauma of Yuli's birth was seared into her own DNA.

TWENTY-SEVEN

Katie slept deep and late. When her eyes finally opened, they filled with tears. Her face was swollen and her throat hoarse. Dragging herself out of the bed and into the bathroom, she washed her face and studied her reflection in the mirror. The streak of white in her hair had gotten thicker and more pronounced overnight.

"Sweet Jesus," she said to herself as she turned her head back and forth in the mirror, surveying the change. "I look like a skunk."

"Pepe Le Pew has nothing on you," Arlo said from the tumble of blankets on her bed that he was currently scraping at with his paws to create his ideal resting place.

"Gee, thanks. Look who's a poet and didn't even know it." She was drained, and she felt weak. "I have to open the store for Yuli, but man, I wish I could crawl back into bed with you." She tugged on a full skirt, a white t-shirt, and white sandals. The outfit was polished and yet comfortable enough for an eight-hour day on her feet.

Twenty minutes later, she parked in front of Kandied Karma and used her key to get inside where Yuli was waiting.

"You're in early," Katie remarked, giving her a quick hug. "You usually like to sleep in."

"I was worried about you, Katia," she said, pulling back and cradling Katie's face with her hands.

"I'm fine. Just a little worn out."

"I have just the thing," Yuli said, returning to the stove.

"Let me guess. Eye of newt and toe of frog?" Katie asked with a grin.

"You know, Shakespeare didn't do us witches any favors," Yuli grumbled. "Those things are just mustard seeds and buttercups, but leave it to a writer to make it sound macabre. No wonder they burned us at the stake." Yuli pulled a kettle off the stove and poured two small servings into tea cups. She added a splash of heavy cream and then a heaping spoonful of sugar before setting one in front of Katie. "Drink it." She held her own cup in her hands. Katie heard her say, "Restoration, innovation, motivation," before she flung the contents into her mouth and swallowed. Katie followed suit. The bitter tang of the tea hit the back of her throat, and she felt her esophagus constrict.

"Keep it down," Yuli advised. "Breathe through your nose and out of your mouth. The nausea will pass."

Katie swallowed the increased saliva in her throat and fought against the heaving of her stomach, breathing into it as Yuli advised. After four long minutes, she felt a warming sensation deep in the pit of her belly. It seeped up her chest and made her heart beat faster before spreading out to her limbs. An intense surge of energy accompanied the warmth, and she stood taller and fidgeted around the room.

"What was that?" she asked. "Whatever it is, we need to bottle and sell it. Forget five-hour energy. That was a whole other level."

"It's poison," Yuli said matter-of-factly.

"What?" Katie exclaimed. "You tried to poison me? But you drank it, too!"

"Yes," Yuli answered. "I have built an immunity to it over the years. You will, too. It will fortify you when your new abilities are too taxing on your physical body."

Flabbergasted, Katie was silent with shock then uttered under her breath, "I have so much to learn."

"That is true." Yuli looked Katie up and down. "The color is returning to your cheeks. Did you want to talk about the journey you took yesterday?"

"I've been turning it over and over in my mind this morning. Do you know why she sent that particular box to me?"

"I have some theories. She's probably using our past to influence you and to create a division between us. No matter what, you need to remember, Zoya always controls the narrative."

"Division between us? That would never happen," Katie said. "You were a helpless baby. Your mother's death was not your fault."

"That is also true, but Zoya has always blamed me." Yuli scowled. "She called me the devil's spawn. On my sixteenth birthday, she gift wrapped the music box. It was the only birthday gift she ever gave me. I was so excited to open it up. I thought after all this time, she was finally beginning to forgive me."

"That's so cruel." Katie thought about the weight of its contents put upon the shoulders of a teenager.

"I cried for a week after I opened it. I was inconsolable," Yuli admitted. "I watched it over and over again, clinging to the memory of my mother holding me in her arms. Enduring the agony of the rest of the journey to indulge in the solitary moment of her love before she was gone." Yuli swiped at the tears in her eyes and then continued, "In a way, it actually *was* a gift. There was always an emptiness in Zoya that I never understood, like her heart had been hollowed out. I tried so hard to fill it and make her happy." Yuli's brow furrowed. "I picked her a bouquet of daisies once, then an hour later, I found them on the ground drying up in the sun. Later, I memorized the words to a song she told me she used to sing to my mother. When I sang it the first time, she said, 'Shut up. You sound like a dog in heat.'"

Katie reached out to squeeze her hand, and Yuli continued. "I always thought if I tried a little harder, maybe she would figure out how to love me, but after I saw the contents of the music box, I knew she never would." Yuli stopped. "That's when I ran away and found my own path."

"At sixteen?" Katie was in shock. "How did you survive?"

"I did what I had to do," Yuli muttered, then clammed up.

"That was her loss," Katie said. "Maybe she's reaching

out now to mend fences?" Her words were twisted up with hopeful yearning.

"I love your heart, Katia." Yuli gave her a sweet, skeptical smile. "I doubt that is the case, but her true motives will be revealed, eventually." She stood and pulled a clean apron from the hook and wrapped it around her body, signaling the end of the conversation.

Katie glanced at the watch on her wrist. "We better open up. There's a line halfway around the block already." Katie pulled her hair back into a high bun and placed a hat on her head, then opened the front door. All morning long, a stream of repeat customers filed into the store. Around eleven, Katie had just returned from her deliveries when she stopped cold. Her eyes locked onto Marisa's. Stunned, she watched a stocky man in his forties pull out a chair for Marisa who quickly settled into it. He was dark-haired and dark-complected, and the line parted to let him cut to the head of it with low grumblings from the crowd.

"Can I help you?" Katie asked.

"Yeah. I need three maraschino white chocolate truffles, a peanut butter and caramel turtle, and two espressos."

Katie folded a box and layered his selections into it, all the while her heart racing. At the register, she reached out a hand for his cash, and the touch of his skin rocketed her back. He was surrounded by black, smudged around his body like a halo. She heard gunshots in quick succession, and then saw a waterfall of blood. It trickled down her face, and she let out a yelp and jumped to shake it off.

The man narrowed his eyes. "What the hell is wrong with you?"

"Nothing. Sorry." Katie apologized and glanced over at Marisa. "Is that your wife?"

"Who wants to know?"

"No one, I was just making conversation. She's a beautiful woman."

"She is."

"I'll bring your order over in a few moments."

She served the rest of the customers in line, eyeing Rocco and Marisa's interactions. Then she delivered the tray of sweets and the espressos to their table. Marisa's eyes refused to meet hers, and an impatient Rocco waved her away. Ten minutes later, she got her chance when Marisa stood up and made her way to the back of the shop to use the bathroom.

Katie intervened and pulled her into the kitchen, where Yuli watched the interaction with interest.

A panicked Marisa looked over her shoulder. "He knows something is up," Marisa admitted in a hushed tone. "I think he had me followed to Davina's office."

"Do you have a plan or a place to go?" Katie asked. "If you stay with him, you will die, and so will your unborn baby."

"How did you...?" Marisa crumpled and wrapped her arms around her belly. Katie glanced through the window in the door at their table, where Rocco was scrolling through his phone. "No. I have nothing and no resources without him. I am alone."

"We don't have much time," Katie stated. "Get away, run an errand, make an excuse, do whatever you have to do. You find your opening and get the hell out. You memorized my phone number, right?"

"Yes," she whispered.

"Send me a pin and I'll come for you." Katie exhaled and offered her a quick hug. "Wipe your eyes. You have to remain calm. Now go."

Marisa nodded and swiped at her tears, then returned to the table.

"Who was that?" Yuli asked.

"Marisa Gabriano."

Yuli's eyes widened, and darted from side to side like she was mulling over a solution to a puzzle in her mind.

"She's in trouble." Katie explained, "One lesson from my freshman philosophy class has always stuck with me: 'The only thing necessary for the triumph of evil is for good people to sit back and do nothing.' And that guy is as evil as they come."

"I know he is," Yuli admitted to a confused Katie. "He comes from a long line of criminals and gangsters. Zoya crossed paths with his family when I was a child."

Katie reeled, trying to understand. "Maybe that's why she's surfaced now."

"Maybe… I don't know," Yuli said, still skeptical.

"Karma sent Marisa here. Isn't this how you said it was supposed to work? When I touched her skin, I saw the flashes. She deserves a rebalance and we have to help her. We can't turn our backs on her now. She's pregnant."

Yuli made the sign of the cross and began muttering prayers under her breath.

Katie pleaded, "The visions were crystal clear and violent. I don't know what it all means, but I know without a doubt, I will never be able to live with myself if something happens to her and I could have prevented it." She ducked back out into the front of the shop, busying herself with adding chocolates to the case. A few minutes later, she felt eyes drilling into her back. She turned around and met Rocco's. Fear cued up and coupled with adrenaline. She couldn't take a deep breath until he left with Marisa in tow. The black energy that hovered around his table left the shop when he did.

TWENTY-EIGHT

Zoya was giddy. At last, it was time. The pear tree's glow turned red, and Zoya pulled the dagger from her bedside table and cut the heavy fruit free from the tree. The tree wrinkled and shriveled up, shrinking and shedding all its leaves to the ground before disintegrating into a pile of ash.

In her hands, the pear was weighty and ripe, the paper-thin skin of it taut against its sweet flesh. It had taken months of nurturing it to allow for the effect to mature. Plump and luscious, it was finally ready to deploy. She took off her gloves and felt the power of it hum through her body. Then she tucked it into a bed of soft cotton napkins inside a wicker basket for safekeeping. The basket sat next to her in the sleek black town car, nestled in the crinolines of her long red skirt.

Her driver parked in front of the apartment that was in the firm's trust to host out-of-town clients. It was the penthouse of a sleek steel and glass building. She waited, tapping her fingers impatiently against the window. A fresh burst of pleasant October air hit her face when Higgins opened the door for Jeff to enter. He slid into the seat next to her with a cunning smile and leaned over to kiss her. She laced her fingers through the thick hair at his temples and tugged, savoring her pleasure when Jeff let out a painful yelp.

A wave of confused thoughts spewed out that Zoya was instantly in tune to receive.

This chick has some weird fetishes. But by God, if she wanted to strip me naked, cover me in honey, and tie me to a mangrove tree in the Everglades, I'd do it.

As tempted as she was to make the man alligator bait, she pushed the desire aside and saw her opening when she heard Jeff's stomach growl in the car.

"I'm sorry to have kept you waiting, darling. You seem to have the tummy rumbles."

That's what happens when you're two hours late for dinner.

"No problem at all. I was happy to wait for you," he lied.

For now. But I'll break you of that habit one way or another. She will learn my time is more valuable than hers. And I will savor breaking this filly down.

His thoughts annoyed her, and she had to fight to push past them and not let anger color her next interactions. "I'm afraid our reservation isn't for another hour," Zoya mentioned and paused, leading him to the water she needed him to drink. "But you're in luck, darling." Zoya plucked the pear from the basket and held it out to him. "I've had the most exquisite pears flown in from Chile."

His eyes locked on the fruit. The glow it emitted was

hypnotic to ordins. "I love pears," he admitted as he reached out to grasp it and then brought it to his lips. He bit into the green fruit, and juice trickled from it and down his jawline. "It's so good. I've never had better."

She watched for visible signs the fruit was working. His skin warmed to the touch as he gobbled down the remainder of the pear. Ravenous for it and unable to stop once he started, in record time, he reduced it to an empty core in his sticky hand. Zoya pressed the button and opened the window, and he threw out the remnants of it. To test its effects, Zoya swiped her hand in a sweeping motion, and Jeff reached up and slapped his own face.

Stunned, it took a full minute before his litany of thoughts returned.

This is trippy.

He held his hand up to his face, wiggled his fingers, and let out a nervous laugh. Then he walked his fingers up her thigh. Zoya leaned in closer, seeing his pupils dilate and nearly black out his irises. She swiftly swiped his hand from her leg, balled her fist, and struck down between her own legs. In tandem, she watched him raise his fist and punch himself in the balls.

Jefferson shrieked in pain and curled his legs up reflexively to protect himself from himself. "I don't know what's gotten into me. Please forgive me."

"Maybe we should try for another evening? If you're not feeling up to it?"

Suck... it up... man. You've been... waiting for... this date for... a month. Set the hook. Reel... the big one in.

His thoughts were slowing down as the pear took effect. Next to him in the seat, she craved physical distance from him as the car barreled to the airstrip. She placed her hands on her knees and, next to her, Jeff mimicked the action. She slid away from him and he copied her, sliding away from her to rest on the opposite side of the car. Pressed against opposite doors, the pair was as physically apart from each other as they could be. Zoya rejoiced. The pear was now in full effect, pairing her movements with whoever ate it.

It rendered him a compliant zombie, and the best part of it was the thoughts in his head stopped. She heard nothing as they drove in the dark for miles. The car finally came to a stop in front of her private aircraft.

Jeff followed behind her, mimicking her movements to a T and climbing the stairs into the jet as Zoya climbed up. She sat down in one of the leather chairs, and he followed suit, buckling his seatbelt the exact moment she did. Thirty minutes later, the plane touched down at the compound, and Jeff was settled at the dining room table. In front of them sat two thick stacks of papers her lawyers had drawn up. She set up a video camera focused on Jefferson, a little insurance policy she wanted to have in her back pocket, just in case.

Zoya raced through the documents, scrawling Jefferson Beaumont on the stack of paperwork, and Jeff mirrored her every move, signing his own bold signature to the documents. A Quit Claim Deed to his home. A Divorce decree granting Katie half of his retirement fund as well as the password to his bitcoin wallet and the twenty-four-word security phrase. He produced the address of his secret safe deposit box and handed over the key from his wallet. In the course of thirty minutes, he signed over fifty percent of his actual net worth to Katia. Her notary verified all signatures and stamped them for approval on camera.

Then she dialed Davina Thorne on the speaker phone. It rang three times before she answered.

"This is Jefferson Beaumont, Ms. Thorne," Zoya mouthed, and across the table, the words came out of Jeff's mouth. "You're the attorney of record for my wife in the matter of Beaumont vs Beaumont?"

"Yes," Davina answered. "What can I do for you?"

"I've put together a settlement and would like you to present it to Katie."

"A… okay," she said. "I'd like to record this phone call. Do I have your consent, Mr. Beaumont?"

"Yes."

"Can you repeat what you just said?"

"I've drawn up a settlement, and I'm interested in closing this matter as soon as possible and getting it in front of a judge. I want to move on with my life and have outlined a fair and equitable division of property and our assets."

"All of your assets?"

"Yes," Jefferson said. "I want to do the right thing. Katie was an exceptional wife and mother that I did not deserve. The least I can do is provide a fair settlement for her to start over."

"What about alimony?"

"I've included that in the agreement as well. Katie deserves to maintain the same standard of living she currently enjoys. She worked just as hard as I did to contribute to the family income and assets, and I shouldn't be the only one who's benefitted from her sacrifice."

"What if she remarries?"

"I will continue the financial support even in the event she remarries."

"That's very... fair of you." Davina's tone was wary. "I have to say I didn't see this coming."

"It's time to do the right thing for once in my miserable life. I've been a selfish bastard, and I want to apologize to Katie for how I've wronged her. I destroyed my family. The blame is mine, alone."

Davina took a long second before responding. "I am happy to hear you say that."

"Good. It's settled then. I've prepared all the necessary legal documents, have signed and notarized them, and will have them messengered to your office in the morning. All Katie needs to do is sign and present them to the judge to be entered into judgment."

"Fantastic."

"Good night."

Satisfied, Zoya ended the call and sat across from Jeff for several long moments. His eyes were black pools and empty, his mind a blank slate. She could do whatever she wanted to him in this condition, and her zeal for justice cried out for release. He was a nippy little Chihuahua. Weak but obnoxious. Always barking for attention. It would serve him right to be condemned into the body of a tiny, annoying dog.

She could do it, but that didn't seem like punishment enough. This one needed to be taught a lesson, and she wasn't sure condemning him to her servitude was the answer. He needed to learn that women weren't objects to be used for his sexual gratification and then tossed aside when their first wrinkle appeared. She had a better idea. Zoya was a believer that the punishment should always fit the crime and come with a killer soundtrack.

From her phone, she cued up music that pulsed through the speakers. Gillette's *Short Dick Man* throbbed from wall to wall, and she couldn't help but groove to it. A mirrored reflection, Jeff rose when she did. He gyrated his hips in tune with hers and the music swelled. His movements matched hers, dancing to the beat, perfectly synchronized. She laughed and shouted the lyrics with glee, and he echoed them exuberantly.

As the music crescendoed, she rubbed her hands together in time to the techno beat. Jeff clapped his large, manicured hands together and rubbed them in unison. Sparks flew as the friction increased, the volume intensified, and she danced around the room filled with glee. She smoothed her glowing hands down her torso from her belly button to the spread of her legs. Three more quick successions and then she pinched her fingers together, leaving only one inch of space between them at the chorus, and the spell was complete.

As the song concluded, she mimed unbuckling a belt and unzipping trousers. Across the room, Jeff went through the same motions. His buckle rang out as it hit the floor. It was a sight that made her laugh hysterically and was made even creepier by Jeff, mirroring her hysterics across the room. Nestled into a tangle of white pubic hair lay a tiny unit, about as big around as her pinky. Zoya laughed until she cried, and seeing Jefferson laugh at his own shortcomings made her grip her sides and fall to the ground on her back, aching in glee. Tears of joy coursed down both of their faces as her revenge was complete.

She reveled in her accomplishment. He didn't deserve to be cast into the body of a dog. This was far better. He'd still have the same insatiable sex drive, but when he went to satisfy his longing, he'd be humiliated time and time again. He'd have to endure hearing his partners ask mortifying questions like "Is it in yet? And, "Is that all there is?" The sheer volume of pure humiliation that was headed his way was mind-blowing, and she was only sad she would not be able to see it firsthand. In a burst of unnatural generosity, she summoned Magnum.

"Yes, My Queen?"

"Show this one to his room behind the kitchen. Then return."

He gathered up a complacent Jeff, who Zoya had redressed before Magnum led him away. She walked over to the bar cart and poured herself a bourbon neat and took a small sip, reveling in her win. Jefferson was reduced to less than nothing. His new micro penis would erode his confidence and make him ineffective in the bedroom *and* the boardroom. He'd never seduce another woman again. It was what he deserved for treating Katia like a slave and disrespecting their marriage vows.

"Impotence comes and goes, but a micro peen is forever," she said, still buoyed by the giddiness of her victory when Magnum returned.

"Yes, for a human, that is a fate worse than death," he readily agreed.

"You've served me well and earned your freedom." At her words, Magnum's tail furiously wagged, and he jumped up and down in excitement. She was drained from her efforts with Jeff, but laughter fed her reserves, and the absolute joy she felt belittling Jefferson had filled her with satisfaction. It was better than any meal she'd eaten in a decade. She knelt down and wrapped her hands around Magnum and chanted indecipherable words. Her eyes glowed silver as she scooped the dog up into her arms and circled the small room. A vortex of energy converged around them, spiraling them together into a blurred circle for several long minutes. The dog cried out as they were ripped apart and flung to the floor.

A naked Magnum found his human feet and took shaky steps to the door, never looking back. Zoya, completely spent, lay where she'd fallen for several hours, dozing in and out, before her maid led her back to her bed.

TWENTY-NINE

Less than twenty-four hours later, Katie was seated in Davina's office.

"It's a good thing you're sitting down because, in my twenty-nine years of being a divorce attorney, I thought I'd seen it all, but this takes the cake."

"What?"

"Listen to this." She punched play on her computer, and Katie heard Jeff's deep voice on the other end.

Stunned, she listened to the entire recording, her eyes welling with tears when he apologized. He'd never taken responsibility for his actions before. The man making an apology to her was unrecognizable from the man he'd become.

Davina handed Katie a box of Kleenex and gave her a few minutes to collect herself. Still trying to understand this crazy turn of events, Davina said, "This kind of thing never happens. You could knock me over with a feather right now. What do you think made him do it?"

"I think he's interested in exploring a new relationship."

"With who?" Davina couldn't resist.

"Look who's the gossip hound after all!"

Davina apologized, "Sorry, that was incredibly unprofessional of me."

"I'll allow it," Katie joked. "He's been jetting off to rub elbows with Florida's wealthiest people. Jeff went to the Autumnal Equinox Ball at the Castanova Compound. Ana Castanova seemed to be quite taken with him, enough that she had a yellow Ferrari delivered to him recently."

"No shit?" Davina's cussing was so out of character and made Katie like her a little more. She always seemed so unapproachable and restrained. It was hard to get to know the woman behind the power suits by design. "Between you and me, Ana Castanova is my idol. She lives her life by a different set of rules. But I'm confused," Davina admitted.

"About what?"

"Why would someone as wealthy and connected as Ana Castanova lower herself to spend time with the pathetic bottom feeder that is Jefferson Beaumont?"

"The heart wants what the heart wants." Katie shrugged as she lied. She couldn't tell Davina the truth.

"He's really punching above his station," Davina said. "She's out of his league, out of his galaxy."

"Maybe we shouldn't tug at that thread?" Katie offered. "Maybe we just take it as a gift from the universe and cut him free so he can pursue his new lifestyle without the weight of the old ball and chain." She snorted. "This ball and chain is ready to pack it up."

Davina agreed and turned to the thick sheath of papers, diving into them. The room was silent as she read to herself, then her mouth flopped open in shock. "This is insane. I can't believe it." She then looked up at Katie and explained, "He's giving you the house, half of his retirement account, and agreed to seven thousand in monthly spousal support in perpetuity, even after you remarry."

"Whoa." Katie was shocked.

"You should sign this decree right now." Davina blinked. "It's a gift."

Giddy joy bubbled up. The massive weight that had been deposited around her shoulders when she filed disappeared as she felt a huge grin break out across her features. She felt effervescent like she was floating.

"I've looked it all over and this is iron-clad. It gives you everything you wanted and then some. Do you have a fairy godmother or something?" Davina asked.

"Something like that," Katie said with a secret smile.

"You should sign it before he comes to his senses and changes his mind. Then I'll messenger it to the judge right away, and you will be divorced within the next 48 hours."

"Really?"

"I can't believe it, either. You are the luckiest woman alive."

Davina separated two copies on the desk. Katie glanced at the stack of legal documents and froze. Three fresh pens lie in wait on the desk for her to sign the sheath of papers, but tears prickled at Katie's eyes.

Davina leaned forward, concern knitting her eyebrows closer together.

"This is dumb," Katie said as she shook off the

emotion that threatened to derail her good fortune. "My marriage has been over for years, but it's one thing to know it's over in your heart and a whole other thing to sign on the dotted line." Katie uttered a sad laugh and a heavy sigh. "I sign these papers and it undoes vows I believed in my whole life."

"Jeff undid them for you when he stepped outside of the marriage," Davina rationalized. "This paperwork is just a formality, like when you turn off the life support of a brain-dead person."

Katie laughed through her tears. "It's a good thing you're not a doctor. Your bedside manner leaves much to be desired."

"Hey!" Davina pretended to be wounded. "I told you I wouldn't candy-coat it."

"You did," Katie agreed with a grin.

"Are you ready to earn your freedom?" Davina asked.

Katie exhaled and nodded. Davina fed her the documents one by one, explaining them as she scrawled her signature at the bottom of each page. Forty-five minutes later, she walked out of the office with her signed copy of the decree and Davina's word she would file it with the court. She floated out of the office to her Beetle, in utter shock it was over. She was fifty and a divorcee. When she cranked up the ignition and her stereo blasted *Free Fallin'*, she sang it louder than Tom Petty and all the Heartbreakers combined because no one understood heartbreak as well as the artist formerly known as Katie Beaumont.

THIRTY

She celebrated her emancipation by inviting the kids to the house for dinner. Her bolognese had been simmering for hours, filling the house with notes of garlic, thyme, and onion. The garlic bread was in the oven, and she tossed a green salad with balsamic. Katie pulled four wine glasses from the rack and uncorked a bottle of pinot noir, pouring it into them. A few moments later, the kids burst through the door together, chattering.

"Mamacita!" Callie was in her arms first. Katie inhaled the clean scent of her smooth hair. Then she reached up to wrap her arms around Beckett.

"I'm starved. It smells great!" His eyebrows waggled, and Katie pulled back to wrap her hands around his face. Her thumbs met the stubble on his jawline.

Lastly, she offered Lauren a sad smile and a hug. "How are *you* doing, sweetheart?" Katie asked, knowing that, of the three, she was the most loyal to her father.

"Okay, I guess. Dad called to let me know it was official."

"He did?' Callie asked, wounded she was left out of the dispersal of important family information. Katie reached over to wrap an arm around her to soften the blow.

"He sounds different. Sadder, maybe. More reserved," Lauren went on.

For a moment, Katie was quiet, glad to hear she wasn't the only one who was affected by the ending. Then she smiled. *Life goes on.*

"I'm glad you're all here," Katie said as they gathered around the island, each sipping on a little wine to ease the tension. "It's true. It's over. Your father and I are officially divorced."

"That was quick," Beckett put into words what they all thought.

"It surprised me, too. I guess he was motivated to move on and wanted to do the right thing," Katie lied, trying to smooth their feelings as she doubted that was true. "I know I'm ready. It's time to start something new."

Callie gulped, and Katie pulled her closer. "We are all going to be okay. I promise you guys."

"How do you know?" Callie asked.

"There's a Buddha quote I heard recently. 'In the end, only three things matter: how much you loved, how gently you lived, and how gracefully you let go of things not meant for you.'"

A silent pall hung over the room while they each considered her words.

"The best result of my marriage, without a doubt, are the three of you. I don't regret being married to your father for one day because it meant I got to be your mother. I love you all so much. You are my heart." Her voice cracked.

"Quick, change the subject!" Beckett cried. "Water-works are commencing in three… two…"

"What's next for you?" Callie offered as a solution to derail the sentimental train. "Are you going to start dating again?"

Katie choked on the wine, which sent her into a coughing spurt where Beckett delivered three solid claps to her back as Arlo barked and reared up on his legs, growling. She recovered, red-faced and laughing. "That's a hard pass," she said, her voice jagged, and she cleared her throat a few more times as Arlo calmed down and lay at her feet. "I think I am going to pick up a few more shifts at Kandied Karma. I want to spend more time with Yuli, and I think I can do the most good there." She didn't want to say anything else, afraid that if the kids knew the truth, they would want to stop her.

"It's a candy shop," Lauren said, confusion knitting up her brow.

"It's so much more than that," Katie said with a knowing smile. "Yuli has a lot to teach me. She's an incredible businesswoman. Your great-grandmother is a force to be reckoned with. After she lost her husband and became a widow, she didn't let it destroy her. She went on to build the most successful candy company in all of Chicago. And even then, she didn't rest on her laurels. She sold it and then doubled down and opened her shop in Aura Cove, and by all accounts, it's even more successful than the Chicago store."

Lauren nodded. "She did." She was proud of Yuli's success.

"And all at a time when women had to fight to have a seat at the table," Katie said. "She's a remarkable woman."

Callie interjected, "She's really getting up there. It's probably a good idea. There might not be much time left."

Katie bit back the truth. Someday, they would have to cross that bridge, but not tonight. Tonight, they were celebrating. She led them to the table, and her gaze landed on each of their faces. She passed the salad and then the pasta and listened to them razz each other and laugh. These were the moments that really made a successful life. The love she felt for the three adults gathered there made her heart swell with joy, and she savored it.

THIRTY-ONE

The next day, she was relieved when Frankie appeared at the door, chasing away the immense silence that had moved into her home. Her mind was quieter now that the divorce was over, and she welcomed the tornado of frantic energy that was Frankie Stapleton.

"I come bearing gifts," Frankie called out with a crazy smile. Inside a Styrofoam container sat deep-fried grouper and oodles of French fries from Walt's fish market. The greasy scent filled the room as Katie pulled out two wine glasses from the cupboard. She held them up in the light to check for cleanliness.

"It's good enough for who it's for," Frankie said, uncorking the bottle with a pop and then not even bothering to aerate the wine. "Tannins for days, but you can't beat four-buck Chuck." She studied her friend. "So, you haven't said much about the divorce. How do you feel?"

"Honestly, I'm still in shock. It doesn't seem real."

"Oh, I assure you it's very, very real," Frankie said.

"It was almost too easy." Katie sighed. "I know Zoya must have had a hand in it somewhere. It's just too big of a coincidence that she invited him to her estate and sent him the car. I don't know if it was all an act to get closer to me, or if there was a more sinister ulterior motive."

Frankie's eyes widened. "Maybe you shouldn't look a gift horse in the mouth. I mean, she's a little old lady. How dangerous could she be?"

Katie shivered and wrapped her arms around herself. "That's the million-dollar question. Why would she move heaven and earth to help *me* when she was so cruel to Yuli?"

"I don't know," Frankie answered.

"Yuli is clamming up and talking in riddles, saying Zoya is evil. I can't really fault her after I learned Yuli ran away when she was sixteen."

"A sixteen-year-old doesn't run away when things are hunky-dory at home," Frankie agreed. "There is a lot more to that story."

"I agree!" Katie said. "And I learned Yuli's mother died during childbirth and Zoya blamed her. To say their relationship is complicated is the understatement of the century."

"Oh my God." Frankie was appropriately horrified at the news. "That's terrible. Poor Yuli."

"Yeah, her mother was Zoya's only child."

"That might explain the resentment and her distance."

"Maybe," Katie muttered. "There are just so many unanswered questions. Apparently, Zoya has lived a very long and colorful life, complete with ties to the Gabriano family."

"Whoa. That's not *The Sopranos*, that's the *legit* mob. Are you serious?" Frankie's eyes skirted around the room, filling with anxiety as Katie nodded. Katie wanted to tell her about Marisa but didn't. It was dangerous to bring any more innocent people into an already treacherous situation. At this point, Frankie would just be a distraction. No, she would handle it privately with Yuli's guidance.

"Can we change the subject?" Frankie begged. "We haven't even gotten to celebrate your good news."

"I guess you're right," Katie agreed. "What did you have in mind?"

"Ooh! Now we're talking." Frankie said, "I'm just spitballing here, but I was thinking of buying tickets to *Thunder from Down Under*."

From his splayed perch on the sofa, Arlo growled. He jumped down and sat on his haunches at Katie's feet, where he pushed his head into her hand. Katie smiled and stroked the soft fur on the top of his head.

"I agree with Arlo." Katie grimaced. "I don't know how I feel about a man Beckett's age rubbing his junk on my thighs."

"Fine, fun hater. You might have a point there." Undeterred, Frankie offered an alternative. "Why isn't there a silver fox version of *Thunder from Down Under*, where discriminating ladies of a certain age can enjoy rock-hard, age-appropriate abs, and Viagra-hardened bulges encased in speedos? Now *that* is a million-dollar idea, right there!"

Katie rolled her eyes. "It's going to be a hot minute until I'm ready to see eye to eye with a stranger's one-eyed snake."

"Don't take too long," Frankie warned. "We're two

single girls now, hot to trot and ready to take Tampa Bay by storm. This is the prime of our lives!"

Arlo howled and lifted his paw, pressing it against Katie's thigh to get her attention.

"You're such a needy little guy today, Arlo." Katie scratched under his chin. "You know you're the only man for me."

THIRTY-TWO

The next day, she lay in bed for a long moment, relishing the quiet of a brand-new day. Arlo's warm body was tucked in tight next to hers. He flopped on his back, and she scratched his belly. His right leg reflexively kicked when she hit his sweet spot. She had nothing on the calendar except her shifts at Kandied Karma.

"Do you think Zoya wants to meet me?" she asked Arlo.

"Why do you ask?"

"I'm just curious," Katie answered. "Yuli thinks she's dangerous and is desperate to keep us apart. What do you think?"

"I'm not at liberty to say," Arlo told her. His brown eyes were warm and ambivalent.

"So, you're going to be Switzerland?" Katie asked. "That's the last time I toss out sweet potato peels for you to enjoy when I'm cooking."

"Come on," he reasoned. "You're not being fair."

"It's just hard to wrap my head around it. Why is she watching me if she doesn't want to be part of my life? Is Yuli right? Is Zoya making a power play to stay alive?"

"Only you can answer those questions."

"I think I liked you better when you didn't talk."

"Don't be like that," he muttered. "My paws are tied."

On the bedside table, her phone jingled, announcing a fresh text. She sat up and pulled on her reading glasses to read it.

Thirty seconds later, she felt a burst of adrenaline. She jumped up and threw on a black hoodie and her tennis shoes as she tapped out a quick reply.

"Where are you going?" Arlo asked as she gathered her purse and car keys.

"I'm not at liberty to say," Katie repeated, and he groaned. "You don't tell me, I won't tell you."

"Oh, dear," Arlo said, watching her run to the garage for her car. "This does not sound good at all."

———

Thank you for reading "Hawt Flash: Midlife in Aura Cove." The series is complete and ready for binge reading! Get the next thrilling installment of this hilarious and heartwarming series! **Flash Mob: Midlife in Aura Cove Book 2.**

ORDER NOW

After discovering she has supernatural powers and has been chosen to conspire with Karma, Katie's first reading is from a desperate pregnant woman and has her tangling with unsavory characters from her great-great grandmother's checkered past.

She unknowingly becomes the target of a dangerous mobster, leading her best friend, Frankie, to take matters into her own hands. Teaming up with Katie's children and her trusty dog, Arlo, they race against the clock to find her.

Meanwhile, Yuli finds herself forced to consider joining forces with her mortal enemy, Zoya, in order to bring her granddaughter home, leading to a showdown between good and evil that you won't be able to put down.

This is book 2 of the Midlife in Aura Cove Series—a little Florida town with big secrets.

———

Like FREE Books? Enter to Win a Gift Card to My Bookstore https://tealbutterflypress.com/pages/join-our-email-list-and-win

There's a new winner every week!

———

ACKNOWLEDGEMENTS

Thank you to my soul sister, Kristi. She took on the monumental task of suffering through the early drafts of this book. Being the most well-read person I know, her early questions and criticisms helped shape it into a story I am truly proud of. Kristi is a brilliant woman, and when she tells me the magic doesn't work or the characters need more definition, she is usually right.

Kristi also has an ear for overuse of certain words, and without her intervention, this story would have been about buttery shoulders. Her insight, editor's mind, and attention to detail are amazing gifts she shares freely with me, and I am forever grateful.

I also want to thank Patrick, my partner in crime. He has cheered me on from the start, even daring to read this book in its entirety so we could untangle plot lines together over pineapple mules. If that isn't love, I don't know what is. I jokingly call him my computer wife because he is the most logical thinker on the planet. I know I hit the lottery with him and I am grateful for his love and endless support while I pursue this career I love.

Finally, I'd like to thank my editor, Kendra. She polishes my words to a shine and talks me off the ledge when I panic about the timeline after editing. Math is hard, and I am grateful she's much better at it than I am.

READ MORE BY THIS AUTHOR
ORDER DIRECT & SAVE 15%

Use code AURACOVE15 at checkout.

Scan the QR code to explore all my books, unlock exclusive deals, and more!

Prefer to tap? Click HERE.

OR Find My Books at Your Favorite Bookseller

Books By Blair Bryan

Books by Ninya

———

Want FREE Books? Enter to Win a Gift Card to My Bookstore https://tealbutterflypress.com/pages/join-our-email-list-and-win

There's a new winner every week!

ABOUT THE AUTHOR

 I've always been a risk-taker, so at 44 I decided to write and publish my own books. It has been a roller coaster ride with a punishing learning curve, but if it were easy, everyone would do it. I write under the pen names of Ninya and Blair Bryan.

I love to travel and a trip to Scotland with a complete stranger was the inspiration for my memoir. I also seem to attract crazy experiences and people into my life like a magnet that gives me a never-ending supply of interesting storylines.

If you love a good dirty joke, a cup of coffee so strong you can chew it, and have killed more cats with your curiosity than you can count, I might be your soulmate.

Visit me online www.tealbutterflypress.com

Let's connect in my facebook reader group, **The Kaleidoscope: Teal Butterfly Press' Official Author Fandom**

Made in the USA
Middletown, DE
20 February 2025

71612997R00178